# BROTHER SLEEPER AGENT

*The Plot to Kill F.D.R.*

JACK O'KEEFE, PH.D.

Outskirts Press, Inc.
Denver, Colorado

Brother Sleeper Agent: The Plot to Kill F.D.R.
All Rights Reserved.
Copyright © 2008 Jack O'Keefe, Ph.D.
V3.0

Outskirts Press, Inc.
http://www.outskirtspress.com

ISBN: 978-1-4327-1745-2

Library of Congress Control Number: 2007943198

Outskirts Press and the "OP" logo are trademarks belonging to Outskirts Press, Inc.

PRINTED IN THE UNITED STATES OF AMERICA

In "Sleeper Agent: A Seminarian's Plot To Kill the President," the authentic voices will stay with you long after you put down this powerful novel. O'Keefe is a champion at telling this well-crafted tale of life in Dingle, Ireland, and the rough Irish community of New York in the 1930's and 40's.

O'Keefe's wit, skill and pacing keep the plot flowing, as the richly developed characters, and their internal struggles are brought to life in this suspenseful story.

-- Helen Gallagher, author: **Release Your Writing, Book Publishing Your Way**


"A well researched and imaginative story that's sure to capture and hold readers' interest."

--Lisa Rosenthal, The Politics of Brie, The Good Harvest, writing coach and writer


... Sleeper Agent is a taut, tight read written with heart and wisdom." Jim Kokoris, author The Rich Part of Life, and a regular contributor to The Chicago Tribune

# Acknowledgements

In gratitude to all the Christian Brothers and former Christian Brothers, both living and dead, who made me a better person.

For help with my writing, I'm grateful to Gordon Mennenga, Jim Kozicki, Brooke Bergan, Cate Wallace, Lisa Rosenthal, Pat Brixie, Cheri Lynn, and Helen Gallagher.

Thanks to my family for putting up with me: Phyllis, Jack and Becky, Kevin, Denis and Therese.

*To Kevin*
*Best Wishes.*
*Jack O'Keefe*

# Glossary of Terms

"poteen"—Irish home-brewed alcohol, "moonshine"

"narrowback"—term of mild derision used by old-country Irish for their spoiled American children who didn't earn the broad backs through physical labor their parents had

"IRA"—Irish Republican Army

""Black and Tans"—British volunteer troops, so called because of their uniforms of tan trousers and shirt; and belt, cap and tunic of dark blue or green; largely undisciplined and cruel, they came to symbolize the English presence in Ireland

"The Troubles"—Irish term for war with the English; later came to signify the sectarian violence between Protestants and Catholics in Northern Ireland

"walloper"—Irish term for big, heavy boy

"shiksa"—Yiddish term of disparagement for Gentile woman

"The Liberties"—slum area of Dublin

"suss out"—figure out

"eejit" Irish slang for "idiot"

"Gardai"—Irish police

"Clann na Gael"—literally "family of the Gaels"; Irish republican organization in America

"townland"—collection of homes, smaller than a village

"vestryman"—Church caretaker

"novitiate"—first year of training in a seminary

# PART ONE

"England's Time of Trouble is Ireland's Opportunity."
(Wolfe Tone 1798)

A Killer in Training

Ballyristeen, Dingle, County Kerry, Ireland, 1936

# Chapter 1

Hold the gun still now, boy. Squeeze the trigger gently, like your first time pattin' a colleen's sweet butt," coached Captain Moore. "Mind the kickback. The Webley is a strong heavy weapon, two pounds of iron and lead. 300,000 of them were turned out during the Great War alone."

In the distance, Mt. Brandon hovered 3000 feet above Dingle, a peninsula in the southwest corner of Ireland. Two miles from the town, the village of Ballyristeen ran up to the raw beauty of the mountains. Mick brought empty tin cans of vegetables and beans from the cottage and spaced them evenly to shoot at during the summer evenings. Mick's Uncle Dan had recruited the veteran of the Irish Republican Army, to give the youngster coaching in firing a gun. The old man had the drinker's face, broken capillaries spreading out from his nose like overripe strawberries.

"Think of each can as a bloody Black and Tan with his khaki uniform and black cap, irregulars, scum the limeys themselves had no use for, swept up from jails and let loose on us while the real soldiers were being chopped up by German submachine guns, or smothered by mustard gas."

"One of the Tans gave me this. Look here to me," said Captain Moore, raising his blue woolen pants leg to reveal a red scar that ran from his knee and ended in a knot of obsidian above his ankle. As Mick bent down to examine the wound, The Drink wafted heavily from the Old Man. "Ruined me, the bastards did. Can't work. Sure, no colleen wants half a man."

"Were you able to get any of them?" the boy asked.

"One. Caught him in the throat, I did. Blood spouting through his fingers covering the wound, and with his eyes begged me to finish him off. Out of kindness I planted a bullet in his forehead."

Mick had auburn hair and skin weathered from the sun and the wind sweeping in from Dingle Bay less than a mile away. Anxious to please his mentor, the boy readied himself to shoot. Captain Moore warned, "These bullets are expensive, lad, so make each one count."

Three cans stood on the sand. Mick pointed the gun at an imaginary Black and Tan. He pulled the trigger, and the gun roared into life. "Oh, Good Jesus, lad, you almost shot your toes off. Sure, didn't I tell you the gun would leap on firing. And you closed your eyes."

Mortified, Mick blurted, "Sorry, Captain. Let me try again. Show me once more."

"Good lad. Right back on the horse." With his trembling hand, the old man lifted the Webley from his side, aimed, and fired all in one motion, sending a tin can rocketing toward the blue sky, a puff of red dust rising.

"Wow," Mick gushed.

"Try again, lad."

Mick's second shot fell just short of one of the cans.

"Better, boyo. Make it personal like. You're gunning for the bastards that murdered your Ma and Da. Mick's last shot nicked the edge of a silver can, smashing it sideways so that it spun in mad circles in the sand. For some time more, the two worked without firing, Mick lifting and sighting the gun, getting used to its heft.

"The drawing and aiming you can work on by yourself," counseled the old man.

When they had finished, Mick and his teacher headed back up to Uncle Dan's cottage, the Old Man leaning heavily on the boy. Encouraged by visions of a glass or two of poteen with Dan, the Old Man perked up:

"A good start. A few more weeks of this will make you a shooter. Your grandfather Denis, now there was a man for 'The Cause.' In the dead of night, pulled a dirty informer out of his house, arrested him, and made one of the firing squad."

As the man and boy entered the cottage, Captain Moore intoned the Irish greeting, "God bless all here." "He'll make a good one, Dan. Please God, some day he'll bring us glory." The old soldier salivated at the sight and smell of the "poteen" awaiting him on the chair next to the hearth. The drink was clear grain alcohol home-brewed from barley, malt yeast, sugar, and water. Raising his glass with a trembling hand, he said, "The first drink out of this hand today."

Mick winked at Uncle Dan.

To be polite, Mick listened for a while to stories of battles long past. Then he retreated upstairs to his bedroom. A schoolhouse desk pitted with scars and a wooden chair next to it were the main items of furniture, along with a three-tiered bookcase choked with Shakespeare, Homer, and other classics. There were no curtains to shield the boy from the rising sun each morning, but no worries about privacy because only the narrow run of sand stood between the house and Dingle Bay.

Mick was pleased with himself. He fell asleep dreaming of killing the English: He was standing on top of a ditch in which lay a bearded enemy, blood gushing through the black bristles from a hole in his throat. Begging to die, the man choked, "Pleesh, pleesh." Trying to finish him off, Mick emptied the Webley into the man, but he still would not die. All the next day "Pleesh, Pleesh" filled Mick's head like a piece of a song that plays over and over.

* * *

Besides Mick's training in shooting, Dan wanted him to develop athletic skills, like swimming, and found an instructor just up the road, Paudy Aherne, muscular from a lifetime of throwing milk cans around. He could swim for miles, and he had time for the boy after his farm work in the early afternoon.

Their classroom was out their back door, Dingle Bay. With a current from the North Sea, the water temperature never reached higher than fifty degrees, so Paudy had to acclimate Mick.

First he taught Mick some basics: "Before you enter the water, check the direction of the currents by determining which way anchored boats are facing and the waves breaking. What do you see, lad?"

"The boats and the waves are bearing west," answered Mick.

"Good, now find the highest point here on shore, so you can read the water," the coach directed.

When Mick found a hillock, Paudy pointed out a narrow channel of brown and bubbly water running from the shore out to sea:

"That different-colored water is sand churned up from the bottom when opposing currents meet and create a swirling motion, a riptide, your worst enemy. Look for a giant mushroom, the 'neck' the channel out to the sea, the 'head' the turbulent water farther out."

"What if I'm trapped in one?" Mick asked.

"It'll drag you to sea, so if you're caught in one, float and tread water. Then swim at an angle toward shore," Paudy advised. "Pick out a landmark and lift your eyes every ten strokes or so to make sure you make a straight line to it."

"I'm scared Mr. Aherne," Mick said.

"As well you should be," said Paudy. "Many a Dingle fisherman has been lost out here. Stay a hundred yards away from piers and jetties where riptides often form."

Side by side, the middle-aged man and the boy hurled themselves into the gray waves. "God, Mr. Aherne, it's terrible cold." After fifteen minutes swimming straight out, they returned to shore.

"Good work, lad. You've a great body for a swimmer. We'll go out on the calm evenings to build your endurance. By the way, what are you shooting at down here some nights? The odd rabbit, is it? We can hear you firing."

"Captain Moore is instructing me in marksmanship with tin cans for targets," Mick answered.

"Poor man. The war did for him right enough. His whole life on The Drink. But why's a young fella like you spending time like that?" Paudy asked.

"I want to be an IRA soldier," Mick answered.

"Oh lad, Garfinney Cemetery is packed with IRA soldiers, boys who never became men. I hope you'll not end up like your teacher, a husk of a man, or his fellows cadging drinks from the old ladies in town," Paudy said.

"Mr. Aherne, there's no harm in preparing myself," Mick replied.

"For what? Killing or being killed? The war's been over these seventeen years. Listen here to me. You're a fine student and an excellent athlete. Let's hope there's more to your life than shooting a gun," Paudy said.

"But my mother and father . . . ." said Mick.

"Grand people, the best. The worst tragedy ever in these parts, but even as an IRA soldier you can't bring them back."

* * *

In addition to honing Mick's shooting and swimming abilities, Dan wanted to add one more talent to Mick's arsenal. Tommy (The Celtic Tiger) Loughran was a former prizefighter, a welterweight who had boxed all over Ireland and even in New York. He had retired from his native Dublin in his mid-thirties and bought a small farm of cows and sheep outside Dingle.

Well-muscled and wiry, Tommy was an athlete, keeping fit by road training and working his farm. He had been a student at the brothers' school in Dublin where Brother Joachim had coached him in boxing and helped launch his career. Anxious to repay the brothers for their help, he volunteered to sponsor the Harriers' club for runners at Christian Brothers' Academy in Dingle, Mick's school. He took all volunteers and worked the hills alongside them.

To the older men in Dingle aware of Tommy's boxing career, he was a mystery because he would never set foot in any Dingle pub even though he was always friendly and courteous meeting them in the street.

"Sure, the great fighter must think himself too grand to share a pint with us," said Captain Moore, a sentiment common among the pub regulars.

"Maybe he wants to put the boxing behind him," Paudy Aherne responded. "He's probably lived enough hurt to last a lifetime."

"But even if he doesn't want a drink, he could at least

come in and have a lemonade just to make one of us," said the captain. "Also he was away in America and didn't suffer with the Tans here like we did."

"Any man who worked as a boxer to earn his daily bread has had enough fighting, and has earned his privacy," replied Paudy, marching from the pub.

"What's with him?" the captain asked to Paudy's retreating back.

Having heard stories of the Celtic Tiger, Uncle Dan urged Mick to ask him if he'd give instructions in boxing: "You're one of his best runners. It would do no harm to ask him if he would train you in how to fight."

One afternoon after cross-country practice, Mick approached his coach: "Mr. Loughran, I was wondering if you have time to give me some boxing tips."

"You're the first boy to ask me. But I won't teach you just so you can pummel some schoolyard bully."

"No, sir. I want to keep fit and I've always liked the grace and beauty of boxing."

"Two conditions."

"Yes, sir."

"First, tell none of the other boys. After a lifetime of boxing, I don't want to be coaching a crowd of you. But you're a good young fellow, so I'll train you in private like, in the gym. Will that do?"

"I'd love it."

"I have punching bags, some headgear and old gloves that I'll bring from home. Get Brother Gerard to find you a cubbyhole in the school to store them."

"Sure, Mr. Loughran."

"The second condition may be harder, and no harm done if you don't accept it. Do you know what a 'pioneer' is?"

"Someone who's taken a pledge to swear off The Drink."

"Right. I'm a pioneer, but I don't put it about because the locals think I'm odd enough already. What do people say about me?"

"That you're standoffish because you won't stop at the pubs with them."

Tommy laughed: "An honest lad. I don't frequent the pubs because they are a source of temptation to me. The Drink destroyed both my parents and three older brothers, none of whom saw forty. When I was sixteen, I pledged to the Sacred Heart of Jesus to never touch The Drink if He would spare my two younger brothers and me, the last of us. He did, and I've never touched a drop since. I retired from boxing and paid for an education in the States for my brothers, who live there soberly and well."

"You want me to take the pledge?"

"God, no. You're too young to commit to it. But I want you to attend one meeting of the pioneers with me and read their literature."

"That's all?"

"Yes."

"Thanks, Mr. Loughran. I'll do as you say. I've already seen for myself the harm that The Drink can cause."

Twice a week, the boy and his instructor worked in a corner of the gym, Mick learning how to keep his hands up to guard his face; and as he punched, to bend his knees and lean with his chest forward over his toes. Mick gradually absorbed the lessons: "A good punch comes from the ground up, from your feet through your legs and hips."

Holding pads to fend off Mick's blows, Tommy instructed him in throwing combinations of punches, always ending with a jab. Light on his feet, Mick soon acquired good footwork, always on his toes, feet spread at shoulder width.

As the school year ended, Mr. Loughran pronounced

Mick a good fighter: "You have the basics: fast hands and quick feet. During the summer find a barn near you where you can hang the light and the heavy bags to work on. I'll give you some tape for your hands when hitting the bags to avoid cuts."

"Paudy Aherne up the road has a big milk shed. I could ask him if I could clear out a corner," replied Mick.

"Fine," said Mr. Loughran. "You have the potential, I think, with time to develop into a professional. But I don't recommend it as a career. It's full of gamblers and other seedy people. When I was a boy, Brother Joachim directed me to honest coaches and managers. I've been blessed by his guidance: no addled brains, no cauliflower ears, and no smashed nose. You stay the same. Any time you want a refresher on technique, or just to talk, you've only to stop by the farm. By the way, what do you plan for yourself when you get older? Manage the farm, is it, and take over from your uncle?"

"No, Mr. Loughran, I want to become a soldier in the IRA," Mick answered.

"But, sure, Mick, there are no soldiers in the IRA, only guerilla fighters with no formal training, many of them bums and layabouts. What about the police, the Gardai, or teaching and coaching?"

"No, sir, I want to fight the Brits," Mick responded.

"But there's no war, only endless hit-and-run skirmishes and revenge murders" the coach replied.

"Mr. Loughran, I respect you and what you stand for, but I wish to join the IRA," Mick persisted.

"Lad, I've watched you work with the other boys in the club. And Brother Gerard tells me you're a terrific student. You have leadership qualities. Don't waste them on clandestine violence, bombings and the like. That's not you," asserted Mr. Loughran.

"Sir, I intend to devote myself to The Cause," Mick said.

"A 'lost' cause, Mick. See these beautiful green hills around us. Underneath they're drenched with the blood of soldiers. Don't add yours."

"Sir, thanks for your advice and your kindness. I'll think on what you've said."

Man and boy shook hands and parted. As the Celtic Tiger watched Mick lope up the curving hill towards home, he said a silent prayer for the boy's future.

# Chapter 2

For a week or more each August, Aunt Elizabeth, the sister of Mick's deceased mother Mary, endured the four-hour train ride from Dublin to Dingle to visit Mick. With her she brought her two sons Sean and Mike, one a year older, the other a year younger than their cousin. Only her love for Mick could overcome her disgust at the dirt in Dan's cottage. He was no housekeeper. Built of whitewashed stone with corrugated panels of tin for the roof, the two-story house was a mess, dog and sheep shit clogging the little courtyard leading to the kitchen.

Elizabeth knew her sister Mary would never have lived in such a foul place. In fact, aware of how unkempt the house was, Dan would allow Elizabeth only in the kitchen, the rest of the cottage off limits. It so desperately needed a woman's touch that Elizabeth had offered to clean the place, but Dan refused.

Elizabeth loved to see Mick grow up, but always a sense of something secretive, not quite right, gnawed at her during her stays. She bunked with the Ahernes, old friends just up the road, now "empty nesters."

Oblivious to the chaos in the house, Elizabeth's boys would make do quartering with Uncle Dan and Mick. City boys, Sean and Mike loved escaping Dublin's congestion each summer. They roamed the hills, swam, and fished from the rocks off the beaches, hopeful for a sea bass, mullet, or flounder. For each of them Dan had gotten a pole and showed them how to dig in the receding tide for the small crabs used as bait. Once he even borrowed the Aherne's horse and trap and took them the fifteen miles to Lough Gill near Castlegregory for brown trout. Thrilled, the boys had ridden home basking in triumph, like Caesar's conquering legions, with three fat brown trout crowding a wicker basket. Dan made a grand fry up of potatoes, onions, tomatoes, and dulse, the red seaweed the Irish used as a vegetable.

Before Elizabeth had arrived, Uncle Dan had warned Mick: "When your aunt comes, there'll be no shooting practice and no talk about it for the duration. Same with her boys. Not a word, mind."

Tall and thin with the coal black hair a legacy of the survivors from the wreck of the Spanish Armada in 1588, Elizabeth had olive skin, what the natives called "dark Irish." She and her husband lived in Dublin where he worked as a truck driver for Guinness Brewery, after some years enabling the couple to move into their own house from their small flat in Dublin's slum, "The Liberties."

The boys out playing, Elizabeth and Dan had tea in his cramped kitchen:

"Now Dan, how are you with raising up Mick?"

"Well enough, I'd say. He's getting strong for a boy of thirteen, he can manage the sheep by himself, and he's a fine student," Dan replied. "He won a medal for English and even reads Shakespeare on his own."

"Grand. I always knew he was bright. I hope there are some fellas up here for him to pal with," she said.

"No, but he has friends in town for football," Dan said. "In the fair weather he'll play until the sun goes down. And he runs cross-country with the boys from the Harriers' club in school chasing up and down the hills. I have Paudy Aherne teaching him how to swim in the bay. With minding the sheep, he's busy enough."

"Sure isn't the swimming dangerous? All those Dingle fishermen drowned over the years?"

"That's why Paudy is teaching him. He's bringing Mick along very carefully—-like his own son. I trust him."

"And what of yourself living up here in this lonely peninsula, cut off even from the rest of Ireland, just yourself and Mick since Eileen's passing, God rest her soul, no woman to keep house for you, to cook your meals, and to comfort your bed?" Elizabeth asked.

"Elizabeth, my life is work and Mick. With John gone, the farm is a double job for me, like. I do both his work and mine," Dan replied. "As I said, Mick gives a hand with the sheep, but it's still too much. We're happy enough. Breda brings us down dinner every evening."

"Sure there's more to life than dinner, Dan," Elizabeth answered.

Dan replied, "I tell you we're fine. And I have no time to be trampin' up and down scouring the hills for a wife."

"Father Long could arrange a marriage for you, like he did for Tom Kevane and Bridie," Elizabeth persisted. "Now they've two sons and a daughter. You're a good-looking man yet with a big farm and a young boy to raise."

"We're fine, I tell you. Besides, I'm too old for courting."

"Aw, get out of here with that. Isn't Tom Kevane older than you and running his farm and raising three young ones. And it would be wonderful for Mick to have a sister and brother or two to grow up with and learn to care for the farm."

"Ah, woman, leave off, will you. Don't I have enough

to be filling my days with the farm and Mick?"

"You need a wife, Mick needs a mother."

Just then the boys barged in looking for their tea, rescuing Uncle Dan from further inquisition.

* * *

That afternoon Elizabeth took Mick shopping to Dingle, walking on the circling road over the hills, her own boys out chasing sheep with Dan. On the way they drew near to Garfinney Cemetery.

The graveyard was overgrown with weeds, the ground uneven, sunken in places, tombstones leaning over at odd angles like an old man's mouth of battered and missing teeth. Holding her hand, Mick warned his aunt, "Be careful now, Aunt Elizabeth. You could break an ankle making your way through here. I've had a few good falls myself when the ground and stones are slick."

"Isn't it odd that we consider this as holy ground and then let it fall into a shambles," Elizabeth commented. "It's a disgrace, a sign of disrespect for those buried here."

The two stopped at the graves of Mick's Ma and Da in the northeast corner of the cemetery near a border wall of crumbling stone. They knelt down in the long grass, and said a few silent 'Hail Mary's,' the only sounds the keening of the wind from Dingle Bay and the songs of the cardinals from the bushes nearby.

Resuming their journey, Elizabeth and Mick turned to thoughts of the dead they had just visited. Because Mick knew his mother only from the few yellowing snaps of her in the family album, he was curious: "What did my Ma look like? It's hard to tell from the pictures."

"Taller, prettier, fairer than I, more like your coloring, and a lot less mouthy," replied Elizabeth laughing. "Your

Ma and Da knew each other from the area like, but met formally the first time at a dance here in Dingle and were married six months later, no arranged marriage for those two. They knew their own hearts."

"I miss them every day," Mick said. "Since I was a little boy, Uncle Dan taught me to go to their grave and pray for them."

"A holy custom. They'll stay in your heart that way," Elizabeth said.

Just down from the cemetery, they reached Garfinney Bridge, supposedly the oldest in Ireland, built in medieval times with dry stone. It spanned the Garfinney River now reduced to a trickle. Built with blocks of stone on top and chinks forming a half circle where the water passed through below, the surface was rough-hewn but passable. Now an asphalt road ran beside it.

"Let's cross the bridge together and come back over," Elizabeth said. "Here, hold my hand. As little girls, your mother and I made this short trip hundreds of times, making a game of it. Many is the time I'm sure she wanted to push me over the edge because I was two years older and bossy."

Mick laughed and grabbed her hand.

Elizabeth said, "It's much harder to walk on this now. The stones have shifted over the years and made it uneven. It brings me back to my childhood. With our father, your Grandpa Denis, away in America, your mother and I were constant companions, our ma raising us by herself with money he sent from the States. We had some cousins in Ventry to the west, but that was miles away."

Mick said, "How can you miss someone you have never even known? Whenever I ask Uncle Dan about my Ma and Da, he shrivels inside himself like a snail and takes my questions as criticism of him. And I have only a little recall of Aunt Eileen. All I can remember is the hacking cough of her tuberculosis. You're the only mother I've ever had, and you live off in Dublin, half a country away."

Mick leaned over and kissed his aunt's cheek, surprising her and bringing instant tears to her eyes.

"Oh Mick, your Ma and Da adored you. I'll send your mother's letters to me about you. I should have thought of it sooner," said Elizabeth.

"Every so often, Uncle Dan will tell me stories about my Dad and himself. Once they were caught stealing peaches from Finerty's orchard and received a fine thrashing. Another time they stole Aherne's donkey for a ride only to be thrown off and earn a beating for that too," Mick said. "But then a black curtain will fall over his face, and he retreats somewhere inside himself."

"The deaths of your Ma and Da were a terrible blow to him. I suppose he can't bear to talk about it. And then his sister Eileen died who would have helped him raise you. Those deaths changed his life," Elizabeth commented. "With he and your Da working the farm, Dan had a good life in front of him, all destroyed."

"But now, Aunt Elizabeth, he's turning to the IRA to make up for his losses. He ransacks the papers every day for IRA tidbits and cuts them out for me to read. Besides The Kerryman, he gets The Irish Echo and The Irish Times. He was thrilled to learn about the boy sleeper agents the IRA sent to England posing as construction workers, the 'boy-bombers.' Never mind that these boys killed innocent people and are now shut away in Borstal prison."

"I never knew Dan would turn so vengeful. Now that you're older, I can tell you what a heartbreak it was to surrender you into the arms of Aunt Eileen and Dan when they came to Dublin to bring back the bodies of your parents. For those few days after the shooting, you were my baby. But I already had Sean as an infant and was pregnant with Michael. And we were so poor living in that one-room flat. As she was taking her last breath, I leaned over your Ma, the blood gushing from her blue blouse, and promised her that I would take care of you. I'm not even sure she heard me. I lost your mother, your father, and you all at once."

Elizabeth began to cry, and Mick took her hand in his, saying, "Not to worry. I understand. Besides, Uncle Dan always wanted me back here to inherit the farm. He would never have let me stay with you in Dublin."

Elizabeth replied, "You're right, I suppose, but giving you up still pains me. Mick, I love you, the same as my own two."

"I know you love me," Mick said. "But sometimes it's difficult at school. I'm the only boy who has no mother. There's a big walloper of a boy in my class, Tim Fahey, who for meanness invented this chant about me: 'Mick no ma, Mick no ma,' as if it was my fault I had no mother. Thank God the other boys didn't join in."

"One day Brother Gerard heard him at it before religion class and dragged Fahey into the cloakroom where he lifted him clean off the floor and hung him from a coat hook: 'That's beyond unkind, Fahey. I'll not have it, mind. If I hear it from you again, you'll have a bruised arse.'"

"Brother Gerard is over six foot with a footballer's build, but is gentle with us. In class a look from him is enough to stop any foolery, no strap or rod. When we went into the yard for recess after lunch, Fahey started in again, 'Mick no ma, Mick no ma.'"

"I rushed the boy, punched him in the belly, and knocked him arse over teakettle, just as Brother Gerard was coming over from behind us to supervise the yard. He heard and saw the whole scene. He walked over to us, and I knew I was done for. Fahey got up rubbing his backside and stomach to wring as much sympathy from the brother as he could. Brother Gerard reached down and hoisted Fahey up by his collar, turning his fat face red. When he had the boy standing, Brother said, 'I warned you' and then clubbed him back down."

"The teasing stopped, but I still wonder was I right to hit the boy," said Mick.

"Only you can decide that," Elizabeth replied. "But a man must stand up for what's right. Brother Gerard's actions supported you."

Brightening, Mick announced, "Uncle Dan has me in military drilling, you know, swimming with Paudy Aherne, taking boxing lessons from Mr. Loughran, running the hills with the Harriers club from school, and shooting with Captain Moore."

"The poor old cripple that's on The Drink?"

"Yes."

"What do you shoot at?"

"Empty cans placed in the sand that I fire at with our revolver, pretend Black and Tans."

"Jesus, Mary, and Joseph, I was hoping Dan had more sense," Elizabeth said.

Mick asked his aunt, "Please don't let Uncle Dan know. He warned me against telling you, but I forgot."

"That he doesn't want me to know means something," Elizabeth said. "But what are you practicing for?"

"To join the IRA. Nothing more grand," he says, "than to be a member of the Irish Republican Army. In a few years I'll fight the Brits and get revenge for us. Uncle Dan goes to meetings in town and has it all planned out."

"Oh, Mick, love, the killing and suffering never end. Revenge begets revenge, Ireland's national pastime. When we get into town, look at all the cripples and war-drunks hanging about the pubs, half crazy, poor things, like Captain Moore. Do you think your Ma and Da would want that kind of life for you?" Elizabeth asked.

"Aunt Elizabeth this is all I know, all we ever talk about."

"Let me tell you a story, Mick. As a young man, your grandfather Denis served in the IRA near Hospital, his birthplace. On duty late one night, he spotted a local man discharged from the British army for drunkenness, Michael O'Mara, informing to the Black and Tans about where the IRA leaders were hiding, especially a commander named Liam Lynch. An informer, O'Mara was trading information for drink."

"A few nights later, my father and a fellow officer, John Keefe, broke into O'Mara's house on Emly Road late at night, arrested him, and took him to Knockadea National School for trial before a jury of eight IRA soldiers who found the man guilty of collaborating with the enemy. My father and his friend were part of the firing squad. They tied the poor soul to a fence post, blindfolded him, and shot him. To the last, O'Mara maintained his innocence."

"While all this was happening, your mother and I were but babies. My father was forced to abandon us and flee the country when news leaked out he was IRA. He escaped to Chicago where an older brother found him a job in the stockyards—-slaughterhouses—-and he lived with other Irish bachelors in a lonely boarding house."

For twenty years he put in twelve-hour days to support us, mailing his pay home religiously. He dared not return until after the war. As children, your mother and I knew him only as an old man who sent us money and some small pictures of himself wearing a straw hat. On his homecoming, he rushed to see us first, but that same afternoon he sought out John Keefe, his fellow officer.

After twenty years my dad's first words to the man were, 'John, weren't we right to shoot that bloody bastard?' Our mother heard the conversation and recounted it to us later."

"His question to his fellow soldier revealed that for all those years your grandpa was still haunted by shooting O'Mara. Whether he had doubts about the man's guilt or whether the enormity of taking another man's life weighed upon him, grandpa never spoke of it again. For the rest of his days, Grandpa Denis never gave us a moment's unhappiness, sweet and gentle to the end. He would even mind the neighbor's little ones, but your mother and I grew up without his love and kindness in our lives."

Mick started to sob, and Elizabeth pulled him to herself: "Oh love, you and my boys are just on the cusp of manhood. I want none of you to be killed, maimed, or carry a tortured conscience around like my father. Young men love thoughts of patriotism and fighting for Ireland, but the reality is different, nothing but loss, suffering, and death. The cemetery we just visited is choked with IRA soldiers who died as boys."

"But, Aunt Elizabeth, Uncle Dan is stuck on the IRA. I don't know what to do."

"Love, at some point you must do what you choose. You don't have to obey a parent who's going to consign you to murder and death. Just pray to Our Lord and ask your own Ma and Da for guidance."

"Let's clean up a bit now and get into town. Have no worry about me breaking your confidence with your uncle. I'll face him in my own way and time without him knowing you told me."

When Elizabeth and Mick reached Dingle, they went first to Masterson's, a clothing store on Main Street, where she bought a shirt for her husband and one for each of her boys, allowing Mick to choose one for himself. He picked a heavy wool shirt of blue and red. "This will go great when I'm out collecting the sheep," Mick said. "Thanks."

They walked by Ned Murphy's saloon where a gang of old men, some of them already drunk in the early afternoon, huddled outside smoking. Their unshaven faces bristled with white. "Captain Moore," Elizabeth said, greeting the old man and pressing a pound into his fist as they shook hands. He still wore the same heavy pants and coat as he had while out shooting with Mick. The captain tipped his tweed cap and said, "Thank you, Ma'am. That's a fine young man you have there with you. He'll make a great soldier." Elizabeth hustled Mick away while Captain Moore and another old man scurried into the pub.

Just off Main Street was St. Mary's, a Gothic church built of the same gray fieldstone that made up the school and many of the other older buildings in Dingle. Elizabeth and Mick went in to say a prayer, the interior opaque except for a vigil light glowing red near the altar. On the side were rows of flickering offertory candles arranged in tiers on a tin tray, below which was a slot for coin donations. Believers lit a candle for the dead or for some special prayer.

A few old women in the back of the church rattled their rosaries against the pews while they whispered their Hail Mary's. Occasionally a moan escaped from one of them.

As they were kneeling, Mick leaned over to his aunt and whispered, "I'll bet some of those old ladies are praying for their husbands drowning themselves over across the road."

"I'm sure," Elizabeth nodded. "But for us this is a holy place, the church where your mother and I were both baptized and later married."

"And my parents buried from," Mick added.

"Yes," Elizabeth said.

23

They left St. Mary's for home, emotionally spent from their talk coming into town. Elizabeth dropped Mick off at Dan's cottage and checked on her two boys, making them happy with their new shirts. No sign of Dan but Elizabeth knew he was lurking somewhere close, avoiding her and her badgering. She continued up the road to Aherne's, the last house on the hill.

* * *

Neat and welcoming, the Aherne farmhouse had a small turf fire, wooden chairs with cane matting around it. The rooms were wallpapered in Jesus and Mary, framed pictures everywhere. A quilt wall hanging proclaimed "God Bless Our Home." The Ahernes were holding tea for Elizabeth, for which she was grateful. The Irish were addicted to tannic acid in tea as much as to "The Drink." Paudy's mother now in her nineties, frail but sharp, lived with them.

They sat in the kitchen. After saying Grace before Meals, Breda brought out from the oven a round loaf of Irish soda bread chock full of raisins and a touch of caraway seed. Still steaming, the brown crust preserved the moistness inside. The Ahernes and Elizabeth slathered dollops of strawberry jam or spoonfuls of soft butter on the bread, and drank the strong tea.

Elizabeth spoke openly to her old friends:

"Did you know my eejit of a brother-in-law has that boy out shooting?"

"Yes," Paudy answered, "we hear the gun on these summer evenings, but not since you've been here. I would have told you before, but didn't want to worry you."

"Captain Moore is his instructor," Elizabeth explained.

"I coach Mick in swimming myself," said Paudy. "It's great exercise, a lifetime sport. He's a fine athlete, but too

24

serious altogether about the IRA business."

"The boy has no home life," commented Breda. "I hardly get a word out of Dan when I bring down supper. Like talking to a turnip. He's never gotten over the killings and grown worse since Eileen passed."

"He's stuck on those deaths, like others on The Drink," Grandma Aherne added. "He'd have the boy killed to get revenge on the Brits."

"Well," Elizabeth said, "Dan's life is his own, but I don't want Mick poisoned by his hate, chained to Dan's vengeance."

"Elizabeth, it's worrisome to us all," Paudy commented. "Worse yet, the boys in town tell me Dan's been meddling with the IRA and their politics, still stirring the pot of violence after all these years. Thank God Mick has you, even if it's only for a short time every summer. And you're only a few hours away in Dublin."

"But I can't be his mother. If I beg Dan, would he let me take Mick back with me and the boys?" pondered Elizabeth.

"No. You can ask, but he'd never allow it," said Breda. "Paudy has tried to talk to Mick about the IRA violence, but the lad's been brainwashed. Dan's built his own small world around that boy, and let everything else fall into ruin. You should see the cut of that house. The sheep live better."

Elizabeth answered, "Breda, what would they do but for you, bringing them meals and love."

"I have to cook anyway, and I worship that boy, sweet and kind despite losing his parents. I pray that Dan would marry and bring a woman to that house," Breda said.

"Sure, didn't I mention marriage to him, and he nearly et the face off me. Hasn't spoken to me since," Elizabeth said.

"He's grown too strange entirely," Grandma

commented. "If he had a woman in his bed, he wouldn't know what to do with her."

"Well, I'm going to ask him about taking Mick to Dublin, and about the shooting practice," Elizabeth said.

"God bless you, Elizabeth, kind and thoughtful like your sister Mary. We'll say our rosary with the intention that Dan listen to you," Paudy said.

\* \* \*

As their vacation was drawing to a close, Elizabeth had yet to challenge Dan. But she had devised a pretext for bracing him about Mick's target practice. Attached to rocks near the shore grew a red seaweed, dulse, a vegetable. Dried, it made excellent eating either fried or ground into flakes or powder. It was a delicacy not found in Dublin, so Elizabeth picked it during her visits to take home with her.

After two days, Elizabeth finally cornered Dan as he chased the flock into their barn, the sheep bawling in a downpour. The yard was a sea of mud and shit swollen by the hard rain. But Elizabeth stood her ground in the muck, the rain lashing her hair into sodden strands of ebony:

"Dan, look here to me. I was out picking dulse from the beach when I stumbled over some cans set up on the hill above the beach. What are they for?"

"Target practice. I bought a gun off an old fella in town for Mick to practice with."

"Why?"

"To learn to be a soldier if he wants."

"You're not dragging this boy into more IRA shit, are you?"

"God no."

"Would your brother John and my sister Mary want a

life of violence for their son? Is there not enough dead from this house already?"

"I'm raising the boy, not you."

"And a fine job of it you're doing, training a boy for his death. This soldier's work is not for John and Mary or for Mick, either, is it? It's for you. Making your own toy soldier. Go off and join the IRA yourself. I'll take him with me back to Dublin."

"Mick is mine. You had your chance."

"We were too poor to keep him, and I thought you'd make a good father, not create 'another martyr for old Ireland.'"

"Mind your own two, you interfering bitch. If you bother us again, we're off to the States and be shut of you entirely. Then you'll have to cross the ocean to interfere with us."

Reaching into the muck at her feet, Elizabeth grabbed some of the mire and hurled a handful of mud and sheep shit right into Dan's face: "If you drag this boy into more suffering and death, may God forgive you. I won't."

* * *

After Elizabeth's visit, Mick became withdrawn, forsaking even the target practice: "Uncle Dan, no more shooting; I've had enough." Not wanting to press the issue, his uncle backed off: "All right, we'll give it a rest for a while."

Mick was in turmoil, torn about Elizabeth's sharp objections to what he had thought until now he would make his life's work. After several days of agonizing with himself, Mick after dinner one evening put his concerns before Uncle Dan.

"Aunt Elizabeth thinks this IRA preparation is wrong."

"Sure she's a woman," Dan replied. "She's never fought."

"Neither have you," Mick retorted. "She's seen what war has caused. The deaths of my Ma and Da and the stunted life of Grandpa Denis."

"Stunted? Sure the man was a hero," Dan answered.

"Not to his family. He missed the raising of his daughters, and felt guilty about his shooting for the IRA," Mick said.

"Not a bit of it. He sacrificed his family life for The Cause. No victory comes without pain," Dan said.

"What victory came from blindfolding and shooting a poor drunk?" Mick asked.

"One step for our freedom," Dan said.

"We signed the treaty with England in 1921, and we're still fighting," Mick answered.

"If you don't believe in this, leave off the soldiering," Dan roared, storming from the house.

Dan realized he was grappling with Elizabeth for Mick's soul, and knew that here in the backwaters of Kerry there was little scope for a powerful blow against the English. America might be a better launching pad for a strike against Britain.

\* \* \*

On the four-hour train ride back to Dublin, Elizabeth brooded about Dan and Mick. As he had let slip during their argument, Dan was desperate to snatch Mick away from her to America so the boy could act as his surrogate.

Elizabeth had lost a father, a sister and a brother-in-law to the IRA. She would not lose Mick.

# Chapter 3

A week after Elizabeth's departure, a package came for Mick, a note from his aunt with letters from his mother, dating from thirteen years earlier, sheets of beautiful script on creamy white paper neatly tied with a blue ribbon. Written during her pregnancy and just after his birth, these were love letters to Elizabeth about Mick. As he read, he cried. It was as if his Ma was by his side in his bedroom speaking to him.

Attached to the letters was a well-preserved picture of a courtly man and his reserved bride with a brief announcement of their wedding clipped from The Kerryman, the local newspaper. Mick reverently placed the letters and picture in his copy of Shakespeare's plays.

The photograph and announcement prompted an idea in Mick. The next day he scuttled off to the Dingle Library. "Miss," Mick asked the ancient librarian at the front desk, "does the library keep old issues of The Kerryman? I need to do some research."

Her glasses magnifying her light blue eyes, the woman asked, "How far back, lad?"

"Thirteen years or so, Miss."

"Yes, we have them downstairs, but you'll have to search on your own because I have to stay at my post here."

Wrapped in a plaid shawl, the lady walked Mick back to the rear of the library, and directed him down a set of stone stairs to a basement gray with dust, newspapers overflowing the oak bookshelves. "You'll find The Kerryman on the right side."

Mick fumbled through the yellowing stacks for 1925 until he found January 6th: "Local Couple Die in Dublin Tragedy." The silent words screamed at him. Below the headline was a black and gray photo of a man and woman lying entwined, blood leaking from them, their faces covered by their coats. Two Dublin policemen stood guard over the bodies.

Stunned by a scene he had pictured a thousand times in his mind's eye, Mick wobbled but grabbed a shelf to keep from fainting. At the time the picture was taken, Mick realized, he was safely in Aunt Elizabeth's arms, unaware that his life had been changed forever. He wanted to howl and cry, not here in a dusty cellar, but outside, where only the Kerry hills could hear.

Mick neatly folded the newspaper, and then inserted it underneath his shirt with a backing of thin cardboard he had brought. Upstairs, he walked deliberately so that the pages wouldn't rustle and alert the librarian.

"Did you find what you were looking for, young man?" asked the old lady looking up from her book.

"No, Miss, but thanks," said Mick as he stumbled his way out onto the street. Mick was forced to reorient himself outside and headed up the hill for Garfinney Cemetery and home. When he reached the graves of his parents, Mick took out the picture carefully, studied it, and retched his gray oatmeal into the grass. "I'll never forget you," the boy cried, as he lay on the graves, pounded the turf, cried, and pounded the turf some more.

\* \* \*

That afternoon as he was minding the sheep, the border collies nipping at their heels to keep them together, Mick gazed up at Mount Brandon surrounded by white clouds, a blue sky revealed as they floated by. The wind from Dingle Bay rustled his auburn hair. How could so much violence and death invade his beautiful country?

Mick didn't know what to do. Should he train for the IRA to get revenge on those who had slaughtered his parents, or follow Christ's way and seek peace? Even the brothers at his school, Christian Brothers Academy, gave mixed messages, divided between a fierce nationalism focusing on British treachery and oppression and Christ's teachings of love and forgiveness.

For a boy of thirteen who had seen the pictures of his murdered parents, Christ's message was hard to accept. But Mick also knew that Aunt Elizabeth loved him and had given him the same counsel.

# Chapter 4

Mick wondered what his parents would wish him to do. As he herded the sheep into the barn, he noticed a caravan of tinkers approaching, a thick brown horse pulling a red wagon with a roof. Out from the van jumped a boy of Mick's age. Mick cut him off before he reached the kitchen. The boy wore dirty brown pants and a blue woolen shirt shot through with holes and snags. His red hair was wild, his face a stranger to soap.

"Would the missus have any pots or pans for us to mend?" the boy asked.

"No," Mick replied. "My uncle is away for the day and will return later."

\* \* \*

When Breda brought down his dinner of lamb stew, Mick asked, "Mrs. Aherne, did the tinkers stop up at your house? They're still parked just down the road."

"Yes, love, they soldered some pans for me," she replied. "Excellent tinsmiths they are, but you can't trust them. Sure, they'd steal the eye out of your head, sheep, horses, and food. Some say the English landlords set them adrift when Cromwell took away our land from the Irish

32

gentry, leaving their retainers no place to live. They've been on the road ever since."

Mick said, "I wonder why they haven't gone."

"Sure, I don't know, love, but keep an eye peeled, she said. "I wish your uncle were here."

"So do I," Mick replied.

Mick read for a while and then got ready for bed, Uncle Dan making a full day of it in town drinking pints with his IRA friends. Mick fell asleep but was awakened by a rustling noise from downstairs. It wasn't Uncle Dan, who moved around with more clatter, especially on a stomach full of Guinness. Whoever this was, was more careful. Slipping from his bed, Mick eased down the stairs barefoot, the kitchen lit by a lone candle flickering atop the hearth. A moving shadow of Mick's size was rummaging through the bureau drawers among Dan's collection of newspaper cuttings about the IRA, the revolver buried beneath them.

"Hey, you," Mick screamed and pushed the intruder away from the drawers. As the two grappled on the stone floor, the thief drew a knife from his belt. Mick knocked him back again, but he popped right back up. Mick yanked the drawer to the floor just as the thief charged again. Grabbing the gun, Mick screamed, "Stop, you bastard." The Webley jumped into life. Driven backwards by the kickback of the gun, Mick lost his balance and smashed his head on the stone floor, out cold.

# Chapter 5

**D**an burst through the door and grabbed the gun from Mick as the tinker was scrambling to his feet: "Please, Mister, don't." Dan shot him.

"Christ, lad, wake up," Uncle Dan yelled as he splashed cold water on Mick's face. "What've you done?"

Mick's head ached, and he had no idea how long he had been unconscious. He grabbed the taper from the hearth and saw the tinker boy looking so pale and small now, with a black and red hole in his chest, arms at his sides. Dan knelt down beside him; and listening for a breath, put his ear first to the boy's mouth and then to his chest. Not a whisper. Mick felt the boy's wrist for a pulse. There was none.

The thief's weapon had been knocked into a corner where Mick picked it up. A silver candleholder that had been in the family for generations. The boy must have snatched it from the bureau and stuffed it into his pants, using it for a weapon when Mick confronted him. "Oh, Good Jesus," Mick moaned.

Staggering to the sink, he vomited a brown mess that had been Breda's stew. Mick sobbed out the story to his uncle and then said, "Where were you all this time? If you had been home, this wouldn't have happened."

"Sure I was having a pint or two in the pub, an IRA meeting," Dan replied. "As I got near home, I heard a shot and ran towards the house. A caravan raced past me, heading back towards town, almost knocking me off the road. They didn't even come back to check on the boy."

"I killed him, God forgive me," Mick moaned, "while you were having a pissup in town with your goddamn IRA friends. Even Breda said you should have been here."

"You made an innocent mistake, thinking the tinker had a knife. And if he had found the gun, it might be you lying there," Dan said.

Mick refused to look at the dead boy on the floor: "Over a candlestick, Oh God."

"It was money for them, either to sell or melt down for the silver," Dan explained. "That's how tinkers operate, scouring the countryside to see what's on offer and then coming back to steal it."

Mick asked, "What'll we do?"

"We won't tell a soul. It means only trouble. Go up to bed. I'll take care of the rest."

Dan went out in back of the barn, and dug a hole of four feet or so in the sandy soil, the only sounds the scraping of the shovel, the barking of his dogs, and the sheep moving around restlessly on the other side of the wall.

Returning inside, Dan wrapped the body in an old woolen coat to prevent blood leaking out, and then slung it over his shoulder. After dropping the corpse into the hole, Dan packed it with sand and dirt. He finished by pushing a heavy iron water trough over the makeshift grave.

The nearest houses were too far away to register the sound of the gun. There were no lights at Aherne's, not a soul stirring. No one would ever know a body had been buried here until the Last Judgment.

Dan realized he could use the boy's death to give Mick

a reason to leave Ireland for IRA work abroad and to get him away from Elizabeth. He would hold Mick's guilt over him.

* * *

Mick relived his terror as he stumbled along the hills grazing the sheep. He could hear no sound but the roar of the gun all day long as he shepherded the flock up and down the mountainside. Everywhere he walked, he saw the boy's pale body spread like a dead Christ on the Cross.

Miles away in Dublin, Aunt Elizabeth had no idea of Mick's misery, unable to console him by hearing his confession and absolving him.

The evening of the shooting Mick dreamed he would again hear the sounds from downstairs, face the boy in the darkness, and blast open the hole in his chest. Then the smell of cordite would choke Mick into wakefulness.

* * *

After two days of watching Mick sleepwalk through his chores, Dan had had enough: "Boy, you've got to stop your mooning about. It's over. The boy is dead and gone. After all, he was only a burglar. We have a right to defend our home. If you want to focus on something, get back into your drilling and marksmanship. You want to learn how to shoot the bloody bastards who killed your Ma and Da. That's something positive, not feeling sorry for yourself over a dead thief."

36

# Chapter 6

**New York, 1938**

The IRA had thousands of followers in New York City desperate to strike a blow against Britain for Irish freedom, "The Cause." But their efforts had been restricted to fundraising, over $18 million raised through the Irish Hospital Fund and Sweepstakes, a blind to hide the real aim of the donations: to buy guns for the IRA in Ireland.

Joe Murphy, a middle-aged dockworker, ran an IRA cell in Hell's Kitchen, Manhattan. They met monthly in a backroom of the Harp and Shamrock, an Irish bar on West 44th Street. Choked with cigarette smoke and the smell of beer, the room had an Irish flag of green, white, and orange in one corner, the walls covered with dusty framed pictures of Patrick Pearse, John Connolly, Thomas Ashe, and other Irish martyrs.

As the three men chain-smoked Lucky Strikes, they swallowed shots of John Jameson with chasers of Guinness beer. "Stifling us, Roosevelt is," declared Joe Murphy. "And he's liable to be President for life. He's going to fire Joe Kennedy from being ambassador to England because he's for the Krauts. Now he's pushing the Lend Lease Act providing free ships and arms to prop the Brits up. He's going to save bloody Britain."

"Too true," agreed Tim Moore, a dockworker. "And all this from a goddamn cripple. The photographers have a tacit agreement never to picture him in his wheelchair. Half a man to be sure but we can't touch him."

"I was wondering, boys, if there's any way we could get at him in Hyde Park," Joe mused.

A subway worker and the final member of the group, Pat Condon responded: "We know the Old Man is up at there on the weekends, especially in nice weather, entertaining royals from the world over, King George VI and Queen Elizabeth of England, Princess Wilhelmina of the Netherlands, and a gaggle of others. Impressed by royals, he is. Even Churchill's been there a couple of times. The Yank papers have a news blackout on his schedule, but we have a Brit source that leaks it to us all the time."

"Is the Old Man always housebound in his wheelchair? I'm wondering if a lone gunman could do us any good when Roosevelt's out of the house," Joe said.

"A good question. He's often out driving on the local country roads showing off his Ford Phaeton, built for him with hand controls, thinking it great fun entirely to give the Secret Service the slip," explained Pat Condon. "He also goes round inspecting his woods, full of trees from the Syracuse University forestry station."

"So, yes," Pat continued, "a lone assassin could nail him if he caught the Old Man outside. As for the place itself, Springwood, it's very well guarded, almost a mile from the main highway. The boys and I have scouted it out a few times. From that side an attack is impossible."

"That leaves only the river side," Joe said. "How close is the Hudson?"

"Three quarters of a mile as the crow flies, a mile and a

half through the woods where the Military Police are stationed. Eighty Secret Service and police live at Vanderbilt's and at the Rogers' estates by him there. Coast Guard boats guard the riverside when he's up there, for fear of them pocket subs the Japs and Germans are on about," explained Pat.

"Jesus, there's no chance at all," Tim complained.

"A lone swimmer with a gun already planted for him near Roosevelt's could get through the patrol boats. Then he would have to carve out a route for himself through the security in the woods. But the reality of it is our man could be captured or killed at any time," Pat said.

"Jesus, it's hopeless," Tim commented.

"Who lives up there by him?" Joe asked.

"Other bluebloods mostly," Pat said. "The Vanderbilts and Rogers, and the Mills. South of him are the Jesuits at St. Andrew's on the Hudson and them seminaries on the far side of the river: Redemptorists, Mother Cabrini sisters, and the Irish Christian Brothers."

"The brothers we had walloping us in school back home?" Joe asked.

"The very same," Pat answered. "This is their American branch. In West Park they have a seminary, a "novitiate" they call it, for recruits. It's almost directly across the river from him, a little north, 5/8$^{th}$s of a mile, a good swim only."

"Say we had a sleeper agent, a fake seminarian like, one of our own posing as a brother up there, could he do us any good?" asked Joe.

"You're both daft, you know. Like that plan from our Clann na Gael brothers to steal an airplane, fly it over the Atlantic, bomb the House of Commons, and crash land in France," Tim laughed.

"Tim, you're wrong. A sleeper agent in the guise of a religious is feasible. There's the element of surprise for one thing. A seminarian gunning for Roosevelt. Who would think it? It could be done," Pat insisted.

Joe asked, "Tim, what are your objections?"

"Sure, your man would have to be a good swimmer, a crack shot, and a fake Christian Brother to boot. Nobody could ever stand that life who didn't believe in it. They'd spot a phony a mile away. Christ Himself couldn't manage it," Tim declared.

"Don't be so sure, boyo," Pat argued. "I've a cousin in Dingle, Dan Slattery, raising up his nephew Mick to avenge himself on the Brits for murdering his parents. The boy has reason enough. He's now in his last year at Christian Brothers' Grammar School in Dingle. He knows the brothers and their life. He would have a leg up on getting admission into Power Memorial Academy, the brothers' school here in Hell's Kitchen. The Old Country brothers there would love to have a smart Irish kid come over and lord it over the narrowbacks."

"But does he have the stomach for it?" Tim asked.

"We'll find out," Pat said. "The wife and myself are going back there on a trip. I'll lay out the plan and sound them out."

Joe Murphy commented, "The brothers recruit new ones, novices, from their own schools. If this Mick is a good lad, and an Irishman, they might well accept him into the order."

"What are the qualifications, I wonder," asked Tim.

"Good marks in school and good behavior," replied Pat. "He'd have to fake the religious part, of course, and put up with all the rules, silence, prayers, and other spiritual gaff. No colleens, of, course."

"Very chancy, indeed," commented Tim. "Smoke and mirrors boys."

"I suppose you have a better idea, Tim. Jesus, what a

wet blanket. Not a good word about anything, always searching for a pimple on an elephant's ass," Joe fired back.

Joe said, "Well, Pat, you and the wife go over and see if your cousin and his nephew are interested. Cutting down Roosevelt would be the greatest blow for the IRA ever. And who knows, maybe the boy could catch old Winston himself in the net if he were up there visiting."

"As for finances," Pat suggested, "we could pay their way out from the hospital fund, money we've raised ourselves. Joe, you could find a job for Dan on the docks and a flat for them."

"Before you leave for the Old Country, Pat, let's the three of us do a reconnaissance of our own up there at Roosevelt's and the seminary to get the lay of the land, like. See for ourselves what the difficulties and opportunities would be like," said Joe. "We might get more ideas."

* * *

The following Sunday the three Irishmen drove two hours north into the Hudson Valley. They reached Poughkeepsie and drove by St. Andrew's, the seminary for the Jesuits, who fancied themselves the Cadillac of all the religious orders. Dozens of seminarians in their black robes were walking on the grounds praying or meditating. "Like fucking crows they are," said Joe Murphy, "all over."

"The rector is a friend of Roosevelt's. In fact he manages a chicken farm next door to the Old Man's dairy farm. He and the Secret Service are used to seeing Jesuits about. If our sleeper were wearing religious garb, it would give him more time, an element of surprise like," remarked Pat, "before the Secret Service caught on."

"Good idea," said Joe. "We could have clothes waiting

41

there for him in the woods with the gun."

As they drove on past St. Andrew's, Pat explained, "Just down here is Roosevelt's. See the stone guardhouse for the Secret Service at the top of the road, perhaps a mile to the house, hidden by those trees."

"By Jesus, that's a lot of open ground to cover," said Tim.

"Right. The only way to get at him is from the back, up from the river," Pat said.

After the three men passed the village of Hyde Park with a library and church made of local fieldstone, they reached Vanderbilt's, the mansion standing like a proud queen on a hill overlooking the Hudson. Clad in white Indiana limestone, the building was fronted by Greek columns. Two stone bridges crossed acres of shaved grass and flowerbeds, and spanned either end of a lagoon. Trees bordered the periphery of the grounds. "Mother of God, an entire village from the Old Country wouldn't fill this place," remarked Joe.

A car of Secret Service men was parked aslant the road blocking the entrance. "Them Secret Service live there," Pat explained. "And in the Rogers' estate below. There's a path behind Vanderbilt's running through the woods to Roosevelt's, maybe a mile. Our man has to use that."

The Irishmen headed over the Poughkeepsie Bridge and arrived at the Christian Brothers. To the left there was a sign for the novitiate. To the right stood a sign for St. Joseph's High School, closer to the river. The Irishmen pulled into a parking lot, a large white statue of the Blessed Virgin Mary welcoming them.

"Let's take a gander round unless someone stops us," Joe said.

In front of the red-brick school, they met an elderly stooped brother wearing a straw hat, white shirt, and shiny black pants. He was fingering his black rosary beads, anxious for conversation and for another cigarette to replace the one that dangled from his lips.

"Good afternoon, Brother," Joe said. "Could we have your permission to tour your beautiful grounds?"

"Of course. Welcome to you. I'm Brother Remegius, retired now, with a brogue like your own. This is the high-school seminary. Across the road up the hill is the novitiate and farm. Would ye have a cigarette or two for me?"

"Yes, take the whole pack, Brother, Lucky Strike. I've plenty," said Joe, and introduced Tim and Pat. The two quickly got the hint and hauled out packs of their own.

"God bless you. Our superior doles them out to us like gold ingots. Up from the city, are ye?" Brother Remigius asked.

"Yes, a bit of sightseeing. Just had a look at Vanderbilt's, which I can see now across the river. We passed by Roosevelt's too," Joe said.

"Bloody bastard. But for him the English would be finished. The Germans would roll over them. They've stomped on us for over four hundred years. Let them have a taste. Would ye care for a cup of tea?" Brother Remigius asked.

"Thanks much, Brother, but we'd like a walk to see the river and then we must head back," Joe answered.

"Just to the left of that back porch is the path to the river where our lads swim. Mind the rocks on your way down. About a quarter mile to a little pier," directed the old brother.

The three men walked for about ten minutes down a route that was steep and sharp until they came to a gray wooden deck. "About 5/8ths of a mile across the river, straight ahead is Hyde Park," Pat explained. "Roosevelt's is a little to the right behind those trees."

"Not a bad run at all. Across and back in an hour or so for a good swimmer," Joe remarked.

"Well boys," said Tim, "you're right. It can be done. But who's going to do it?"

The conspirators agreed that Pat Condon would lay out their plot to his cousin in Dingle. Tim warned: "They've got to know the risks, like that poor dago Zungara electrocuted within a month for shooting at the Old Man in Miami."

"One thing in our favor, boys," said Joe. "We have someone on Roosevelt's domestic staff who can plant a gun and clothes for our man."

# Chapter 7

**Dingle: 1939**

A month later Pat Condon and his wife Therese left on their trip to the Old Country. Both their families lived in Dingle close to Ballyristeen. They had tea with Dan and Mick in their cottage, Therese doing her best to ignore the untidy house. At the end of tea, Pat whispered to Dan, "Could I have a private word with you in the Skelligs pub tomorrow night? IRA business."

"Sure," said Dan.

The following evening the two cousins settled with pints of Guinness in the pub, a smoky peat fire smoldering opposite the bar. They sat well away from the local farmers and old men smoking their pipes.

"Pat," Dan complained, "Kerry is a graveyard for the IRA. The Civil War has beaten down the people. But my own life has been destroyed by the British, and I want revenge. If John were still alive, the two of us could enlarge the flock and make a real go of the farm. But that's all lost to me now. That's why I've had Mick preparing to become a soldier."

"You've done well with the boy," Pat complimented Dan.

"Thanks, but Mick is feeling very low. In self-defense he shot and killed a tinker boy robbing us one night. We kept it to ourselves, and I buried the body. But it's stuck on his mind, like. And his Aunt Elizabeth nearly et the face off me before that for having him learn to shoot. She even screamed at me for training him for the IRA."

"Strange you should mention that because it's the very reason I asked you here this evening," Pat said. "We may have IRA work for ye both in New York, maybe the biggest job ever. Can the boy fire a gun and swim?" Pat asked.

"God, yes. He's trained in shooting, swimming, running, and boxing. What's this job?"

"The biggest ever. You'd both have to move to New York where we'd get a job on the docks for you and a flat. Mick would enter the Christian Brothers' high school, Power Memorial Academy. After graduating, he'd apply to join them as a novice brother, really an IRA sleeper agent for us in disguise as a seminarian. Roosevelt lives only little more than half a mile almost straight across the Hudson River, and the boy would have to swim over and use a gun we'll have placed there. He'd live as a novice brother until the time came to assassinate the Old Man and Churchill if he's up there," Pat explained.

"Jesus God, you aren't serious," exclaimed Dan.

"Very," Pat replied. "For the boy, he would have to sneak out from the novitiate to learn the route. We'll not tell him the target until he's up there, just that it's somebody important. The chief danger will be the attempt itself. He could be captured or killed. He's got to know that going in, scary for anyone, let alone a young man."

"Good God, the real thing. Not chasing after moonbeams. I've been waiting and working on this for years," said Dan.

"Be fair with the boy, Dan. He'd be putting his life on the line. Sound him out and let me know before the week is over because we'll have to move fast before school in September. Mind you keep this to yourself and Mick," Pat warned.

\* \* \*

The next evening after tea, Dan said, "Lad, we've got big news. An offer to move to the States for the IRA."

"What's that?" Mick asked.

"In New York the IRA want you to live as a sleeper agent, in disguise like, going to the Christian Brothers' high school and then entering the brothers' seminary," Dan explained.

"Why?" Mick asked.

"Some American big shot in the war lives right across the Hudson River from their novitiate, the one behind the deaths of your Ma and Da. He's been giving ships, arms, and money to the Brits. If you were a sleeper agent, you could swim across the river to gun him down, " Dan explained. "There would be terrible risk in it for you. You could be caught or shot."

"After shooting that boy, I feel so bad I hardly care. I'm already a killer," Mick said.

"The brothers take new applicants for the order from their own schools. With good marks and good conduct in school, you'd tell them you have a calling to be a brother, a vocation," Dan explained.

"What about Aunt Elizabeth?" Mick asked.

"This is soldier's work. Besides, she could visit you over there," Dan responded.

"This is what you want?" Mick asked.

"Lad, this is the opportunity of our lives. But it's what

47

<u>you</u> want that counts. If you succeed, it would be a great IRA triumph, and we'd get back at the real leaders," Dan answered.

"I'll do it," Mick replied.

"Good lad, I knew ye would," Dan said.

\* \* \*

The next few weeks passed quickly. Mick wrote Aunt Elizabeth. Dan leased out the farm to a young man from Ventry. But Mick had one last task. As he knelt down in the dewy grass at the graves of his parents, Mick spoke to them:

"I'm leaving you now, perhaps never to come back again," he sobbed. "I hope I'm doing the right thing, what you would want me to do. I love you and will never forget you."

# PART TWO

# Chapter 8

**New York:, 1939**

A s Pat Condon had promised, the IRA brought Dan and Mick to New York, finding Dan a job as a longshoreman. The two moved into a flat on West 48<sup>th</sup> Street in the middle of Hell's Kitchen, an Irish enclave on Manhattan's west side, close to Power Memorial Academy, the Christian Brothers' high school. Thousands of people, many of them immigrants, were compressed into blocks of brownstone apartments, more people than Mick had ever seen in his life.

At first the city terrified Mick, always wanting to be outdoors, heedless of traffic lights and cars. One afternoon he tore across Amsterdam Avenue, almost getting clipped by a taxi: "Dumb bastard kid, watch where you're going," screamed the cabbie.

One of Dan's first tasks was to register Mick at Power Memorial Academy. After ringing the doorbell, Dan and Mick were escorted into the office of the principal by a secretary. Brother Hendry, a bald, brick of a man barely contained by his black habit, welcomed them. An American flag stood in one corner; the Irish tricolor of green, white, and orange in the other.

After introductions, Brother Hendry got down to business: "So, you're both brothers' boys from Dingle, uncle and nephew, are you? I was raised in Emly, near Limerick. We're glad to have you, young man, but you'll have adjustments to make. Because we're so close to the Columbus Circle subway, we draw boys of every nationality from all over the city: Puerto Ricans, Polish, Italians, Negroes, Ukrainians, as well as our own. And you'll have to get along with them."

"Yes, Brother," Mick nodded.

His clear blue eyes peering through glasses with wire-framed lenses, the principal leaned forward and asked, "Are you an athlete, boy?"

"Yes, Brother. I love to run, swim, and box. I ran in the Harrier's club and was coached by Tommy Loughran in cross-country and boxing."

"The Celtic Tiger?"

"Yes, Brother."

"A good one. I saw him beat Tony Varillas in Madison Square Garden not a mile from here. We have fine track and cross-country teams here too, so you'll run for us and fit right in. We practice in Central Park and in the armory close by. I was a coach myself until they saddled me with this," the principal said, pointing to the papers piled high on his desk.

"We have a good school here, fine teachers and discipline. But I know you're used to that. Tuition is five dollars a month with a five-dollar registration fee. If you like, I can sign you up for a job cleaning the gym. That would cover your tuition. We take care of our own here."

"Fine, Brother," Mick said. "I want to pay for my own education."

"That leaves only the registration fee."

From his pocket Dan pulled out a crisp five-dollar bill,

which Brother Hendry buried deep into the folds of his habit.

Mick was now officially enrolled in Power Memorial Academy.

\* \* \*

As Pat Condon had predicted, the Old Country brothers at Power were thrilled to have Mick come to them straight from the land of their origins and from their own school in Dingle.

For Mick the transition to an American high school was not so difficult because he had always been a keen student and knew the ways of the brothers. Even with his Irish accent or "brogue," he got along well with the first-generation Irish Americans, "narrowbacks," who because of their education had been spared the physical labor their parents had performed. This group made up the majority of the student body. Mick was a rookie, a "greenhorn."

By joining the cross-country team and cleaning the gym after practice, Mick worked off some of his restlessness, but always in his mind's eye was the body on the cottage floor.

Like the city teeming with immigrants, Power was crowded, especially because of its ten-story funnel shape. It had originally been built as a hospital in the 1880's with only one central staircase winding around an elevator reserved for faculty and boys on crutches.

\* \* \*

"Out of my way, greenhorn," yelled Billy Flaherty as he jammed his elbow into Mick's side. Grabbing him from behind, Mick slammed the older boy against the wall, and then buried his fist in his gut with the corkscrew punch Tommy Loughran had taught him. "Christ," the boy cursed. Mick didn't say a word. Billy would never bother him again.

The incident left Mick shaken because without any warning he had lost control, simply exploded. Uncle Dan had warned him to keep a low profile, and Brother O'Connor, a natural spy, had observed the scene from the top of the stairs.

* * *

After his shoving match with Flaherty, Mick's next two years at Power were marked by academic success, always on the "A" Honor Roll. And by his junior year, he had become the school's best long-distance runner, bringing in many blue ribbons to adorn the trophy case.

Bounding down the stairs one afternoon on the way to cross-country practice, Mick met a sobbing Terry Kelleher, a Hell's Kitchen neighbor and friend. With a head of wild red hair, and a face covered with freckles, the freshman was easy to be with. Huddled against the green wall in the sixth floor stairwell, Mick handed him a handkerchief.

"Terry, what in the name of God happened?"

The boy was trembling: "Brother Irving al-always m-mocking me for st-stuttering."

"But you're on the honor roll. Why should he pick on you?"

"D-d-don't know, Mick. I h-hate him." In frustration the boy hurled his books to the floor.

Helping him gather up his books, Mick explained, "He's a creep, Terry. He spent all last year making fun of my brogue. I never met a brother like him, some kind of sadist."

54

"C-c-can't take it anymore. Should I tr-transfer out, Mick? They'd t-treat me b-better at H-Haaren across the street." Haaren High School was the local public high school in Hell's Kitchen just across the street from Power Memorial.

"No, sure you're a good student. You belong. Give me a couple of days to work on something. What period do you have him for math?"

"Last. I spend the w-whole day dr-dreading it. C-c-Can't even keep d-down my l-lunch."

"All right, just hang in there. Don't let one jerk spoil your education and make you miserable."

"Th-thanks, Mick."

The next afternoon Mick hung around outside Brother Irving's seventh-floor classroom as the students scrambled out, Mick winking at Terry as he passed.

Knocking on the classroom door, Mick said, "Good afternoon, Brother. May I have a word with you?"

In a rush to leave, Brother Irving was stuffing his black-pebbled briefcase with papers, the last one The Daily Racing Form, with its easily recognizable red logo of a horse and jockey. Tall, skinny, nails chewed to the quick, fingers stained brown from nicotine, Brother Irving looked as mean as he was, a brother in name only. Unlike the other brothers who were hard-driving teachers and wanted the students to learn, this man wasn't really interested in teaching. No chalk marks ever smudged his black habit, his blackboard untouched.

"What do you want, Slattery?" Irving demanded. "I had enough of your Irish mouth last year."

Walking right up to his desk, Mick told him, "You've been making life miserable for one of the freshmen, Terry Kelleher, torturing him about his stuttering. Because of you, he wants to transfer to Haaren. Not very fair jumping all over a new kid with a speech problem. At least I knew the score when you spent last year mocking my brogue instead of teaching us."

Standing directly under the wooden crucifix above his desk, Irving replied, "What's it to you Slattery?"

"But, Brother, if you were kinder to the boy, his stutter wouldn't be so bad. You make it worse."

Striding under a pale blue and white statue of the Blessed Virgin Mary, Brother Irving got right into Mick's face and spat out, "Slattery, I'll teach the way I want. Get out!"

Mick turned away as if to leave, but instead he slammed the door. As he did so, he saw through the window in the door boys milling around outside hoping for a confrontation. Standing toe to toe with Brother Irving, Mick whispered conspiratorially, "Brother, you're heavily in debt to your bookie Al from the barbershop on 57th Street. With your vow of poverty, I'm wondering where you get the money to put on the bangtails. I see The Daily Racing Form poking out of your briefcase. Surely you aren't turning over to Al our donations for the black babies in Africa."

"What do you want, Slattery?"

Mick continued, "As you know, Principal Brother Hendry plays cards with a bunch of Old Country Irish, friends of my uncle, at Sacred Heart. It would be a shame altogether if during the course of an evening, one of the old lads let slip word of your gambling problem."

Brother Irving recoiled a step. Mick savored his victory, taking time before finishing him off.

"And, Brother, just to be clear, don't even look cross-eyed at Terry again."

"You Irish bastard," Brother Irving choked.

"And the most important thing, Brother. The city runs a

free speech therapy program for students in parochial schools. See that you get Terry enrolled this week. Good afternoon, Brother."

And with that Mick opened Irving's classroom door and looked straight ahead, wading through the knot of boys in the hallway who were disappointed with the lack of fireworks. Mick was satisfied.

# Chapter 9

Launching a black and green bowling ball from a school window seven stories above West 61$^{st}$ Street almost ended Mick Slattery's espionage career. The ball, cheerfully donated by a classmate on the bowling team, exploded into a mushroom of fine black dust not ten feet away from Tony Recite. The bomb turned his black pants wet brown. In his panic Tony's instincts made him look up for further threat, only to find the face of Mick Slattery smiling directly above him: "Warned you, guinea bastard." Tony never set his foot inside Power Memorial Academy again, transferring to All Hallows in the Bronx the next day.

Earlier that day Mick had accosted Tony, his huge gut overlapping his belt. They met on the stairs: "Give Tim Brady back his lunch money, you bloody thief. He needs to eat"

"Fuck off, foreigner. I want money for a sure horse today." After all, what had Tony to fear from this skinny kid with the strange accent like those cops in the cartoons? He was only a displaced person, a "D.P." just off the boat. But niggling at a corner of Tony's mind was the question of why the freshman had sought out the skinny Irish kid for help. What did the Brady kid know about Mick that Tony didn't?

Catholic all boys' schools bubbled with gossip, and soon most students had learned of Fat Tony's departure and were gladdened for it, many of them past victims, remembering long slow afternoons endured with growling stomachs, their lunch money extorted. Eventually news of the incident reached even the brothers, always the last to know anything important in the school. Twenty-four brothers and six laymen taught at, and administered the school of 800 boys, the religious living in a community on the top three floors of the ten-story building. The story of Tony and Mick was the chief dinner-table topic for the brothers that night.

Brother Irving said, "We must punish him. He could've killed that kid."

"Get out of here with that. Isn't Mick from our own school in Dingle, an "A" student and a fine runner? Haven't you seen how straight he kneels up at Mass and how devout he is after receiving Communion? And Brother Sloane tells me Mick always contributes to the missions."

"But Brother Hendry," Brother Irving objected, "a few feet the other way and the boy would be dead. As it was, he literally scared the shit out of him. You should fill out a police report."

"Bring the police into school business? And mind your language, too. I won't do it. We'll take care of our own," Hendry roared.

Brother Irving persisted, "But Brother . . ."

"But my big Irish arse. Mick wouldn't do such a thing. Sure, didn't I register him myself? Besides," he continued, "wasn't this Tony a bully, taking money from the wee freshmen? Sure, we're well rid of him."

Long-used to Brother Hendry's prejudices, some of which they shared, the other brothers knew the issue had been settled. Whenever Brother Hendry met Mick in the hallways, he beamed at the boy like a proud father.

But a different interpretation of Mick's action was voiced at home. When he arrived home from the docks one evening, Uncle Dan confronted Mick: "What's this you've done at school? Joe Murphy tells me you almost pulverized a boy with a bowling ball. For Christ's sake, is that how you keep a low profile, dropping a bowling ball out a goddamn seventh story window to scare some kid?"

"But he was taking Tim's lunch money, and I warned him," Mick replied.

"I don't care. What about our plans? You'd throw it all away on some punk? They could put you out of the school, even bring in the police," Dan yelled.

"Bullshit," Mick retorted. "It's been four days now and not a word. The bastard transferred. Besides, Hendry likes me. Didn't I buy him a bottle of John Jameson at Christmas?"

"You did that? Without even telling me? Where did the money come from?" Dan asked.

"From cleaning the gym. You give me no credit atallatall. Sure, I'm only a right eejit to you, but I'm the one to do the job," Mick warned.

Dan mellowed: "Well all right then. But no more stunts, mind."

Mick didn't bother to answer, but both he and Dan knew that his stay at Power Memorial Academy was his ticket of admission to the brothers' seminary where, in time, he would have access to the Yank big shot across the river. Because the brothers recruited new members from their own schools, there was a self-screening process. In addition, because Mick had attended the brothers' school in Dingle, he had a leg up from the Irish connection.

# Chapter 10

Nellie Keyes had been working for the Roosevelts for over twenty years. A talent scout for the family had plucked her out from dozens of other applicants from the Mission of Our Lady of the Rosary for the Protection of Irish Immigrant Girls, a Catholic organization in New York that screened prospective employers. Nellie had a grammar-school education, a strong work ethic, and fluency in English, which made her desirable to a New York aristocracy seeking domestic help.

Nellie was brought to the Roosevelt estate in 1921. The property of 800 acres was heavily wooded, the future President having supervised the planting of over 400,000 trees in a program co-sponsored by the Forestry Department of Syracuse University. Springwood would later become the "Summer White House."

A stone terrace enclosed by a white balustrade lay in front of the house and was the site of Roosevelt's acceptance speeches on election night. During his Presidency, Roosevelt would return to his birthplace over 200 times. He never tired of it:

"All that is within me cries out to go back to my home on the Hudson River."

On either side of the original farmhouse, Roosevelt had

added fieldstone wings, one for servants. Though a patrician's house, Springwood was comfortable and lived-in, with American furniture throughout, no imported Italian marble or carved German woodwork as graced the Vanderbilt Mansion to the north.

Nellie's arrival in 1921 came at a time of crisis for the Roosevelts. Franklin had been stricken with polio and was to be cared for at home. Sara, the matriarch, had always managed the estate with rigid authority, and was exasperated with Eleanor, her daughter-in-law, who went to pieces after her husband's illness.

Severe-looking, with a mannish face, Sara had interviewed Nellie herself:

"Nellie, if we hire you, your responsibilities will be heavy. You can sense the chaos around us while I care for my son. To install a trunk elevator for him to go between floors, we must rearrange all the furniture. You may be called on to do more than cooking and cleaning. Are you up to doing more than your share in our time of need?"

"Yes, Ma'am. I am sorry for your troubles and will give you every assistance."

"That's a good, honest answer. Your salary will be $15 a month with one day off every two weeks. Do you have any questions?"

"Yes, Ma'am. I'll need an hour off every Sunday morning to attend Mass."

"Fine," Sara said. "You have a right to practice your religion."

"Secondly, Ma'am. My given name is 'Nellie,' and that is how I wish to be addressed, not 'Bridie' nor 'Mary' nor any other of the common names assigned to Irish serving girls."

"'Nellie' it shall be. You have some spunk. Good. You may start immediately."

"Yes, Ma'am. Thank you."

* * *

Nellie Keyes had a history of her own. From Ventry, a village just west of Dingle, she had left Ireland with a hole in her heart. She had been engaged to an IRA leader, Thomas Ashe, a teacher. Along with the future president of Ireland, Eamon deValera, Ashe had been imprisoned in England for treason. Under a general amnesty, he was freed and returned to Ireland. As they lay in bed at the Blennerville Hotel in Tralee after months apart, Nellie begged her lover to stop the crusading: "You've done enough for them now. Arrested twice. Under a death penalty. You're thirty-two, I'm twenty-five. Time for us to start our own family."

"They've asked me to give only the odd speech now and again. I'll lay low, I promise you," he replied.

"Sure, you won't stop. It's not me you love but Mother Ireland," Nellie said.

Kissing her again, he said, "Hush now, you know it's you that's in my heart."

"No, you're determined to make a martyr of yourself," Nellie answered.

She was right. Arrested once again for treason after a speech, Ashe was sentenced to Mountjoy Jail in Dublin where he agitated to be given prisoner of war status. In protest he began a hunger strike. As he grew weaker, he was placed in a straitjacket and force fed by a trainee doctor who accidentally pierced his lung with a feeding tube. He died in a Dublin hospital shortly after. Nellie's lover had died a hero's death, and was buried with full military honors, a crowd of twenty thousand in the funeral procession, the eulogy given by IRA leader Michael

63

Collins, small consolation to Nellie.

After Sara Roosevelt had died at eighty-six in 1941, Franklin wore a black armband for a year and would allow no changes in the way his mother had managed the house, so Nellie remained a fixture. Years before, she had been vetted by the Secret Service.

Nellie's workload burgeoned with the invasion of White House staffers and security once Roosevelt became President. Like old lady Sara, Nellie was unimpressed with the strangers in her life, except for Mike Reilly, chief of the President's Secret Service team, whose parents came from County Cavan. The two became good friends.

Joe Murphy, leader of the IRA cell, and his wife Mary were life-long friends of Nellie from the Old Country. Nellie spent some of her days off with the couple. Joe was interested in her not only because of their friendship, but also because she fed him information about the President.

"So, Nellie, how's life with the high and mighty?" asked Joe Murphy during tea on one of her visits.

"Just work, even with the old lady gone. She ruled that place her whole life, Franklin and Eleanor, the kids and grandkids. She'd spoil the grandchildren to sabotage Eleanor. After she died, Eleanor said, 'It's hard to imagine living with someone for so many years and having no feelings at her death.' When Franklin wanted a divorce to marry that Mercer woman years ago, Sara threatened to disinherit him, putting the kibosh on the romance. They've had separate bedrooms ever since, more a partnership than a marriage."

"What's the security like up there?"

"Always underfoot, Joe. Sure, you can't draw your foot without stepping on one of them."

"Have you seen old Winston himself up there?" Joe asked.

"Yes, indeed. Three times."

"We hear he's coming up again in August before they go up to Quebec for some conference," said Joe.

"Could be. They don't bother to inform the likes of me."

"What's Churchill like, Nell?"

"A head on him like a ham. Full of himself. Every hour of the day a cigar in his puss and a drink in his hand. He thinks himself so important he carries around a suicide pill in a pen for fear of capture. He walks around the house barefoot. Old lady Sara would have had a fit."

"He's a drinker then?"

"Joe, sure he'd drink the River Shannon dry."

"How does your man stand him at all?"

"Oh, Franklin likes his drink—'martinis'---but can't abide the long evenings. Churchill works at night because of "the black dog," depression if you please. He wakes in the morning to a brandy. 'Winston hours' the Old Man calls them. Wears him out like."

"How's Roosevelt himself?"

"The lord of the manor now his mother's gone. He moves about in his chair and hides being crippled, a shawl over his knees to cover the wheels."

"Is he ever out of the house?" asked Joe.

"Most often in fair weather. He gets around so well you forget he's disabled, inspecting the rose garden, supervising tree planting with those men from the State University, and even driving his roadster with the hand controls," Nellie said.

"Does he obey his minders?" Joe questioned

"Not a bit of it. Often he pulls pranks on them like making a sudden u-turn on a country road to have the Secret Service chase after him. Or he'll ask an agent to inspect the roof and then order a servant to take the ladder away, all for foolery," Nellie said.

"How does the Great Man treat you, Nellie?" Joe asked.

"Like part of the furniture. I've been there so long that I have the run of the place now."

"That's grand, Nellie, because we have a little job for you in Tom's memory like."

"What's that?"

"To hide in the woods somewhere close by a canvas bag with some equipment for one of ours, a place he can find it straightaway," Joe explained.

"'Tis easily done, but I'm better off not knowing what's to be in the bag then," said Nellie.

\* \* \*

Some weeks later Joe gave Nellie a blue canvas bag with a zipper like construction workers use. The inside was lined with a plastic sheeting to protect a Webley revolver wrapped in oilcloth, and a priest's cotton cassock. No fool, Nellie guessed that the "equipment" the bag contained might bring harm to the Old Man. Well, that was his worry. She had given the family the best years of her life. Let them take care of themselves.

She knew just the place. A few hundred feet down a path at the edge of the woods gurgled a man-made waterfall that fed an ice pond in winter. To the right of the falls stood a large brown boulder. Behind this, she dug a hole with a garden trowel, covering the dirt with leaves and twigs. For weeks Nellie had been making this walk part of her routine.

"Hi Pete," she yelled to a Secret Service agent patrolling the woods. "There will be tea waiting for you in the kitchen when I get back."

"Thanks, Nellie," he shouted back. "You're a lifesaver."

# Chapter 11

After 8:00 Mass one Sunday morning while her parents were chatting with neighbors outside Sacred Heart Church, Mick Slattery worked up his courage to speak to Katie Muldoon:

"Katie, would you like to go with me to the Power Memorial dance Friday night and maybe get an ice-cream soda after?"

"Yes, Mick, it sounds like fun."

"I don't know how to dance, but maybe I can learn from you," Mick said.

"Sure I'll teach you, but I'll bet you're better than you think. You're a runner, so you're athletic enough."

"Yes," Mick answered.

"What time?"

"Is 7:00 okay?" Mick asked.

"Here's my address," Katie replied.

Mick made a pretense of writing it down, but he had known it for weeks, having scouted the house dozens of times hoping for a chance meeting.

For months Mick had received Communion early to give himself more time to check out the girl with the raven hair and the pale face dusted with freckles as she walked back from the altar rail with her parents, her breasts just beginning to plump out the top of her dress. She was as Irish looking as if she were walking down John Street in Dingle.

All day Friday, butterflies fought in Mick's stomach. His first date with Katie called for his one suit, bought too large for him to grow into, which draped around him like a blue airplane hangar. Worn to all the Irish wakes in Hell's Kitchen, in Mick's imagination the suit gave off the scent of roses from the flower memorials he had stood next to.

Promptly at seven o'clock, Mick rang the bell for the Muldoon's flat, the third floor of a brownstone on West 46th Street, and was buzzed in right away. Carrying a bouquet he had bought at the Italian florist on 57th Street, Mick walked up the stairs carpeted in a threadbare red where a miniature Katie still wearing her Catholic school uniform of blue skirt and white ruffled top greeted him. Even though dating was new to him, Mick understood that the ritual called for his inspection by the family, so he had checked and rechecked that the zipper of his pants was firmly in place.

He was admitted to a cloud of sweet blue smoke from Mr. Muldoon's pipe. Giving Mick a resigned wave, signaling that she had to take care of the little kids before greeting him properly, Mrs. Muldoon was shepherding two small girls and their younger brother into the kitchen for cocoa and a snack as they gawked and giggled at the newcomer. The front room was neat but lived in: A sofa of blue mohair, a rocking chair with a caned yellow seat, a cathedral-style Zenith radio emitting Walter Winchell's staccato tones, and finally a plush chair covered in lace in which sat the king. Clutching his straight-stemmed pipe, Mr. Muldoon rose to shake hands with Mick. A block of a man in his forties, Mr. Muldoon had close-cut black hair veined with streaks of gray. "Welcome," he said. "Have a seat why don't you?"

"Pleased to meet you, Sir," Mick said, occupying the rocker and immediately regretting it because the chair might move on him, one more thing to worry about.

"Old Country, then, with a brogue like the wife and myself. Where from?"

"Ballyristeen, Sir, a town land outside Dingle."

"I've heard of it. The wife and I are from Listowel, just east of ye," Mr. Muldoon said, as he plunged his pipe into a pack of tobacco. Tamping the tobacco into the bowel with a tin spoon, he lit it several times before it caught, giving Mick time to glance around. Mick was familiar with the religious art on the walls. In his mind he imagined a giant warehouse of Irish religious statuary and art somewhere in the city churning out copy after copy of the same artifacts: pictures of the Sacred Heart with the heart itself flaming red and crowned with thorns, a sad-faced Blessed Virgin stomping the snake under her bare feet, and on top of the radio a statue a foot high of the Infant Jesus of Prague dressed like a doll, a scepter of gold in his tiny hand, clothed in a bright-red robe, a crown of gold perched atop his head. There was one large picture of an Irish country scene, white cottages amid green hills dotted with cows and sheep, reminding him of home.

With the kids temporarily held at bay in the kitchen slurping their cocoa, Mrs. Muldoon entered the room and formally shook Mick's hand. She was beautiful with dark hair and pale, freckled skin, a care-worn Katie.

"To a dance, you're going, is it?" she asked.

"Yes, Mrs. Muldoon, at Power Memorial Academy, my school," answered Mick.

"Those brothers have a great reputation for the discipline," Mr. Muldoon remarked.

"Well earned," answered Mick, smiling. "I had them in Dingle too."

"Had priests myself at St. Michael's. They weren't shy with the stick either," Mr. Muldoon said. "But they were dedicated teachers. Well here's herself," as Katie floated into the room, her ebony hair complemented by a dress of light green.

At sight of her Mick almost slid from the rocker. Heart hammering at her loveliness, Mick still managed to croak, "We'll go for an ice cream after the dance, and I'll have Katie back before 11:00, if that's all right."

"Grand, grand," Mr. Muldoon answered. Katie kissed her parents goodbye.

As they left the apartment, Mick said, "I hope I passed the test."

"You must have. You got me out," Katie replied laughing.

The couple began walking the five blocks up sooty Amsterdam Avenue to Power Memorial Academy, factories on the east side of the street, Haaren Public School and a rusty ten-story tenement on the west side. Realizing he didn't know what to say to Katie, Mick panicked. He had never talked to a girl before. Finally he asked, "Do you like school?"

Katie attended Cathedral, an all-girls' Catholic school next to St. Patrick's Cathedral, staffed by teaching nuns: "I like it well enough," she replied, "but a couple of those old nuns would just as soon smack your hand with a ruler as look at you."

"What for?" Mick asked, shocked to learn that Catholic girls suffered some of the same indignities as the boys.

"Not sitting up straight in class or missing your homework," she said.

"Good God," said Mick.

"It doesn't take much some days. Peggy Ryan got smacked across the hand with the ruler today for giggling in Sister Prudentia's American History class," Katie explained.

"Some of our guys smart off to the rookie teachers, making teaching hell for them. Those lads would be murdered in the Old Country," Mick said.

"Yes, but if the hard nuns catch them at it, they're given Saturday detention, scrubbing stairs all day with a toothbrush," Katie said. "And if a girl is always in trouble, she's expelled. Her parents must come to pick her up at the school and escort her home, a disgrace to her family."

"At Power Memorial, Brother Hendry makes a big production out of kicking a boy out and then sneaks him back in the next day like nothing ever happened," Mick said laughing.

They reached the school gym and Mick paid their admission. Blue papier-mâché streamers crisscrossed the ceiling of the darkened gym in an attempt to make the place more inviting. As they approached the dance floor, Mick cautioned Katie, "Be easy on me now and show me what to do. I feel a fine fool out here."

Katie laughed, "Go slow, Mick. One small step forward with the right foot and then close with the left. One small step back with the right foot and then close with the left. There's a rhythm to it."

"Maybe for you," Mick quipped.

"You'll be fine."

To his relief, Katie ignored Mick's occasional crushing of her toes.

After a couple of dances, Mick was feeling more comfortable as he held Katie when he felt a tap on his shoulder. "May I have the next dance?" asked Mike Scarfuri, a short Italian with slicked black hair.

Mick was so surprised that he gave way to the boy. And to make matters worse, Scarfuri was a smooth dancer. Mick had to stand aside and watch the little rat glide across the floor with Katie, sure of himself, not counting steps to himself like Mick.

When the dance was over, Mick stepped back in. Thinking Katie's head was turned, he jammed his elbow into the Italian's side, whispering to him, "Last time, Dago."

When the band took a break, Katie and her girlfriends went downstairs to the bathroom for gossip. Mick made a beeline for his enemy, pushing him out one of the doors into the empty courtyard. The boy said, "Nice looking girl, Slattery, but not much in the boobs department. I'll get my hands on them and let you know for sure."

Mick's fist cracked the smart-ass over his right eye, knocking him to the concrete: "You even look at her again, you're a dead dago."

After the dance Mick and Katie walked over to Cerasoli's ice-cream parlor on Ninth Avenue with its pink vinyl stools and small booths with white marble tabletops veined with purple. They each had chocolate malts crowned with a puff of cream, vanilla cookies by the side of the glass.

As they finished their ice cream, Katie asked, "Mick, is Ireland as badly off as they say? My parents talk about babies dying of sickness, having little money for food, and the cruelty of the Black and Tans."

"All of those things but beautiful too. I lived with my Uncle Dan on the family farm near the town of Dingle, the ocean at our feet, hills and mountains surrounding us. But there's no money. We raised sheep, which is a full-time occupation with little profit. The Yanks would call the place 'backward,' but at least people weren't stuffed into tenements as they are here. The worst thing in Ireland is that there are no jobs," explained Mick. "That's why everyone comes here or goes to England."

"My Uncle Mike Quinn hires Irish to work for the subway. Half of all the workers in the Transport Workers Union are Irish, like my Dad," Katie explained.

"Thank God for your uncle," Mick replied. "He's famous for helping us out. Gets jobs on the docks for us too."

"My grandma sends home packages of clothes with money sewn in behind the labels every Easter and Christmas. Once a canned ham smothered in clothes," Katie said. "But she said she'd never go back herself even for a visit."

"As kids we loved getting those packages. That's where I got most of my clothes, hand-me-downs from cousins in Chicago. Dollars go a long way back there. We'd race to the sweets shop in town. For a lot of older Irish here, the memories of Ireland are so harsh they can't face them again, especially after the civil war in which Irishmen fought each other, brother often killing brother."

"Would high school kids go on dates like this?" Katie asked.

"God no. The culture is so different. Parents don't trust a boy and girl going out alone," Mick explained. "Many marriages are 'arranged.' The local priest finds a single woman for a bachelor with a farm, introduces them to each other, and then negotiates an agreement between them. Often the woman must bring a dowry, like a cow or money."

"But I've heard my parents talk of dances," Katie said.

Mick laughed. "Yes, but the whole family goes to them, the men drinking, the women gossiping, the little kids playing tag, and the teens sneaking looks at each other. Even the dancing itself is done in groups, ceilis, something like barn dances. A boy and a girl don't dance holding each other. I never thought much about it before, but teenagers aren't allowed to do much on their own, always under the eye of their parents or the church."

As they were leaving Cerasoli's, in strolled Mike Scarfuri with a smile on his face, a red bump over his right eye, and a blonde on his arm. "How are youse?" he asked.

"Goddamn dago bastard," muttered Mick.

"Mick, don't use that language or racial slurs around me. If you do, you can find yourself another girlfriend," Katie said. "And don't be giving him a hard time, like that elbow you shot him. He was polite and nice."

Mick didn't dare reveal what the boy had said in the courtyard. Embarrassed, Mick answered, "Ah, Katie, I was just jealous because he bumped me off and is a good dancer while I'm so awkward. I didn't mean anything."

"No matter, if you're going to swear and push people around, find someone else. I mean it," she said.

"Geez, I'm sorry. I won't do it again. I'm just not used to being around girls, and I wanted you to like me, not him" Mick replied.

"All right then," Katie said.

"May I hold your hand?" Mick asked.

"Sure," Katie answered.

When they reached the vestibule, a trysting place for teens in New York's brownstones, Mick asked, "May I take you out again?"

"Of course. I had fun," Katie replied. "But I hope you're not one of those boys who makes promises they don't keep."

"Katie, I like you and you know it. You needn't be teasing me," Mick said, a red spot of anger like a small strawberry rising on his cheeks. Then he surprised himself by kissing her.

She returned his kiss: "Only joshing. I like you too."

With that she scurried up the stairs to her apartment where her parents, Mick knew, were monitoring the amount of time the couple were spending downstairs.

Mick was thrilled. His first date had been a success. Pretty and friendly, Katie had let him hold her hand and kiss her. But he was surprised at the steel in her: She hated racist remarks and bad language. He would change.

\* \* \*

On December 11, 1941, the atmosphere in the back room of the Harp and Shamrock was somber:

"Well, that Dutch cripple in Hyde Park has got his war," intoned Joe Murphy. "Sure the Japs made it easy for him, a surprise attack."

"Poor Ireland," added Pat Condon. "Now the Brits will have the Yanks do their fighting for them."

"'Tis a shame. The Germans would have done for them right enough," Dan Slattery said. "The bombing already had them demoralized."

"More pressure on us to top the Old Man, like," said Joe, "while his death still means something. A year and a half before Mick goes to the seminary, right Dan?"

"Yes, his full senior year at Power Memorial. Let's pray that will be time enough."

\* \* \*

"Mick, isn't the news about the war awful?" asked Katie.

"Yes, the Power Memorial seniors are getting ready to be drafted as soon as they graduate."

"I'll be scared for you, Mick, if you have to go. I'll pray for you every day."

"Thanks, Katie. I know I'd miss you."

The Circle Line boat tour, three hours around the island of Manhattan, was the kind of date Mick wanted, inexpensive and long. As the two walked hand in hand by the factories and brownstones lining the streets of Hell's Kitchen, Katie asked, "You're a historian, Mick. Why is our neighborhood so looked down upon?"

"When the Irish came here because of the Great Potato Famine, there were jobs that men could walk to in breweries, brickyards, slaughterhouses, and the docks. Then during the Civil War many poor Irish were drafted to serve for the North, while rich men could pay a $300 commutation fee exempting themselves," explained Mick.

"That wasn't fair," Katie said. "The Rich bought their way out of death, the Poor couldn't."

"Exactly. The injustice caused 'The Draft Riots.' Because Blacks were hired as longshoremen, threatening their jobs, the Irish lynched eleven black men, the women tearing up railroad tracks so men couldn't be taken to war. Many impoverished Irish did terrible things, like burning down the Colored Orphan Asylum. Thank God the kids escaped. The rioters battled the police and the army with so many deaths they had mass burials on 11^{th} Avenue."

"I never heard this in our American History class," Katie replied.

"History texts present only a cleaned-up version of events," Mick explained.

"Is that why our neighborhood is called 'Hell's Kitchen'? Some of the girls at school from Queens and the East Side snicker about where we're from," Katie said.

"Many homeless kids formed the first gangs, mostly poor Irish. One day two cops were watching a riot. One said, 'This place is hell itself.' His partner replied, 'Hell is a mild climate. This is Hell's Kitchen.' The name stuck."

"But surely things are better here now," said Katie.

"Thank God," Mick said. "The city improved the housing codes. Schools and churches helped, but an air of violence still clings here as if The Ghosts of the dead stalk the streets."

As they walked to the boat dock on West 50<sup>th</sup>, Mick pointed to one of the shipping bays:

"That's where Uncle Dan helps unload cargo ships. Dockworkers sometimes put in three days in a row with no time off, a man-killing job."

"My parents tell me, like you said, that there is no work in Ireland," said Katie.

"According to Irish inheritance laws," Mick explained, "the oldest son inherits the farm, and the siblings have to leave for jobs here or in England."

"That's why my parents came, my mother working as a domestic for Jewish families on the East Side," Katie explained. "She even had to mind their kids."

"That's why we have to get an education for ourselves. That's a nice Aran sweater," said Mick.

"Thanks, a gift from my gram. Why do you call it 'Aran'?" Katie asked.

"Those sweaters came from the Aran Islands off Galway where they have hardy sheep and wonderful knitters," Mick answered. Mrs. Aherne up the road knitted me one to wear for Mass on Sundays," said Mick.

"I've seen you wearing it, not that I was looking or anything," smiled Katie.

"The designs in them come from illustrations in the Book of Kells, a medieval Bible copied by Irish monks. Two myths: one that a knitting pattern was used for a family or for a village so that the bodies of fishermen drowned at sea could be identified. Real Irish morbid," said Mick.

Katie laughed.

"The second legend is more romantic. A young woman would knit a sweater for her fisherman lover to demonstrate her domestic skills. Once he accepted it, they would be married, and the groom wore it on his wedding day."

"That's pretty," said Katie.

As they neared the dock, a wolf whistle echoed down the concrete canyon.

"Who's that?" Mick asked.

"Tommy Corcoran, a harmless fool. Don't mind him, Mick."

Mick bolted after him and yanked him by the collar.

"You're making fun of my girl," Mick yelled.

"It's only Katie," answered a skinny boy with a face dented by blue and purple acne.

Catching up to them, Katie ordered, "Let him go."

Choking the words out, Tommy couldn't resist: "Now, listen to the little lady, why don't you?"

Mick tightened his grip, and Katie yelled, "Stay here and make Tommy your date." She began to stomp back the way they had come.

"He insulted you," Mick insisted.

She kept walking.

Giving Tommy a parting shove, Mick said, "All right, all right."

Resuming their walk, Katie explained, "Both Tommy's parents are drunks. He's a dropout with no job."

"But he embarrassed you," Mick complained.

"No, you did. He's a sad case, you're not. Now let's enjoy the tour," Katie said, reaching for his hand.

The Circle Line boat was a red and white double-decker with a bottom section enclosed by glass and an upper deck open to the air. Across the Hudson the oil refineries in Jersey City were belching black clouds, a backdrop for seagulls wheeling around the boat. Mick paid for their tickets, and they climbed the stairs to the upper deck.

Mick and Katie stood by the rail, the wind strong enough for Mick to put his arm around her.

"Want a hot chocolate or a soda?" Mick asked. "I had no idea it would be so cold up here."

"Cold enough to put your arm around me?" Katie teased. "I was hoping you would."

"You're bold," Mick said.

"I'm bold? You're ready to pick a fight with any boy who asks me to dance or whistles at me," Katie replied.

As the boat sailed south, passing the tip of Manhattan and Wall Street, Mick gestured to all the great houses of finance: "There are the New York Stock Exchange and the Federal Reserve Bank where all the gold is stored, where the Great Depression started."

"You've a good sense of history," Katie said.

"My real love is Shakespeare. Too bad he's English," Mick said.

"What's the difference?" replied Katie.

"The English are bastards. Made slaves of us and starved us," Mick shot back.

"But, Mick, that's over. My Uncle Mike always quotes Yeats, 'Too long a sacrifice can make a stone of the heart.'"

Stung by Katie's use of an Irish poet to refute him, Mick flared, "What do you know of it? Have you lived in a country where a million of us starved in The Great Famine?"

"Mick, you're screaming at me," replied Katie. "I'm sick of talk about hate and revenge."

"God, I'm sorry for blathering so, Katie. I've been raised to hate England."

Katie said, "Nothing good can be raised from hate."

"You're sweet and kind. Please forgive me," begged Mick.

"I forgive you, Mick," Katie said. "but you have to write your own history."

The tour continued up the East River past the Gracie Mansion, the mayor's residence, and then the towers of the rich East Side, followed by the slums of Harlem. The cruise cut west to the Hudson near the George Washington Bridge and made its way back to the West Side.

This was great history, but Mick's outburst had left an uneasy truce between the couple. Why did he blow up with Katie? Didn't he want her to like him?

\* \* \*

Desperate to make peace with Katie, Mick realized he loved her. Hell's Kitchen was a narrow world with no better spies than the Irish watching each other. Because of that Mick had a difficult time finding places to take Katie that were both inexpensive and away from the neighborhood. He decided on the Empire State Building, the world's tallest building because New Yorkers took it for granted.

Katie and Mick took the cross-town subway to 33$^{rd}$ and Fifth Avenue and walked a half-block. On each side of the entrance, a stone façade of an American eagle stood guard. In the lobby hung a sculpture of the building in metal relief. They took one of the elevators to the observation deck on the 86$^{th}$ floor. As they stepped off the elevator, Mick froze, the breath sucked out of him, his back riveted against the door.

"What's wrong?" Katie asked.

"I can't move," Mick replied.

"Are you hurt, Mick?"

"No, right petrified."

"Do you want to take my hand?" Katie offered.

"Thanks, but I feel lost," Mick answered.

"Maybe you have fear of heights, acrophobia," Katie suggested.

"God, all my life on a mountain top," Mick said.

"Want to go back down?" Katie asked.

"No, you go have a look," Mick replied.

At the edge of the deck was a wall three feet high with spaced iron bars above. For closer viewing, every few feet there were permanent binoculars requiring coins.

Handing Katie some coins, Mick said, "Here. Get a good look."

"No, that's fine. Look south and to the right. New York Harbor, the Statue of Liberty, and Ellis Island," Katie pointed out.

Mick dared only a tentative peek from his post on the wall.

"Let's go down," Katie said. "You're still so uncomfortable."

Mick said, "I feel so silly. I could look down a bit, but when I looked up I became disoriented."

"Acrophobia is pretty common," Katie said. One group that doesn't have it is the Mohawk Indians from upstate New York and Canada. They're ironmongers, doing the high steel work on bridges and skyscrapers."

"They have it all over me. How about we walk to Cerasoli's for some ice cream? Maybe the walk will do me good," said Mick.

"Ok," Katie agreed.

Once they were settled in the ice-cream parlor, Katie attacked her banana split, unusual for a girl so prim in other ways, Mick commenting, "An old fella in Dingle told me that the girls with the smallest stomachs eat the most."

81

Katie laughed: "What about you skinny runners?"

"Yeah, I eat a lot, mostly my own food. There's so much more food here. I make chicken and ham for Uncle Dan and me."

"Mom's a great cook, usually roast beef or chicken on Sundays with mountains of mashed potatoes for the kids to carve craters in as lakes for the gravy," Katie said.

"Do you cook, Katie?"

"Sometimes. Mom has taught me a few things. I've tried her buttermilk biscuits, but she makes them 'by eye,' she says. I'm not sure she wants me to learn," Katie laughed.

As they left the ice-cream parlor, Mick bought a bag of penny candies: "For the wee ones. Maybe someone in your family will like me."

"Oh sure, buy off the kids ones with treats."

In the vestibule of Katie's apartment, Mick kissed Katie, and she responded. "I'll call you soon, ok?"

"Sure," she said, and gave him a kiss of her own.

Mick floated home.

\* \* \*

The following Sunday Mick and Katie walked to the Tivoli Theater to see <u>Gone with the Wind,</u> a movie Mick had purposely chosen for its length. As they sauntered home, Katie asked him,

"Did you like Scarlett?"

"No, she's beautiful but a schemer," Mick said. "She uses everyone: Ashley, Charles, even Rhett, until he figures her out."

"But she had to survive during war in a man's world," Katie countered.

"She sure is different from the long-suffering Irish

women that I know, except for my Aunt Elizabeth, my mother's sister. She's pretty and feminine, but strong and direct. She once told my Uncle Dan he should get a wife," Mick explained.

"You still close to her?" Katie asked.

"I love her, the closest to a mother I've ever had," said Mick. "But I haven't seen her since we left Ireland. She writes for my birthday and holidays, always sending a few pounds."

"We've all got to have someone," Katie said.

"She really got Uncle Dan mad when she bawled him out for having me in drilling," Mick said.

"For what?" Katie asked.

"To be an IRA soldier. A veteran taught me military tactics and shooting," Mick explained.

"Shooting at what?" Katie asked.

"Tin cans," Mick said.

"Practice to kill people?" Katie asked.

"The English if there were to be more fighting," Mick said.

"Jesus, Mary, and Joseph," a rare oath from Katie. "Your aunt was right. Do you mean there hasn't been enough killing in Ireland?" Katie asked.

"What do you know of it? Our people starved, not even citizens in our own country," fired back Mick.

"I know plenty. But that's a hundred years ago. I have five older cousins, each maimed by the war or consumed with The Drink because of it," Katie said. "I'll not love any man filled with hate."

"Sure, you'd rather some Yank with no sense of history," Mick retorted.

"I'm a Yank too," said Katie. "And what about the innocent kids and old men killed by the Irish boy bombers?" she yelled back.

"Bloody English bastards," shouted Mick.

"You're like the old Irish obsessed with the past. I'll not be close to you," Katie said.

"You would not love me?" Mick asked.

"Not if you think like that. I want a life, not a replay of Ireland's tragedies," Katie said.

"Do you want to go to Horn and Hardarts for a bite to eat?" Mick asked.

"No. After listening to you, I can't eat," Katie said.

"I'm sorry, Katie. I'll walk you home," Mick said.

"No, I prefer my own company," Katie said.

"But I told you I'm sorry," Mick said.

"Sorry doesn't do it. Good bye," Katie said and charged off.

Crestfallen, Mick repeated their conversation in his head to see where he had gone wrong. He realized he had ruined almost every date they had had, yet still she went out with him.

\* \* \*

When Katie came home from the movie, her mother sensed something was off:

"You're home early. Anything wrong?"

"Oh Mom, Mick is driving me crazy."

"Not too fresh, I hope."

"No, that would be easier."

"Let's go into the kitchen, love, for some tea and privacy. Dad is out with the kids, but they'll be back soon."

While her mom fussed with making the tea, Katie sat at the kitchen table crying softly. Her mom walked over to Katie and kissed her on the forehead, the two of them looking like a before and after picture of what the years had done to her mother and what they would do to her daughter.

Her mom poured for them both. With the kids out of the house, the place was quiet.

"Mick's not a groper, Mom. He respects me. He doesn't hang out with the hooligans on 57th Street ogling all the girls who walk by. He has his job at school to pay for tuition. He got Terry Kelleher out of some jam at school. In small ways, too, he's nice. He buys candy for the kids and tobacco for Dad."

"But then what's the matter, love?"

"He's so angry. He elbowed a boy who asked me to dance, and he was choking Tommy Corcoran for whistling at me. He's nuts against the English, even Shakespeare, an old bald guy who's been dead three hundred years. When I mentioned the English victims of the boy bombers last year, he snarled and said they were just 'British bastards.'"

"Katie, there are a lot of Irish like him. Look at your poor cousins, not a one of them who hasn't been poisoned with the same disease, The Drink, or both."

"I told him that," Katie said. "Then when he sees how mad I get, he's full of apologies. These rages are so scary; he's like a different person. I told him I wouldn't love a boy consumed by hate."

"But you've only known him a few months. Isn't it early to be talking about love?"

"Ma, that's the pain of it. I do love him. He's been so hurt by whatever happened to him in the Old Country and so angry, he's beyond reach sometimes."

"You know I don't put much stock in Old Biddy O'Hearn across the street gossiping about the two of you in the vestibule. But she does hint of some tragedy in Mick's family back home. Maybe you could ask him about it and get him to open up to you."

"Good idea, Mom. I got so mad at him today ranting about the Great Famine and making slaves of us that I walked home alone."

"But, love, 'tis true for him. The English did all those things. Just pray that he grows out of it. When I first met your father, he was a drinker and great for the IRA. I told him, 'It's either The Drink or me. Make your choice.' Your Uncle Mike settled him down about the IRA. By the time we were married, he'd given up both The Drink and the IRA, and look at the fine husband and father he is now."

"Dad's a good man."

"So there's hope for your Mick. Don't give up on him." Katie's Mom kissed her on the forehead again. "You're sensible and make good decisions. If anyone can bring him round, it's you."

"Thanks, Mom," Katie said, and hugged her mother.

# Chapter 12

As Power Memorial students waited for St. Patrick's Day marching practice outside the 12<sup>th</sup> Regiment Armory just a block from the school, a crazed gunman burst upon them and shot seven students, killing sophomore Tom Beasley, and wounding six other boys.

Coming upon the horror just as it unfolded, Mick charged straight at the gunman, "Stop, you bastard!" The man fired at Mick, but his gun jammed. The shooter then turned and fled, leaving bodies all over the sidewalk. Brother Hendry and other students joined Mick and then some policemen alerted by the shots and screams. The killer dashed into a tenement, Mick and a young policeman the closest pursuers.

"What's he done?" the policeman shouted.

"Shot some Power kids outside the Armory," Mick yelled back.

"Good Jesus, I went there myself," the cop answered.

When more police came, the young officer took charge, shooing Mick back and finally cornering the killer on the fifth floor.

The man who had unleashed such terror was a crazed sixty-five-year-old Serbian immigrant whose only child had died of a cerebral hemorrhage some years before. He blamed Catholics and Italians for his loss, and on this day took revenge on students from Power Memorial. At his arraignment, the man was judged criminally insane and sentenced to life in Mattewan Prison, close to Hyde Park.

The St. Patrick's Day Parade was the most important day of the year for New York Irish, a chance to display their heritage to the world. There were prizes for the best marching band and the best-drilled school.

The six wounded boys eventually recovered, one of them going on to become a brother. Power Memorial Academy took part in the parade, drums muffled in crepe. Because of his heroism, Mick was conscripted by Brother Hendry to lead the Power marchers. As they passed the reviewing stand, the President of the United States summoned Brother Hendry over to offer his condolences to the families of the victims and to the school.

As terrible as it was, the tragedy elevated Mick even more in the eyes of the Power Memorial teachers and students. "You're a courageous young man," Brother Hendry told him in his office the following week.

"Thanks, Brother, but sure we would all have done the same. Once I saw Tom go down, I didn't even think," Mick answered.

"You may have saved the lives of other students by rushing at the man," Brother Hendry replied, tears leaking from behind his wire-rimmed glasses. "We're all grateful."

But when Uncle Dan heard of the tragedy and saw pictures of his nephew in all the New York papers, he was furious with Mick:

"Jesus, is this your idea of a low profile, all over the newspapers, chasing a maniac?"

"Goddamn you, Uncle Dan, my friends shot, would you have me run away? Is that what men of "The Cause" would do?" retorted Mick. "Is that what you would have done if the Black and Tans had shot someone in the village?"

"But our mission. . . ." Dan answered.

"Fuck your mission," Mick screamed. "Tell your IRA friends to shove it. I'm not a puppet."

"Now, lad, hush. Mrs. Daley next door will be repeating every word to the neighbors. I didn't mean any harm. I just meant you're not supposed to draw any extra attention to yourself like with that guinea boy," Dan said.

"If you mention that boy or this shooting one more time, you'll have seen the last of me. I'll find a place to live on my own. I'll not take it," shouted Mick, as he heaved the kettle off the wall.

"Please settle down, lad. I wasn't criticizing you. Sure I can't say a word to you anymore," said Dan.

"That's right. Not another Goddamn word. I'm the sleeper agent, not you, nor any of your drinking mates at the Harp and Shamrock," Mick answered.

# Chapter 13

After Mass at Sacred Heart on Sunday, Katie rushed up to Mick to congratulate him for his courage in chasing the lunatic shooter: "Oh Mick, how brave to help chase and capture that murderer."

"Thanks, but there was no thinking in it atallatall, just pure reaction. Poor Tom Beasley, a really nice kid. He had just gone to confession at school."

"But weren't you scared with the man shooting at you?"

"Honest to God, Katie, I was so mad I just wanted to get him. Say, how about we take the kids to Central Park this afternoon and then for an ice cream after? It's a good excuse for a date."

Laughing, Katie replied, "The kids would love it, my parents too. My mom is stuck with them all the week round."

When Mick arrived at the apartment to pick Katie and the kids up that afternoon, four-year-old Eddie ran to greet him: "I want chocolate, Mick."

"Don't be so bold, Eddie," scolded Mrs. Muldoon. "Don't mind him, Mick. We have him spoiled silly." She tried to shove a few dollars into Mick's hand, but he'd have none of it: "This is a little treat on me."

They set out for their walk to Central Park, Katie and

Mick making sure to detour around Cerasoli's ice-cream parlor, which they would visit on their return. They entered Central Park, an oasis of trees and ponds amid the concrete of Manhattan. At Columbus Circle, a column honoring the Italian navigator dominated the landscape, a statue of Columbus and a reproduction of the Nina, the Pinta, and the Santa Maria perched on a plinth. From there they turned east, making their way down paths canopied by trees reaching across and shading the pavement. Bicyclists rode by, parents pushed baby buggies, and horseback riders cantered on the nearby bridle paths. Rows of benches lined both sides of the path with wrought-iron fences protecting the grass.

Each of the kids had a brown paper bag filled with bread crumbs for feeding the waterfowl on The Pond: ducks, geese, and even a few swans, Bridget and Mary parceling theirs out while Eddie exhausted his in fistfuls. The geese fought the other birds for the breadcrumbs, and the kids enjoyed the squabbling. "Mine's all gone," Eddie yelled. "Bridget and Mary, give me some of yours."

"No," Katie ordered. "That's not fair," and halted the whining.

From The Pond they walked west to the Hecksher Playground, jammed with kids and parents from the exclusive apartments on Fifth Avenue. Many of the children were being cared for by Irish nannies, their brogues unmistakable to Mick and Katie. These women were doing the same work Katie's mother had when she had first come to America. "There's a job I'll never do," remarked Katie. "I don't mind taking care of our own, but I won't make a career of raising the children of others."

"You won't have to," Mick replied. "You're smart, so you'll go to college and carve out a career for yourself— like I'll do."

Bridget and Mary waited their turn for the slides and swings, avoiding the sandbox for fear of getting dirty. Eddie wanted to cut the line, but Katie kept him in check. Mick and Katie each took a hand in pushing Eddie on the swings when a ball decorated with white stars escaped from a knot of children and landed at the feet of Bridget, at six the youngest of the Muldoon sisters. She bent down to retrieve the ball and toss it back when a plump hurricane came charging up. The mother yelled to a young boy in her wake, yarmulke atop his head: "Abie, snatch the ball from that thieving Irisher before she runs off with it."

Bridget dropped the ball at her feet and burst into tears, Katie rushing over to hug her. "You should be ashamed of yourself teaching your child prejudice," Katie shouted at the woman as she kicked the ball back. "How proud of yourself you must be embarrassing a little girl. She was going to throw the ball back."

"You little shiksa, how dare you speak to an adult that way," the mother snarled.

"If you were really an adult, I wouldn't have to talk to you like that. You're mean-spirited and ignorant," Katie replied. "Take your precious ball and over-protected son and learn some manners!"

Picking up the ball, the mother slammed it into her son's stomach, as if he had been the cause of all the trouble. She screamed at him: "Stay with your own friends and keep away from these low-class Irish."

Still hugging Bridget, Katie shot back, "The only one low class here is you."

A balding, curly-haired man with a yarmulke chugged across 59th Street. Dressed in a black suit with a white shirt, he shouted to the woman: "Bertha, what's the matter?" Dodging cars, the man was almost hit by a yellow taxi whose driver yelled, 'Hey fatso, get your ass off the street.'"

His wife was dragging their son when she stopped and pointed back to Katie, Mick, and the kids: "Hit them, Samuel, hit them. They stole Abie's ball and insulted me. Hit them."

"I'll call a policeman," the man assured his wife.

"No, hit them," she insisted.

By this time the couple with their bellowing had attracted a small crowd watching the scene play out. With her husband as support, the mother and son turned face and advanced on Katie and Mick, as they were about to leave the park.

"Hit them," the mother screamed.

The husband was striding towards Katie, Mick, and the kids when Mick stepped in front of the man: "Rabbi, a word please." That this boy had discerned that he was a rabbi and was respectful gave the man pause.

"Rabbi," Mick said, "your wife is creating a scene here. She screamed at an innocent little girl. May I suggest that you stop all this commotion and get them home so your wife can calm down," Mick said.

"Hit them," the wife shouted again.

The rabbi turned around and gripped his wife firmly by the elbow: "Shut up, Bertha."

The wife meekly accompanied her husband, and the family marched home to their apartment.

The crowd cheered.

Mick came over to give Bridget a hug: "Don't pay any attention to the mean lady. I think it's about time for some ice cream, Bridge." The little girl nodded, "Yes," and the group set off for Cerasoli's at 59th Street and Ninth Avenue. The anticipation of the treat had dissipated some of the sour mood from the park. "I'll have chocolate, please," said Eddie to the genial, balding Mr. Cerasoli, an apron enclosing his ample midriff. Bridget and Mary shared a banana split, even dividing the maraschino cherry that crowned the puff of whipped cream. One wall of the store held a long mirror below which were glass cases of Mary Jane's, root beer barrels, and buttons, giving the children something more to think about.

When the kids had stuffed themselves, Mick gave them a dime each to barter for their penny candies. "I admired the way you stood up for Bridget and fended off the screwy lady," Mick said to Katie. "Thanks," she said, giving his hand a squeeze. "And I loved the way you treated the rabbi, so diplomatic."

On the way home, Mick stopped at a Walgreen's and bought a pouch of tobacco for Katie to give her father. When they reached the vestibule of the apartment, Mick wanted to kiss Katie but knew it would spark no end of hilarity and giggling with the kids. "Tell Mick thanks," Katie told them, and then surprised Mick with a kiss.

# Chapter 14

During Mick's courting of Katie, Dan had said nothing. He also wouldn't bring up the dating to his IRA comrades. But the Irish world of Hell's Kitchen was small.

One day at work, Joe Murphy approached Dan: "I'm just after hearing that Mick has been squiring the Muldoon girl about. A bit late in the day for romance with his mission less than a year away."

"Sure, he's seen the girl a few times. 'Tis nothing," Dan said.

"Don't be so sure. Old Biddy O'Hearn spied them kissing in the vestibule last week. The boy should be concentrating on our business rather than fooling with a colleen," Joe remonstrated.

"Jesus, Joe, I'm sure you're right. Maybe I could lock him up in a closet," Dan replied. "Would that suit you?"

"No need for sarcasm, Dan."

"In a year he'll be up in the cold Novitiate where there'll be no colleens," Dan said.

"That's all very well for you to talk smart when we've got so much invested in you——bringing you over, finding a job, and getting an apartment."

"We're well aware of your generosity, Joe. Besides,

there must be dozens of other lads here in New York besides Mick who would be willing to make this sacrifice for The Cause."

"All right, enough of your mouth, Dan. Jesus, I'm sorry I brought the matter up."

"You should be. Do you mean to tell me our IRA cell has been reduced to bearing tales from the likes of Biddy O'Hearn? You should be ashamed of yourself. Mick and I are in this for the duration," said Dan.

# Chapter 15

Dan confronted Mick when he came home from school one afternoon: "The IRA fellas are just after asking me if you're still holding true to our mission."

"No, I won't go up there and hide myself among those brothers to kill some Yank big shot--or get killed myself," Mick screamed.

"But you promised," Dan yelled back.

"Yes, when I was thirteen and didn't even know my own mind. The IRA was all you ever rammed down my throat. Tell your boyos at the Harp and Shamrock to shove it," Mick roared. "I'll not destroy my life for you or for them."

"But they brought us out, sure, and paid our way," Dan reasoned.

"For their own dirty ends, not for any kindness to me," Mick fired back, slamming the door and leaving the apartment.

\* \* \*

In a panic, Dan called Joe Murphy for an emergency meeting of the IRA brethren that evening. As usual the back room of the Harp and Shamrock was a fog of tobacco smoke mixed with the smell of stale Guinness. After Dan told them of Mick's rebellion, Joe Murphy pounced:

"I told you that his chasing that little bitch would come to no good. Now that he has her to fool with, he's lost interest in our business. You should have put a stop to it."

"Yes, sure it's easy to lock up a boy of seventeen going to school every day and having a job," Dan replied.

"Enough of your bloody mouth," Joe yelled.

Waving one of his Camels, Tim Moore interjected, "Is there anything we can hold over him, like, force him to do this? You told us he felt guilty after drilling the tinker when you covered up for him."

"Yes," said Dan.

"Well, then, threaten to reveal the tinker shooting unless he goes up there to the seminary and carries out our mission," continued Tim.

"There's an idea," said Joe. "He sure doesn't want his hussy to know he's killed a boy. The body is still there and can be dug up."

"Yes," answered Dan. "And the best part of it is 'twas me that shot the tinker. Mick was out cold from the kickback and thinks he did it."

After bringing in another round of Guinness from the bar, Pat Condon said, "But that will bring trouble with the Gardai to you too, Dan, for hiding the body."

"I'll lie," Dan said, "and put it all on Mick, that he shot the boy and buried him while I was in town. His word against mine."

Pat said, "You'd do this to your own flesh and blood? Blame the killing and hiding the body on your innocent nephew?"

"'The Cause' is everything," Dan insisted.

"But we're really messing about with his mind. He was only a boy, after all," said Pat.

"The devil take his mind," Tim commented.

"It just might work," Dan answered. "He has never said a word about the shooting."

Joe said, "Go ahead and try it on then. We've nothing to lose. Nellie Keyes is up at Roosevelt's and will plant the bag with the gun and the priest's robe. We know the boy has the swimming and shooting skills."

"Dan, you've got to stick it to him," insisted Tim.

Wiping the tan froth of Guinness from his lips with his sleeve, Joe summed up:

"It's all on you, Dan. I warned you about the little wench. Let's finish our pints and head home. We'll pray for your success."

Dan waited a few days to pick his moment. Mick had made them a supper of fried liver with onions and boiled small potatoes, which they had eaten in silence. As Mick rose to make tea, Dan said, "You know, the IRA are going to force you to go up to the seminary and carry out your task."

"How?"

"If you don't go, they'll reveal that you killed that boy," Dan replied. "The Dingle Gardai will dig up the body where I buried it behind the barn."

"But how would they know that—-unless you told them?" Mick said.

"I did," Dan answered.

Mick screamed, "You bloody cold bastard," and heaved the silver kettle at Dan. It bounced off the table, and the spout thumped Dan in the chest, scattering broken dishes and water everywhere. "You'd blackmail me, your own nephew?"

"For The Cause," Dan shouted back.

"Fuck you and fuck The Cause," Mick screamed as he flung himself from the apartment.

Seething, Mick tore east down 57th Street. When he reached 9<sup>th</sup> Avenue, his feet took him north. He wanted to be alone and walk off his fury. He came across St. Paul's Church. Built of gray stone in 1886, its twin towers dominated 9<sup>th</sup> Avenue. Behind the heavy oak doors the church offered solitude and peace, the ceiling of the church painted a deep blue, a representation of the midnight sky. Seeking refuge in its comforting darkness, Mick slid into one of the oak pews, the last of the day's light filtering in through the stained glass windows high above. There were just a few people in church, three old ladies praying their beads and a line of four women and a man waiting for Confession.

Mick rose from his pew and walked to the end of the confession line, a priest sitting in the middle compartment, penitents in the boxes on either side. Mick hadn't been to Confession for four years, ever since killing the intruder. Confession could be a liberating experience, freeing himself from sin, or a harrowing one, if he happened across a stringent priest. Mick had witnessed several times back home a priest loudly ejecting a young penitent from the confessional for not remembering the Act of Contrition.

Mick didn't know what had prompted him to go to Confession. How could he explain to someone he didn't even know—the wooden nameplate above the confessional door said "Father Ryan"—what he had done on a dark night years ago in another country. Uncle Dan had concealed everything. He hadn't even known until an hour ago that Uncle Dan had buried the boy's body behind the shed.

When the wooden door of the confessional creaked open releasing an old lady with a lace covering for her head and a pair of black rosary beads in her hand, Mick was invited into the darkness of the box to replace her.

The priest slid back the wooden grill as Mick knelt

facing him through the cloth covering, the only light coming from behind the man as he sat listening to the penitents. As nervous as he was, a strange thought hit Mick. What do claustrophobics do in the confessional? He had heard stories of penitents rushing from the confessional sobbing and of drunks hauled from the box by a beleaguered priest. Mick began the ancient formula: "Bless me, Father, for I have sinned. Oh Father, I killed a boy."

To Mick's surprise, the voice of Father Ryan was young, and the priest asked softly, "How old were you?"

"Thirteen," Mick answered.

The priest began gently to probe the circumstances of the death, which Mick unfolded easily: the break-in by the tinker youth, his rummaging in the drawer where the revolver lay hidden, the flashing of the candlestick which Mick had mistaken for a knife, the boom of the gun, and the body lying spread-eagled on the floor. As he finished his account, Mick cried, "Oh, Father, I feel so terrible."

"You were a young boy, not yet a man, " the priest consoled Mick. "You were acting in self-defense. That wasn't murder. What did your parents say?"

"I have only my uncle," Mick said, and then recounted the story of his parents' deaths and of his being raised to become an IRA soldier for revenge. Mick continued: "I feel bad, Father, because my uncle covered up the shooting, and we came to this country shortly after," explained Mick.

"I have a lawyer friend who'll help with the self defense," the priest said.

"Father, that would be great. But now my uncle is blackmailing me into an IRA plot, to join the Christian Brothers as a sleeper agent."

The priest gasped: "If there is sin here, it's not yours; it's your uncle's. He has abused your conscience for his own purposes. In Christ's name, I assure you that you've committed no sin. Do you see that?"

"Yes, I understand, but what's so awful is I've lost my faith. I wasn't even sure about coming to confession. I can't understand how a merciful, loving Jesus could rip my parents away from me and then pile this heartache of the boy's death on top of everything else. How can I trust a Jesus who does this to me?" Mick asked.

"How old are you now?" the priest asked.

"Seventeen," Mick answered.

"You're a good man forced to grow up too fast. Don't worry about your faith. That will return. As for the suffering you've endured, Christ knows every minute of it. For now, face up to your uncle. Whatever you decide will be right. Christ loves you personally. Come back soon and we'll talk again. I am giving you no penance, you've committed no sin," the priest said.

"Thanks, Father," Mick said and recited his Act of Contrition.

As he left St. Paul's, Mick felt as if a stone weight had been wrenched from his chest. He would confront Dan and tell Katie. When Mick reached home, his uncle was sleeping. Mick ripped off the blanket and woke him: "Get up, Dan. I've just been to confession at St. Paul's, and the priest told me what I should have known all along. You're the one responsible for concealing the death of that boy, not me."

"You shot him," Uncle Dan replied, still groggy from sleep.

"You covered it up to have a hold over me."

"Sure I was only protecting you from the Gardai," said Dan.

"Bullshit," screamed Mick. "Protecting your own bloody plans."

"Hush now, boy, the whole building will hear you," Dan said.

"I don't care. I confessed everything to the priest, including your IRA blackmail," Mick answered.

"Oh Jesus, what if he tells?" asked Dan.

"He won't. He has the Seal of Confession. Not the same as you a bloody mean gossip like Biddy O'Hearn spilling my secrets to your IRA pals," retorted Mick.

\* \* \*

Mick's revelation called for another meeting of the IRA cell. The four conspirators marched by the main bar of the Harp and Shamrock with its sign "But for whiskey the Irish would rule the world." They sat in the dank back room while Dan explained what Mick had done.

"By Jesus, he's going off the rails altogether on us," Tim Moore said. "First the girl, now the church. The only good thing the priests ever did for us was to invent whiskey. How do we know that priest will keep his gob shut?"

"The Seal of Confession. Every fool knows that," Pat Condon answered.

"Seal, my arse. What if he tells the FBI?" Tim yelled, a glass of Guinness in one hand, a Camel in the other. "Then where will we be?"

"Who is this priest?" asked Joe Murphy.

"He didn't say. Only that it was at St. Paul's last night," answered Dan.

"It should be easy enough to track him down. Whichever of them has night confessions on a Thursday. Pat, you're the religion man. Go nose around St. Paul's and get his name," Joe ordered.

"All right, but then what?" Pat asked.

"We'll send someone round to threaten the bastard and tell us what he knows," said Tim.

"We'd get at the priest if Mick doesn't go the seminary?" asked Dan.

"Jesus, I don't like it, messing with a priest and the Church," replied Pat.

"The Cause," said Joe. "We're doing it for The Cause."

\* \* \*

At their next meeting of the IRA cell, Pat told the group that Mick confessed to a Father Ryan: "He's a young Paulist priest, a Yank, the regular confessor on Thursday evenings."

"Good," Joe said. "Now, Pat, you go to this priest for confession, find out what he knows, and put a fright into him."

"Not me. I won't feck with the Church. Send Tim. It's his idea," said Pat.

"All right, you coward, I'll go," barked Tim. "I'll straighten your Father Ryan out."

\* \* \*

The following Thursday evening, Tim Moore was ready for his role as priest basher, carrying with him to St. Paul's a short-handled blackjack of leather covering a lead weight, not trusting himself to carry a gun. At 240 pounds and over six feet tall, he was an imposing size, used to throwing his weight around, but he wasn't in shape, his most frequent exercise walking to the pubs.

Since his mother's funeral Mass in Dingle forty years ago, Tim hadn't seen the inside of a church, but he adjusted quickly. At the front of the church stood a marble altar with a canopy of gold, twin marble columns on either side. Mounted high on the stone walls were windows of stained glass. Buckets of money wasted on hocus-pocus and superstition, funds the IRA could have used for guns and bombs to kill Brits. The place must have cost a fortune. The church was in semi-darkness with scattered lights from the blue ceiling, a lone red vigil light in honor of the Eucharist on the altar, and four rows of flickering votive candles encased in cups of red glass.

The church was empty except for one old biddy in line for confession rattling her black beads, so devout Tim wanted to punch her. Chewing gum furiously to mitigate the smell of the shots of John Jameson he had thrown down on his way, Tim waited for the priest to pull back the wooden grill: "Bless me, Father. It's been forty years since my last confession."

The priest interrupted him, "Have you drink taken?" The gum hadn't worked.

"It doesn't matter, you little bastard, because I'm really here for your confession. Look here to me. A young man came to you last week with a tale about the IRA. I want to know what he told you," Tim ordered.

Startled, the priest said, "You'd better leave. I'll tell you nothing. The Seal of Confession is sacred."

"Bullshit," yelled Tim, "give it out right now, or I'll pull you out of that box, black dress and all, and beat the bloody hell out of you."

"Do what you will," the priest replied. "I'll not say a word."

Tim burst out of his side of the confessional and lunged for the door knob to the priest's compartment, but Father Ryan was too quick for him, and flicked the lock on to give himself a few seconds to get ready.

Yanking furiously on the doorknob, Tim shouted, "Open this door, or I'll tear the whole feckin thing down."

Father Ryan timed it so that just as Tim was pulling his

hardest, the priest flicked the lock open and Tim shot backwards, landing on the marble floor. The priest was right on top of him, knocking the blackjack from his hand, and shooting hard lefts and rights into Tim's soft belly. Tim had only enough breath to curse: "I'll kill you, Goddamnit!"

Tim's curses and the thuds of the punches attracted the attention of the old vestryman who was cleaning the sacristy, the priest's dressing area, before locking the church for the night. The old man took one look at the struggling men and ran by them to open the church door onto busy 9th Avenue and shouted: "Help! Help! A man's attacking the priest!" A husband and wife about to enter a yellow taxi and the driver ran up the steps to assist.

But the priest needed no help. Grabbing Tim around the neck, he yanked him to his feet, and shoved him through the church doors the vestryman had left open: "Don't you ever come to desecrate the house of God again," he yelled, and pitched him down the stone stairs. Tim bounced once and landed on the pavement surrounded by a crowd of onlookers. Getting up painfully, he hobbled off into the darkness, desperate to avoid the police whose sirens he could hear approaching down 9$^{th}$ Avenue.

* * *

The conspirators met the next evening at the Harp and Shamrock:

"Well, Tim, what did you learn from the thumping you got?" Joe asked.

"It's all right for you to be sarcastic. How was I to know the bastard priest would be the next Joe Louis?"

"According to the papers, you had drink taken," Joe said.

"A lie. Not a drop," Tim replied.

"What next?" Dan asked.

"I'll go again next week, scatter a few shots over his head, and scare the shite out of him," Tim answered.

"No drink, mind," Joe warned. "Shoot a priest and we're all done for."

# Chapter 16

Katie, Mick and Terry Kelleher were sitting on her front stoop watching her sisters play jacks on the sidewalk while little Eddie harassed them.

"Let the girls be and join with Paulie down the street," Katie said to Eddie.

"But he's a dago," Eddie whined.

"Eddie, come here," Katie ordered.

The boy climbed the steps of the stoop, and Katie said, "That's a bad word, making fun of someone's nationality."

"Dad says it," Eddie blurted out.

"It's wrong for him too. Go across and play with Paulie or it's up to bed," Katie told him. Eddie dashed over to Paulie's.

Terry asked, "Did you see the story in the News today? Some thug tried to beat up a priest in the confessional at St. Paul's last night."

"What happened?" Mick asked.

"Some guy tried to yank the priest from the confessional, but the priest was too much for him and tossed him out into the street," Terry explained.

"Wow!" said Katie. "Did the police catch him?"

"They just missed him, and the priest wouldn't say anymore, something about an oath," Terry said.

"The Seal of Confession?" Mick asked.

"Yeah, that's it," said Terry. "A promise priests make when they're ordained to keep confessions secret."

"I know a priest from there, Father Ryan, a nice young guy," Mick said.

"That's him. That's the name of the priest," Terry said. "The paper said he walloped the guy good. Those priests and brothers are all good fighters. They must train them for it in the seminary."

"I don't think so," Katie said laughing.

After Terry had gone home, Mick said to Katie, "That trouble at St. Paul's may have been over me."

"What do you mean?" asked Katie.

"I've been so afraid to tell you about this. I'm pretty sure it's the IRA using a tragedy that I was involved in as a boy." Mick then gave Katie a full account of how he had shot the poor thief, Dan's cover up, his recruitment to be a sleeper agent, and the uproar his confession had caused.

"Why is your uncle behind all this?" asked Katie.

"He's crazy altogether with taking revenge on the Brits, trying to blackmail me into the IRA."

Katie kissed and hugged him, all in full sight of the Widow O'Hearn recording the scene from across the street.

Little Eddie Muldoon stopped running long enough to say to them, "Are you going to have a baby or something? You're always kissing." Without waiting for an answer, Eddie returned to his game with Paulie.

"He sure says interesting things for a little fella," Mick said to a blushing Katie. "God knows, I'd love to put my arms around you and make you part of me."

"Mick," Katie exclaimed as she hugged him, "that's the most romantic thing you've ever said to me."

"I'd love to say a lot more along those lines, but don't want to offend you."

"Well, then, don't. There'll be time enough for that in our future," Katie replied.

"Yes. Getting back to my troubles, I've told Father Ryan the whole story, and he's found a lawyer to help with the accident."

"That's wonderful. You're so young to be dealing with all these problems. I love you, Mick."

"I love you too. You're the best thing that's ever happened to me."

Katie called the kids into the house and sent Mick off with a goodbye kiss. Across the street the Widow O'Hearn was probably sewing the Scarlet Letter that very moment.

# Chapter 17

A week later, Tim was ready for Father Ryan. Often priests would arrive in confession early to pray their breviary as they waited for penitents. With Joe Murphy in his car on West 59<sup>th</sup>, Tim had his escape planned. His blue work overalls concealed the bulky Webley as he sat hunched over close to the side altar of the Sacred Heart.

At 5:30 Father Ryan walked the length of the church to the back and entered the confessional, clicking on the red light that signaled he was open for business. Tim rumbled by two old biddies kneeling in separate pews muttering their beads. As he got near the confessional, over his face he pulled a Lone Ranger mask snatched from a neighbor's kid who had left it on his stoop. Then a tall boy with auburn hair entered the church from 9<sup>th</sup> Avenue and headed straight for the confessional. Mick Slattery. Perfect. Tim ducked behind a stone column. He would scare the shit out of both of them together.

Mick knelt for his confession: "Bless me, father, for I have sinned. It has been two weeks since my last confession."

Boom! Boom! Two shots like cannon bursts filled the emptiness of the church, raining down splinters of red oak and chips of plaster on Mick and the priest from the empty confessional on the other side.

"Get out and stay low," the priest yelled.

Both burst from the confessional diving for cover on the floor behind the nearest pews. On the far side of the church, a thick man in overalls and a mask was limping toward the door. Mick and Father Ryan were ready to give chase when the shooter turned and fired twice more over their heads. The priest yanked Mick down: "Keep low and creep along the wall."

The two of them reached the open door and peeked out just as a black Ford tore west.

"Father, you ok? There's blood on your face," Mick said, shaking the dust and plaster from his hair.

"Scratches from the splinters. They'll wash off," answered Father Ryan.

Breathing hard, the two of them sat side by side in a pew trying to make sense of it all.

Soon the police arrived. "Somebody sure seems to have it in for you, Father," said a tall officer as he swept through the cops setting up yellow tape to mark off a crime scene. "I'm Captain Miller. Please find us a room so we can talk."

The priest led them to a small conference room near the sacristy. While the priest went to a bathroom to wash his cuts and scratches, Captain Miller questioned Mick: "First give me your name and address." When Mick did so, the officer asked him to detail step by step what had happened.

"The gunman was big and overweight, and he could only hobble away like someone on a tear with drink. He wore a black mask. We chased him, but he turned around and fired twice over our heads. He got into a black Ford, which may have been waiting for him."

When the priest returned, the policeman asked him, "Father, was this the same man who attacked you before?"

"I didn't get close enough to see. The man I fought was very heavy, drenched with whisky, with a thick brogue like my mother's. The vestryman mentioned it too."

"But why come after you?" the captain asked.

"I can only think it was something said in confession or the act of a religious nut."

At first the mention of the brogue had rolled over Mick, but then it hit him like a hammer. Without thinking, he had told Dan that he had gone to confession at St. Paul's, only now realizing he had placed this kind priest in the IRA crosshairs.

The police captain noticed that Mick was in a daze: "Mick, you okay? You may be in shock."

"No, Officer. I'll be fine."

"Were you in church the night of the first attack?" the policeman asked Mick.

"No, Sir."

"Father, how soon after the boy's confession was the assault?"

"A week to the day."

"So tonight would be the second week, correct, Father?"

"Yes, I have night confession only on Thursdays."

"And no other priest has been targeted?"

"No, Captain. I would have heard."

"This shooting was premeditated because the gunman fired into the empty confessional, which he knew because the light wasn't on. Then he purposely shot over your heads. We need to find out why he wants to frighten you. For the present both of you be very careful. We'll increase our patrols around the church. I'll interview you again when I learn more. If you think of anything else, here's a card with my number for each of you to call."

When the officer had left, Mick was near tears: "Father,

I brought this on you. I told my uncle that I had gone to confession here. The IRA is behind this and sought you out, wanting to know what I had said in confession."

"Not to worry," the priest assured Mick. "I would never tell; and if it hadn't been me, it would have been some other priest. You couldn't anticipate what your uncle would do. By the way I've talked to a lawyer, an Old Country man, about the tinker's death in Ireland. A good friend of mine, he's volunteered to represent you. He thinks the death would be ruled accidental, but your uncle would have responsibility for covering it up."

"Thanks, Father. That's a right weight off my shoulders."

"What's important now is to say nothing to anyone. Because of the Seal of Confession, I can't relate to the police what you or that thug revealed about the IRA. Keep out of sight for a few days. Then come and see me at the rectory, the back door where there's less chance of being seen. Here's the phone number. We can both think of what to do next. You're a good man. With God's help things will work out."

# Chapter 18

Two nights after the shooting, the conspirators met again. "Slainte, Good Health, God bless us all," Joe intoned as they bounced their emptied shot glasses off the scarred table.

Tim Moore bragged, "I sure scared shite out of the goddamn priest and the boy too. That'll keep him from confession for a while. I'll go and yank off the 'Father Ryan' sign from the confessional, slash a line through the name, and write 'R.I.P.' Dan can bring it home to him and put it on the kitchen table."

"Good idea," said Joe. "But you can't go back there again, Tim. Dan, that will be your job. Lay low for a few days first."

Dan asserted, "We need to guarantee that Mick commence his assignment. We've used the death of the tinker and now the shooting at St. Paul's. The little bastard won't talk to me, so we still don't know if he'll go. We should up the ante and force him."

"How?" Joe asked.

"The girl," Dan replied.

"I warned you about that bitch," Joe shot back.

"Shut it for once, Goddammit. The fool loves her. If he refuses to go, we'll break the girl's legs like those dago thugs. I'll do it myself. We already have the priest to hold over him. She'll be our clincher."

"I like it," said Joe.

"Jesus God," Pat swore. "Cripple an innocent girl?"

Dan retorted, "If the bastard does the job, no harm will befall the priest or her. It's his choice. He's fecked around with us long enough. Just remember it's our arses on the line too--like those six Germans executed in Washington. Do we want to end up like them buried in unmarked graves?"

Pat screamed, "You'd do this to the only child of your dead brother?"

"He's as good as my son. I raised him and schooled him for revenge. That's my life."

"What about his life? You're worse than the dirty English," said Pat. "You put him in the frame for a killing he didn't do and now you threaten a slip of a girl? Your plans are the devil's own."

"He's mine. I'll do what I want with him," Dan retorted.

"Congratulations, Dan. By the time you're done, you'll have destroyed the last of the family—-mother, father, and now son."

Heaving back his chair, Pat swept all the bottles, cigarettes and ashtrays onto the wood floor: "You make me ashamed to be your cousin. I'm through."

To his retreating back, Joe mocked, "Sure you won't turn informer on us now, will you, Pat? You're part of this too."

"I wish to God I'd never laid eyes on any of ye," shouted Pat as he charged from the room.

* * *

116

Mick returned home from school to find on the kitchen table the "Father Ryan" sign scratched through with a screwdriver, the letters "RIP" carved into it.

As soon as Dan came come home from work, Mick grabbed him and flung him against the stove: "You bastards. That was your doing at church. You could have easily killed me or the priest."

"We shot to miss, to scare that priest into keeping his gob shut and for you to join the brothers' seminary. We're safe."

"Not for long. I'm going to Captain Miller and disclose all your plots including the tinker boy. The priest is getting me an Irish lawyer who'll defend me about the accidental death. You were responsible for covering it up."

"Christ, you've done that?"

"Yes, and I'll face whatever consequences I have to, just to be shut of you forever. Fuck your seminary!"

"The boys were right. Warned me you might betray me like this. I didn't believe it."

"Believe it."

"Well, boyo, you've backed us into a corner. Figuring you might do this, we've upped the ante."

"What?"

"If you don't go, we'll slaughter the priest and crush the legs of your girl. Complete your task, they'll be untouched."

Mick smashed Dan in the face, sending him reeling onto the linoleum floor: "Touch a hair of her head, and I'll go and slaughter the lot of you myself."

"September 15th, boyo," Dan groaned from the kitchen floor. "That's the date of your first rendezvous. We'll have a map drawn for you. Mind you be there."

# Chapter 19

The policeman arrived at the Slattery apartment unannounced: "Mr. Slattery, I'm Captain Miller, here to see Mick. That's a nasty bruise you have."

"Run in with some dago on the docks. I'll fetch Mick. He's studying."

As he brought Mick into the kitchen, Dan asked, "Officer, do you want me to stay?"

"No."

After debating with himself whether or not to try to eavesdrop, Dan decided to leave.

Mick and the policeman sat on heavy wooden chairs around the kitchen table.

"Would you care for a sup of tea?" Mick asked, knowing that the ritual would get him out from under the policeman's stare.

"Great."

As Mick was putting the kettle on and getting the milk and sugar, the policeman asked "Have you thought of anything more since that night?"

"No, Officer."

"Can we assume that the shooter was trying to scare Father Ryan and not you?"

"No one's after me."

"No gang from Power or the neighborhood?"

"No, Sir."

Mick poured the tea and sat down and faced the man.

"Good tea," the policeman remarked.

"We use loose tea, not the bags, makes it stronger."

"When the priest mentioned the other evening that the attacker had a brogue, it seemed to throw you."

"I thought I might know the guy from the neighborhood, but I didn't get a close look. He looked like a dockworker right burly. But the man said nothing," Mick answered, absently massaging the bruised knuckles of his right hand.

"Why would someone assault the priest?"

"I don't know, Sir."

"How long have you known Father Ryan?"

"I met him only in confession."

"I'm Catholic, so I know what's said in Confession is sacred, but is there anything you told Father Ryan that could have provoked these attacks?"

"No," Mick lied.

"Did you tell anyone else what you said in confession, like a friend or your uncle?"

"No, Officer," Mick lied again.

"Mick, if you know something that later brings harm to Father Ryan and don't tell me, you're going to feel very, very bad."

Mick said nothing.

"I talked to Father Ryan today, and he appears not to be worried. We added extra men to our patrols of the church."

"Good, he's a kind man," said Mick.

"You have my card in case you think of anything else."

"Yes, Officer."

"Have you seen Father since?"

"No, he told me to call on him at the rectory."

"Good. The two of you together might come up with something. Thanks for the tea."

"Goodbye, Officer," Mick said as he opened the door for the man.

Dan had been pacing up and down at the end of the block near 10th Avenue and rushed home as soon as the policeman had departed: "What did he want?"

"Go ask him yourself."

After going outside, the policeman slipped into the shadows of a brownstone a few houses away. He watched the uncle race home. The uncle and the boy had fought. Why?

\* \* \*

Father Ryan was at a loss at how to counsel Mick. Because his own parents were Old Country, he knew something about the IRA and was surprised at their recklessness, especially in New York where they had always been very quiet.

The priest would have loved to inform Captain Miller about the IRA connection, but knew in his role as confessor that he was on treacherous moral ground. The content of Mick's confession was sacred, excommunication the punishment for the priest breaking his oath.

But at least he had formed a plan to get himself out of harm's way and to liberate Mick from worrying about him.

\* \* \*

The next afternoon Mick called Father Ryan. The priest met Mick by the kitchen door and took him past the industrial-sized black oven flanked by butcher-block cutting boards and a walk-in refrigerator. The priest got them two bottles of Coca-Cola while they talked in a parlor stuffed with plush but aging chairs, the ever-present crucifix hanging on the wall. When they were both settled with their cokes, Mick began:

"Thanks for seeing me, Father. If it's all right with you, I'd like to confess what I'm going to tell you. That way the Seal of Confession will protect you from revealing it."

"Fine," Father Ryan said. "I have a stole for Confession here." The priest draped the purple cloth around his neck while Mick recited the penitential formula: "Bless me, Father, for I have sinned. It has been three weeks since my last confession. You've been good to me, even placing yourself at risk. I only hope that what I'm going to say doesn't put you in more danger."

"It won't, Mick. I'm safe." He smiled, and Mick knew it would be all right.

"I've told my uncle that you've gotten a lawyer to defend me for the shooting of the tinker boy at home, so the IRA can't blackmail me any longer about that. Now they've warned me that they'll kill you and break the legs of my girl Katie if I don't enter the Christian Brothers' seminary."

"Why?"

"To become a sleeper agent for the IRA."

"To do what?"

"Father, this is the most dangerous thing I could tell you. A year from now, the IRA wants me to assassinate some American leader."

"But that's crazy."

"My uncle has prepared me for this all my life. He's mad altogether for this."

"But you'll be captured or killed."

"For my uncle and the IRA, I'm cannon fodder," Mick explained.

"I don't see how you or anyone could ever manage this," said the priest.

"During the novitiate I'll have months to practice swimming the Hudson. The IRA has another sleeper agent for me to meet, with a gun and clothes and details of the mission."

"They're vicious."

"Irish hate is forever," Mick said. "The worst, my own uncle. The attack on you and the shooting could have gone wrong in a thousand ways."

"What if you went to the police?"

"I've thought of it, and the police captain suspects something. But if every member of the IRA cell weren't caught, that would still leave Katie and you at their mercy."

"Mick, I can relieve you of some of your burden. In two weeks I'm going to Rome for a year to study theology. But then you'll be facing them by yourself."

"I'll miss you because you've been so kind to me, but you'll be out of danger," Mick said. "You've helped me to bury the ghost of the tinker boy. I'll have to go up there to keep Katie safe and buy me twelve months to find a way out."

"You're taking so much on yourself, Mick. The novitiate will be difficult for you with a strict schedule of lights out, and they'll keep a close eye on all the novices. And you're going to find it lonely and boring."

"I've got to handle that," Mick said.

"What will you tell your girl?"

"That I'm going to the seminary, but not why. The less she knows, the less danger for her."

"Mick, you're a good, good man."

"Thanks to Katie and to you. Just pray that I can figure a way out of this."

"We'll be in each other's hearts till this is done. I only

wish that I could do more for you."

The two men embraced.

* * *

Mick's departure for the novitiate was less than a month away, and he still had not told Katie. For days he hadn't called her. He owed Katie the respect to tell her personally. He asked her to lunch one day at Horn and Hardart's. Butterflies crowded his stomach, and he knew he wouldn't be able to eat. As soon as they sat down, Katie asked, "What's the matter with you? You're green."

Instead of answering, Mick retched. The dry heaves. He choked twice more, scattering customers close to them. Katie grabbed his hand, and they fled the restaurant to Eighth Avenue where he spat green bile into the street.

"Do you have the flu?" Katie asked.

Mick shook his head "No," but couldn't stop retching foul air. They entered Central Park and found a bench near the statue of Columbus on 59th Street. Mick was finally able to speak: "I have something to tell you."

"What's this? The last-date brush off?"

"No, there's no one nicer than you. In July I'm planning to enter the Christian Brother's novitiate in West Park, New York."

"Become a Christian brother? So that's what has been going on with you lately? Not a call or a word for days. You've been afraid to tell me."

"I didn't want to hurt you."

"Nice try, Mick. You mean you didn't have the guts to face me."

"Oh, Katie."

"What's this really about, Mick? You no more want to be a brother than I do."

"I want to see if I have the call."

"I can save you a trip. You don't."

"But I want to try it out."

"You're lying. For months you tell me you love me, want to hold me and kiss me. That's no sign of a vocation."

"But, Katie, I have to follow my conscience."

"Mick, you have no vocation. What's behind this? The IRA, your uncle, and the St. Paul's shooting?"

As Mick had feared, Katie was spot on, but Mick had to keep up his charade: "I thought someone as religious as you are would understand."

"To use your vocabulary, Mick, 'Bullshit.' I hope you make a better brother than you do a liar."

Katie ran from the park in tears.

In an attack of self- pity, Mick wondered if she would ever know that he was doing this for her, protecting her from his uncle and the IRA bastards.

\* \* \*

When Katie arrived back home, her Mom knew there was trouble because Katie didn't come to kiss her. Instead, trembling and crying, Katie ran into the bedroom she shared with the girls and ripped the "Power Panther" pennant from her wall. "Now he says he's going to be a Christian Brother," she screamed to her mother. "The boy who loved me a month ago."

"Mick a brother?" her mother asked.

"In a few weeks he's leaving for the novitiate up in New York State."

"But, love, if he has the call? Even the Blessed Mother had to give up her own Son."

"Ma, he has no call, he's lying! This all started after the trouble in church, something with the IRA." Katie sobbed into her mother's arms.

"Katie, you know we love you. I have a feeling that life will work out for you both. Why not get a wash before your Da and the kids come home. We'll talk again later."

# Chapter 20

On Sunday, July 1, Mick rose after a sleepless night and got ready to leave for the seminary. Having packed his two cardboard suitcases the night before, he had one piece of business left. He went to his uncle's bed, grabbed him, and lifted him against the wall. "I loved you once as my father, but you've destroyed that. If you lay one finger on Katie, you're dead men, the lot of you. That's a promise," Mick said as he shoved Dan against the wall and left the apartment.

Mick attended Mass in a daze, so lonely he felt like the only man in the world. He prayed that Jesus would allow him to come back to Katie free of murder. A number of young men and their parents were already in front of the school waiting for the bus that would whisk them away to West Park.

"Where's your uncle, lad?" boomed Brother Hendry as he walked over and shook Mick's hand.

"He had to work today, Brother."

"Well, at least I'm here to see you off. It doesn't seem like four years since I first enrolled you, and here you are to become one of our own, having saved other boys from that killer. Mick, I'll say a prayer for your vocation every day." Into Mick's hand, he slipped a medal of St. Patrick. "Now

126

mind that you pray to him every day. He'll take care of you the same as he did me."

Surprised by the tear that leaked from the Irishman's eye, Mick felt his own eyes moisten.

On the outside of the group, Brother Irving was skulking around, and Mick walked up to him: "Thanks, Brother, for your help with Terry Kelleher. His speech has really improved."

"Who will protect the stutterers and other unfortunates from Hell's Kitchen when you've gone, Slattery?"

"None of them will have any trouble from you, Brother, because at any time one of Brother Hendry's card-playing friends could slip word to him of your gambling."

"You little bastard," Brother Irving whispered, "you'll never last in West Park."

"I'm neither little nor a bastard. As to whether or not I'll make it, we'll see. Attend to your own spiritual life."

After all the kisses and farewells, thirty-six young men trooped onto the yellow school bus. The kind words of Brother Hendry and the verbal sparring with Irving had at least distracted Mick from thinking about Katie if only for a few minutes.

# Chapter 21

## Hyde Park, 1942

T he patrol of the Hudson River as a protective measure is ridiculous," President Roosevelt declared to Mike Reilly, Chief of the Secret Service. But Reilly was unconvinced, especially after two German U boat submarines had landed spies on Long Island and on Ponte Vedra, Florida. Four Germans had made their way to New York City with $175,000, American uniforms, bombs and detonators. In all, eight saboteurs were caught, all but two of them electrocuted and buried in unmarked graves in Washington.

# PART III

Brother Mick

# Chapter 22

Sitting on 960 acres in Ulster County's Hudson Valley two hours north of New York, the brothers' novitiate, Santa Maria, had been purchased by the Irish Christian Brothers in 1921. To Mick, who had never been out of New York City since coming to America, the place looked like Kerry with its rolling hills and the green haze of the Catskill Mountains in the distance. His first view of the Hudson, shining like a new dime below, surprised him. The steep angle from the grounds to the river made it seem as if the Hudson was just below his feet, an endless sheet of green. Was he strong enough to make it over and back?

After a short look around, Mick was shown his bed and a place to store his clothes. He bunked in a dormitory with twenty beds, which spanned the width of the second floor. Four smaller bedrooms accommodated four men each. He would find little privacy here, no front stoop on which to chat with Katie and Terry. A bell summoned them all to the chapel for the welcoming talk from the Novice Master, Brother Chapman, the religious in charge.

Once the trophy room of some minor Rockefeller, the building had been converted into a chapel. Built of stone, it lay separate from, and below, the main house. Criss-crossed tiles of black and white marble covered the floor; oak beams traversed the ceiling. There was an odor of sanctity in this residence from the Gilded Age, transformed to train Catholic brothers to teach the poor and middle-class sons of immigrants, people and a religion the former owners had despised.

"Why hast thou come?" the Novice Master intoned. "Look into your hearts for the answer." Mick had intended to dismiss this homily, mentally tuning out the man while wearing a mask of attention on his face. Each of the thirty-six young men pondered the question to discern whether or not he had a vocation, a call from God to serve Him as a Christian Brother. The question jolted Mick into attention. Looking into his heart, he asked himself, "Why have I come?"

Every Sunday morning after Mass, Uncle Dan had taken him to the graves of his parents and reminded him of the tragedy: "Sure, lad, the murdering bastards never gave your ma and da a chance, two innocents. Riddled with bullets just for being there. But you and me will get revenge for them." In his mind's eye Mick saw himself later sprawled out on the grass near their graves, sobbing, while he clutched the yellowing newspaper photo of their bodies congealed in their own blood.

While listening to the Novice Master, Mick fastened on the image of the tinker boy as he lay spread-eagled on the stone floor of the cottage, a candle flickering capriciously. Now here he was a continent away, hidden among these brothers, pretending to be one of them, and pretending at the same time to be an assassin. His act had to be played out for two different audiences: the ruddy-faced Novice Master now preaching to him, and his uncle and the would-be IRA heroes at the Harp and Shamrock.

But what did he want for himself? Surely not to be a celibate Christian Brother. He lived for Katie and a teaching career, free from the yoke of avenging his parents. What would be his mission across the river, less than a mile across the Hudson from this chapel? What if he were captured or killed during one of his practice runs. As each young man left the chapel, the Novice Master shook his hand and introduced himself. Middle-aged, handsome with graying hair and clear blue eyes, this was the man Mick had to fool, no easy task he feared.

\* \* \*

Church law stipulated that the novitiate, the first year of a candidate's training, be a time of immersion in the spiritual life and of withdrawal from the world-—except that they had to write home every Sunday. The Novice Master did the same, sitting with his charges in the classroom. He screened all outgoing and incoming mail, Mick surmising that the censoring was directed at removing love letters from old girl friends, a problem he would not have because Katie was mad at him and would never lower herself to write. For show, Mick wrote a few letters to his uncle, snippets of news about their work and games. To Aunt Elizabeth, he sent messages from his heart.

Father Ryan had warned him that the novitiate would be boring and lonely. The priest had been correct on both counts. They said more prayers than he could ever have imagined. After rising at 5:40, the novices had morning prayers, meditation on some spiritual topic, and Mass, all conducted during The Great Silence, which began after night prayers the previous evening. It was during one of the periods of silence after breakfast that Mick made his first enemy among the novices.

One morning when Mick was putting pans away during cleanup, Ambrose asked, "Mick, where does this big frying pan go?" "Under the bottom drawer of the stove," Mick answered. Vincent, a graduate of the high-school seminary, pounced on Mick: "Hey, we keep the silence here."

"Who put you in charge?" replied Mick.

"Rules are rules even for you backward Irish," Vincent said.

"No one from Brooklyn should call anyone else backward. You talk like you've got a mouthful of rocks. And you're a narrowback with Old Country parents. You should show some respect for your heritage. We're called the Irish Christian Brothers."

"Listen, rookie, you're supposed to use the Great Silence to recall God's presence, not jabber away," Vincent said.

"Sure, isn't that what you're doing right now, jabbering?" Mick retorted.

For the rest of wash-up, Mick feared that the little rat might go running to the Novice Master and report him for breaking the silence.

When the novices were out cutting grass in the cemetery the next afternoon, Vincent came over to inspect Mick's work: "You missed a spot."

"You'd make a right 'informer.' Ask your father what that word means in the Old Country," replied Mick.

"At least my family comes for visiting day, unlike yours," goaded Vincent. This was a sore point for Mick. The Novice Master had asked why his uncle hadn't visited. Mick put him off by telling him his uncle had to work on those Sundays.

\* \* \*

"Mick, you know we don't allow novices to receive pictures of girlfriends," the Novice Master had said, slapping four photos on his desk. Mick stared at the snapshots of Katie in her school uniform, his heart pounding loud enough to hear.

Mick said, "That's a girl I dated before I came here, Katie, but she would never send these. She's a Catholic and understands the seminary rules."

"The pictures are candids. She's oblivious of the photographer. What's this about?" asked the Novice Master.

"Brother, I don't know. I haven't got any friends who would do this for a lark," Mick explained, but he knew exactly who had sent the pictures and why.

The IRA were right eejits, not realizing that all mail was screened by the Novice Master and that young men had been sent home from the novitiate for such an offense, the opposite effect of what they had intended. If they hurt Katie, all bets would be off, and he'd turn The Harp and Shamrock into an abattoir.

"Calm down, Mick," the Novice Master said. "I believe you." Mick knew his face had revealed too much.

* * *

Mick hit a hard line drive between left and center for a double. Robert hit a grounder off the shortstop's glove, and Mick tried to score, but the ball arrived at home ahead of him. Vincent held it in his mitt blocking home. Instead of sliding, Mick lowered his shoulder and crashed into him, knocking the ball loose.

"That's a dirty play," snarled Vincent.

"That's baseball," yelled Mick. "If you don't want to get hit, don't block the plate."

For all his bravado, Mick was suddenly glad that the Novice Master wasn't there. He had already gotten himself noticed when the photos came.

* * *

Mick had honed sharp edges for survival, first in Dingle where he was the only boy at school being raised by someone other than his parents, and later in Hell's Kitchen where he was a "greenhorn." He was quietly aggressive and took no guff as Billy Flaherty had learned when he had pushed Mick on the stairs. But those same qualities that had made Mick street-tough were not suited for a follower of Christ in the Novitiate, and were easily spotted by the Novice Master. Mick knew it, but couldn't stop himself. He seemed adept at making enemies. When the novices took on the "mission monks," those brothers already out teaching, in a basketball game, Mick had undercut Brother De Sales from behind, slamming him to the floor, a needless and dangerous foul.

When the Novice Master told the novices of theTurkey Trot, a Thanksgiving novitiate tradition, Mick practiced for days the four-mile course around the perimeter of the property.

On the day of the race, Mick broke out easily and was leading with less than a mile to go. As he rounded the last turn entering a long chute with thick trees on both sides, he saw Ambrose, his Newfoundland swimming pal. Allowing him to catch up, Mick yelled, "Sorry, Ambrose" and smashed his right elbow into his chest.

Mick thought he had pulled it off when Dominic accosted him after the race: "That was dirty. You won by cheating." Mick was his own worst enemy, fighting with everyone as if that would help him against his real enemies.

That night at recreation, Mick went to Ambrose and apologized: "I was wrong to thump you. You're the real winner of the race." The two shook hands, Ambrose grinning and saying, "Wait until hockey. You're going to need eyes in the back of your head to watch out for me."

\* \* \*

Walking back from the farm one day, Mick met an old brother, tall and bony, whom he knew by name only, Brother Quinn, a retired teacher from the Old Country. The man was out praying on his black rosary beads.

"Brother, I'm Mick Slattery. I haven't met you yet." The two shook hands.

"Is that a brogue I hear?"

"Yes, Brother."

"So you're our Irish novice? There are too many of you to get to know at once, and they keep us old ones up on the third floor away from everything. Where are you from?"

"Ballyristeen, just outside Dingle."

Delighted, Brother Quinn brushed the few graying strands of hair on his bald pate. "I'm from Ballyferriter right near you. Christian Brothers School in Dingle?"

"Yes, Brother."

"Do you miss the Old Country?"

"I do. It's beautiful."

"I've a sibling, a brother also, principal of our school in Limerick. I'm the eldest of eight, the quiet one. Three of my brothers are dead, shot by the Tans, and I had to be away from there. I've always ached to do my bit for The Cause. I have a brother head of the Transport Workers Union in the city and a sister."

"Is Katie Muldoon your niece?"

"Yes."

"She's a lovely colleen. I knew her from the parish. I admire your courage to volunteer for America teaching Yank kids."

"Yes, thirty years at Rice in Harlem, but I haven't lost my Irish."

For a few minutes, the two conversed in Gaelic, the language the British tried to extirpate from the country. Because Kerry was a backwater, the English had their least success there.

"Do you have people over there still?" Brother Quinn asked.

"An aunt and two cousins in Dublin."

"How's the novitiate going?"

"Well enough, but some of the days are boring."

"Just hang on till your first vows. You'll have more freedom then."

"Out for a good walk?"

"Yes, but I'm hoping for some kind brother to run me over to Roosevelt's."

"I'm surprised you'd be a fan of his."

"Indeed I'm not. The man has saved the dirty Brits. I don't want to scandalize you, Mick, but once a year I make a pilgrimage over to pee on his property, my own little way of getting back at him. And if he dies before me, I'll make water on the devil's grave."

Mick burst out laughing: "Brother, you're a man after my own heart. That's the best laugh I've had since I've come here. I've enjoyed meeting you."

"The same here, Mick. God bless."

\* \* \*

The novices went two or three at a time to see the dentist, Dr. Green, a farmer who doubled as a veterinarian.

They would joke among themselves about where the man's hands had worked last, pulling a tooth--or a thorn from some cow's ass. The office of the dentist was an addition to his farmhouse with a small waiting room just outside his surgery.

Jogues was in with the dentist while Mick and Vincent were waiting their turn: "Turkeybird, this the first time you've ever seen a dentist?" needled Vince. "They ought to make false teeth for you as kids. Save them the trouble later."

Mick retorted, "Always stirrin' the pot. I can't believe your parents are Irish, spawning a nasty little runt like you."

Reddening, Vince launched out of his chair: "I'm going to save the dentist some work and take out some of your teeth right now."

Mick said, "Go ahead and try it on."

Just then, Dr. Green popped out of his office, and yelled, "What's the matter with you two? In all my years of treating the brothers, I've never seen this. Fighting in the waiting room! Aren't you religious brothers?"

Blushing, both novices mumbled apologies.

"If you act this way in public, I'd hate to see what you're like back home," the dentist continued.

The two novices had scandalized even an outsider. Mick realized their sparring had spun far out of control.

# Chapter 23

**B**esides the thirty-six young men living in the rambling three story novitiate, several retired brothers lived in their own quarters on the top floor. Every Sunday afternoon in good weather, the older men would make their way down to the wide front porch and tell the stories of their lives. The novices would gather around and listen, especially Mick and Dominic. Brother Angelus, now in his late seventies, still taught college math. He was strict and demanding, but personable and friendly. Brown as a berry, he had a thin halo of white hair caressing his baldhead. He had a severe limp from a broken ankle playing handball in his sixties, but got around with the help of an Irish black thorn stick, actually a wine-red cane with mean spurs topped with a yellow knob. He had a unique style of teaching. Instead of lecturing, he held a mini-conference with every student every class. When the attention of one of his students began to flag, he smashed his cane on the battered teacher's desk.

Of all the aging brothers, Angelus was the one most interested in the novices, especially in their baseball games when he would sit in a lawn chair along the left-field line observing the action. He was the oldest brother on campus and delighted in telling about his early days of teaching: "I was sixteen, a raw rookie sent from Dublin to teach in St. John's, Newfoundland, so cold that icebergs often drifted by. The temperature would drop twenty degrees in an hour. But our people had emigrated there and we brothers followed. My first year I taught Grade 2, eighty-three boys tumbling out of their seats like puppies. Their parents and grandparents were survivors of the famine. Some of them even spoke Irish. After school we supervised hockey games. I fell in love with the sport myself."

Mick asked, "How did you control so many kids, a strap or a ruler?"

"Neither. The eyes. It's all in the eyes," responded old Irishman. "Edmund Rice, the founder of the brothers, had two hundred boys the first year he started. From the streets of Waterford, Edmund collected these poor wild kids denied an education by the English and rented a barn and hired two teachers to help him, but they quit."

Dominic asked, "How did he survive?"

"He finally got two volunteers who stayed. He used his own money from his business as a ship's chandler or supplier to build Mt. Sion School." The Brothers' schools were so crowded that Edmund adapted what was called the Lancasterian method of instruction in which classes were broken into sections supervised by monitors, themselves under the guidance of a master teacher. At Mount Sion in Waterford, Edmund's first school, the brothers taught religion, spelling, reading, and arithmetic to the younger boys; bookkeeping, writing, navigation, and other practical subjects to the older students. With a bakery for feeding the boys and a tailor shop for clothing them, Mt. Sion was self-sufficient and became a model for the new schools founded by the brothers.

After the Diaspora created by the Famine, the Irish Christian Brothers followed emigrant Irishmen to England,

Australia, America, as well as Newfoundland.

"I thought Catholic schools were outlawed in Ireland," Dominic said.

"They were. In 1829 The Duke of Wellington had told Edmund his schools would be closed because they were illegal. But the Penal Laws against Catholic schools were finally repealed in 1832,"explained Brother Angelus.

"How did Edmund himself get an education?" asked Mick.

"His mother, even though a parent was forbidden to teach her own child," replied Angelus. "Then hedge schools, illegal schools held outdoors in the country, the teacher and students hidden behind thorn bushes or hedges."

Dominic asked, "Any Protestant schools?"

"Yes, Church of England, but Catholics had to convert to attend them," Brother Angelus replied. "Those who converted were rewarded by being made landlords. They became known as the Protestant Ascendancy. And the Quakers set up a school in Clonmel, so the vast majority of Catholics received no education."

As time passed, Mick found himself getting more and more interested in Brother Angelus. Mick had gotten off to a bad start in math class with the old man when he had been reprimanded for giggling, but the incident was soon forgotten and Mick was grateful. The old brother held no grudges. Mick began to notice small things about the old man. He was always first in chapel each morning despite his limp. Leaning his black thorn stick against the end of his pew, he squirmed over to the corner against the wall and began praying: "My Jesus, mercy" and "O Sacred Heart of Jesus, I place all my trust in Thee." These short prayers were called "aspirations" and though silent, were often whispered loud enough to be heard by the other brothers. Occasionally, the old man uttered a deep moan as if wrestling with God about some inner pain, unaware that the sound carried. When community prayer began, the old brother would enter into it fully, his private prayer postponed until after Mass.

\* \* \*

One Sunday afternoon the older brothers were again gathered on the front porch, the novices absorbing their every word. Dominic asked Brother Quinn, "Why is there so little knowledge of The Great Famine? I never heard about it from my grandparents or the brothers at school."

"Denial," Brother Quinn said. "It was so awful the Irish wanted to deny it happened and the English denied their role in it. The English thought us savages, life unworthy of life. During the famine a writer for the <u>Edinburgh Review</u> blamed the disaster on us: "the heedlessness and indolence of the Irish has brought [the famine] on themselves."

Brother Theodore, a Canadian, interjected, "The man was right. It was their own fault for relying on one crop."

Brother Quinn explained, "From 1841-1845 a million of us died, starved in our own country or infected by typhus and cholera either here or on the famine ships, rotting hulks once used by the English as slave ships. The <u>London Times</u> rejoiced at our fate: 'An Irishman in Connemara will soon be as rare a sight as a red Indian on the shores of Manhattan.' Sure, a hundred years earlier the Protestant priest Jonathan Swift in 'A Modest Proposal' wrote that 'half of the revenues of Ireland were taken out of the country and spent in England.' Absentee English landlords, some of them members of parliament, received grain, barley, oats, butter, cows and pigs while the Irish starved."

Brother Theodore, a Canadian, objected: "'Twas their

own fault for relying on one crop."

"Their other crops were snatched away by the English," Brother Quinn retorted. "The rest of Europe suffered the potato blight but only Ireland had the famine. Where do you think Irish calves, butter, grain, wheat, oats and barley went? In ships protected by soldiers to England for rent to the landlords while a million of us died and another million fled the country. For poor Irish farmers the potato was their crop of subsistence. Even during the famine years Ireland was a net exporter of food. Every ship bearing grain into the country passed by six going out. One of every four Irishmen died to feed the English. Some villages used one coffin to bury all the dead, a 'drop lid' coffin with a hinge of the bottom to release the body into the grave."

"Now wait a minute," exhorted Brother Theodore. "Many Irish middle class survived and did little for their countrymen. Also, the English set up workhouses to help the poor. There were 130 of them by 1845."

"Have you seen those workhouses, Brother Theodore? I have. They were houses of death. One quarter of Irish deaths in the famine took place in the workhouses. Families were torn apart, fathers, mothers and children living in a separate area. Men breaking rocks and women knitting for twelve hours a day for two meals of stirabout, a soup made of ground Indian maize. And then Charles Trevelyan, the Englishman in charge of famine relief, and Prime Minster John Russell halted even that under the economic policy of laissez-faire, that is, keep the status quo. If the Irish have to starve to feed England, so be it."

"What did you Irish bring to Canada? Cholera and Typhus. Infected a beautiful island three miles long, a mile wide, just thirty miles east and down river of Quebec," Brother Theodore retorted. "You brought typhus to Quebec and Montreal, killing priests, doctors, and nuns. Tell me this. For all your talk of famine, were any of you Irish brothers ever personally affected by the famine and quarantine?"

Unusual for him, Brother Angelus had remained silent during this exchange, but no longer. He turned blood red and two tears to which he gave no notice leaked down his leathery face. "When the ships were quarantined at Grosse Isle for weeks for health inspection by Doctor Douglas, the chief surgeon, people previously healthy contracted typhus. Some were sent to hospitals, others lived rough in tents and lean-to shacks on shore. But many had to stay on board because there was no room for them on the island."

"Thousands spread the disease to each other in the holds. No one would carry out the bodies of the dead from the ships because of fear of infection. Several priests, doctors and nurses had already died. A giant fishhook impaled the bodies of one couple from the Viginius intertwined in death while a kind priest held back their ten-year-old son from touching his infected parents. Lifted by a winch against the gray sky above the gray water, the bodies of the boy's parents were dumped into a wooden horse-drawn cart and driven to a mass grave. Imagine the poor lad seeing his parents naked, gaffed like fish, and then dropped into a mass grave a half-mile away."

"Like thousands of others, the couple had been evicted from their small farm in Connemara and carried off in a coffin ship, an overcrowded rotting hulk, a former slaver. Already starving, the poor souls drank water and ate food contaminated by human feces. Many had already died at sea on the crossing, perhaps as many as 20,000, and their bodies dumped into the Atlantic. Between twenty and thirty thousand Irish are buried in mass graves at Grosse Isle, among them the parents of this boy. That day he and the priest were the only mourners."

"All on his own, the child managed to catch a job working on a timber ship to Liverpool, made his way back to Connemara, and raised a family. I was his oldest son and still remember the screams he made in nightmares about my grandparents speared like fish and now lying in an anonymous grave in Grosse Isle."

The old brother had given this account as if in a trance, and his audience listened with a reverential silence. Head held high, leaning on his black thorn stick, Brother Angelus struggled to his feet and moved off towards the chapel, unashamedly bearing the tears still glistening on his cheeks.

# Chapter 24

Dominic awoke in the dorm slightly fevered and sweating as he had so often lately. Walking to the bathroom, he glanced out the window into the darkness and saw someone flash by outside, making his way from the house. It was Mick. Where would he be going this hour of the night? Novitiate lore held stories of novices seeking a beer at Bennie's, a tavern down 9W, but Dominic couldn't believe Mick so desperate for a beer.

He watched Mick's flashlight disappear and then reappear, flickering on the path that led to the Hudson. Dominic went cold with fear. Should he go after him, or go and get the Novice Master?

\* \* \*

Mick had memorized the map Dan had given him. The blackness of the river seemed to stretch forever. He slid into the Hudson from the wooden deck, guided by the running lights of a Panamanian oil tanker anchored a few hundred yards away. The water temperature was still in the sixties, even at night, but he had to set off diagonally across the river towards Hyde Park to allow for the tides.

Using his long windmill stroke, Mick sliced through the

water, glancing up occasionally to keep focused on the lights of the Hyde Park railway station on the east side of the Hudson.

The Hudson was an estuary, an arm of the Atlantic Ocean extending inland to meet the mouth of the river flowing from Lake Tear of the Clouds in the Adirondack Mountains in the north, the land a drowned valley. The water was smoother here in the mid-Hudson Valley than it had been in Dingle Bay. From all his practice in the old country, Mick had learned to breathe away from the currents and swells, lifting his head for navigation.

When he neared the eastern bank, Mick turned south for a short distance until he reached the shore. Putting on the sneakers that he had tied around his neck, he clambered up the steep bank of stones and cinders and crossed over the New York Central tracks. It was a mile and a half curling through the woods to the site of his meeting. As Mick made his way east through the trees and wetlands, he stepped softly, staying close to tall bushes for cover.

After fifteen minutes, he reached the brown boulder at the edge of the Mill Pond, just as it had been drawn on the map. Scraping away dirt and leaves, Mick uncovered a blue bag lined with plastic. Inside were pants, shoes, a priest's cassock, and a Webley revolver covered in oilcloth. As he held it, a shiver ran up and down his spine. Repacking the bag, Mick covered it with dirt and foliage.

# Chapter 25

So you're the one. So young," the voice of a middle-aged woman speaking with a brogue spoke from the shadows. She wore her blue-gray hair tied in a bun on the back of her head. "Ten years younger than my Tom. How did they get a lad like you stuck into this?" she asked.

"Miss, are you the lady I'm to meet for my mission?" Mick asked.

"Mission? Is that what they're calling it? Shooting the leader of the free world," said the lady.

"What, Miss?"

"You mean the devils didn't tell you?" asked the woman.

"No, they told me to meet you here," answered Mick.

"You're a quarter mile from President Roosevelt's, lad."

"Oh, Lord, no," replied Mick.

"Sending a lamb to do this. And you're Old Country, not a Yank. They're mad altogether. Not to be worried today, lad. There's no military police or Secret Service around with the Old Man away for two weeks in Warm Springs."

"Who are you, Miss?" Mick asked.

"Have you heard of Thomas Ashe?"

149

"Yes, Miss, one of the martyrs for The Cause, from Lispole, just a few miles from us in Ballyristeen. The Brits punctured his lung force-feeding him during his hunger strike. His picture hung on our wall all my life."

The lady nodded approvingly: "Well, you know your man. That bag you're trying to hide, 'twas I who put it there—-for Thomas Ashe. I hope it won't mean a death sentence for me some day, or for you."

"What do you mean, Miss?" Mick asked.

"Don't be play acting with me. They wouldn't send an eejit up here. This isn't a game we're playing. 'Twas the Old Man himself behind the executions of those six German spies. You'll need to be sharper, lad, if an old woman like me can come upon you so unawares," said the lady.

"Oh God," Mick moaned. "I should have sussed it out for myself."

"By the way there's one of them over there watching your every move. Religious indeed! God bless," the woman said, returning to the path towards the house.

"But what's your name?" Mick asked.

With a wave of her cigarette, the woman dismissed his question and kept walking.

Mick retraced his steps back to the river for the return swim. The mystery lady was right. She had caught him napping, maybe because he had been distracted by the contents of the bag. Her warning had been stark: Death for them both. He had until August for his mission, not quite a year.

As he swam back over the river, the tanker was still swaying gently in the breeze, its lights leading him to the dock. He was tired, but the danger wasn't over. He still had to go back up the hill and sneak into the novitiate under the nose of Brother Light, the cook, prowling the place like a cat at all hours of the night, and the Novice Master who seemed to know everything. On the third floor where the retired brothers lived, there was a light in a corner window, but Mick could see no one.

He thought he had made it when a voice from the shadows of the washroom whispered, "Where have you been? I saw you leave."

"I went for a swim, Dominic. Get to bed," Mick said. "I'll talk to you tomorrow."

Would Dominic go running off to the Novice Master?

\* \* \*

From the corner room on the third floor, there was a phone call made: "Joe, it's me. The boy made the trip and is back. An hour and a quarter for the whole thing."

"Good work. Keep your eyes peeled. God Bless."

\* \* \*

The next day just before lunch, the Novice Master approached Mick as he came out of chapel: "Mick, let's take a walk."

"Yes, Brother," Mick replied, terrified that someone had seen him sneaking out the previous night.

As they walked past the Brothers' cemetery, the Novice Master said, "Mick, you seem preoccupied, worried, always a frown on your face."

"Brother, I'm having trouble with my faith. I'm not sure Jesus dwells in the Blessed Sacrament. I receive Communion and wonder if anybody's there. Sometimes I don't even believe He exists."

"A crisis of faith comes at a time when your own personal life is in trouble, like deciding whether or not to take vows in the fall. Did those pictures of the girl bother you?"

"Yes, Brother, as memories of home. But it's more than that. I ask myself how a gentle, loving Jesus, could allow my parents to be killed and Tom Beasley shot down in front of me at Power. And then when I come up here, I look off at night and see Mattewan Hospital lit up. That's where Tom's killer is, as if I needed a reminder."

As they approached the large statue of Christ the King guarding the cemetery, His arms stretched out to embrace the world, the Novice Master consoled Mick: "I have no answer to explain why you're suffering, but I do know you are trying hard. Christ knows it too. You're going through a trial of faith. Christ loves you personally and will help you through this. It's like walking through a fog and then you reach the end."

They walked back to the novitiate for lunch, the conversation releasing some of Mick's tension. He had felt guilty and ashamed about his lack of faith. Now he had admitted it to the Novice Master, and the man had understood.

* * *

Each novice had a daily "charge," or job. Dominic's was to clean the room of Brother Angelus, one of the retired brothers living on the third floor of the novitiate. As he was dusting, Dominic heard one side of a phone conversation from next door. The speaker was overly loud, perhaps from deafness, and had a brogue:

"The first trip he left about 11:00 and returned a little past midnight. He sneaks out and returns by the back door of the kitchen."

"No, no one else, only Mick."

"The Novice Master. If he caught him, he'd punish him or send him home."

"I will, Joe. God bless. It's all for the IRA."

The call ended with Dominic trying to piece the conversation together. "The first trip" perhaps referred to Mick's crossing the river when Dominic caught him coming back. But to whom was the brother reporting and why? The next day Dominic would learn the name of the brother.

That evening at recreation Dominic asked Mick, "What's going on with you sneaking out at night?"

"Pipe down, will you? This is between you and me. When we get some time alone, I'll explain."

# Chapter 26

At the beginning of supper during silence, the religious custom was for one of the novices to read the Martyrology, a summary of the sufferings of the martyrs who had died on that date in history. On this night, Lane was reading when a visiting priest, late and not wanting to disturb the silence, crept across the room towards the faculty table. With a shock of blown white hair, the priest took mincing baby steps, like an electrified white mouse tiptoeing around a cat. His appearance prompted smothered giggles among the novices anxious for a laugh, especially during silence. Stammering slightly and focused on the page, Lane did not see the priest and assumed the laughter was being directed at him. "Goddamnit," he yelled, and flung the heavy book to the floor. He ran from the room, slamming the heavy oak doors of the refectory behind him. All were paralyzed, except for the Novice Master, who raced after him.

The next day Lane was gone, whisked home to New York by the Novice Master, driven home before the rest of the novices even rose for morning prayers. The young man departing had been enjoined by the Novice Master to tell no one, as if he had committed some sin. Lane had simply disappeared. What a strange attitude, to pretend like no novice ever left, as if he had an infection that might spread. In such an insular system this attitude was cultivated to preserve the institution by making it harder to abandon it. The sacred Christian tenet of freedom of conscience, like Thomas More's refusal to obey king rather than God, counted for little.

Discussing Lane's breakdown later, Mick and Dominic tried to make sense of it:

"He was nervous and high-strung, Mick, but he was friendly and good-natured."

"He must have bottled his feelings up to explode the way he did. The Novice Master and Berchmans took turns watching him all night. Probably afraid he'd top himself. What will become of him, Dominic?"

"His parents may have to put him in a psychiatric hospital, what a shock to them."

"All because a silly-looking old priest sneaked through the refectory and started the giggles in us?" Mick asked. "It doesn't make sense."

"He must have a history we don't know about. I liked Lane, Mick. He was forever chewing his fingernails, but I had no idea he was so troubled."

"Me neither. It's scary," said Mick.

After Lane's blowup, Mick worried about himself, the tensions of pretending to be what he was not and the constant nagging of Vincent. Would Mick crack up too or lose it and someday wallop Vincent his nemesis, putting Katie at risk by getting himself thrown out?

# Chapter 27

B rother, I'm Jim Kozicki and this is Bill Stone, my assistant. We're Secret Service agents guarding the President in Hyde Park, and we have some questions."

Showing their credentials, Mr. Kozicki continued, "Brother, we're worried about spies, especially after the capture of those Germans dropped from U Boats off Long Island and Florida. They had $175,000 and may have been planning at attempt on the President's life up here. Also, there are rumors about one-man pocket submarines coming up the Hudson and landing near Hyde Park."

"How can we help?" asked the Novice Master.

"We'd like to interview any foreign nationals among the young men for a background check," said Mr. Kozicki. "Do you have any living here?"

"Yes, three Canadians and an Irishman. There are also five older brothers, in their seventies, from Ireland, who are on our faculty," said the Novice Master.

"We wish to speak to only the young men," Mr. Kozicki said. "But our first concern is that every morning for months we've been seeing a car with its headlights on coming down this road and crossing 9W. Because you're almost directly across from Hyde Park, it's been worrying us."

Thinking a minute, the Novice Master said, "At 6:30 every morning, Brother Light drives Father Barry down from here to say Mass for the high-school seminarians below Road 9W. It could be those lights you see. If you wish to confirm this, you could join Father Barry and Brother Light in the dining room right now for a cup of coffee."

"Thanks, Brother, we'd like that," Mr. Kozicki replied.

Ever starved for news, the novices spread the word about the Secret Service agents within minutes, jolting Mick who had swum the river only two nights before. Maybe somebody had seen him.

"It's something about spies and foreigners," Vincent said. "Those Germans probably got them worried."

When the Novice Master brought the two men into the dining room, bile rose in Mick's throat, the acid burning his gorge. They walked straight to his table but continued past him to sit with Father Barry and Brother Light. The Novice Master introduced them all, and Mr. Kozicki explained, "Every morning from the President's house, we see headlights coming from here down to the main road. We're afraid of an attack on the President from this side of the river."

Father Barry said, "Brother Light drives me down every day at 6:30 from here to the high-school seminary below 9W. The driveway is semi-circular followed by a sharp left on the other side. It could be our headlights you see."

"That explains it," replied Mr. Kozicki, "and sets our mind at ease."

Then Mr. Kozicki was to interview Ambrose from Newfoundland, Canada, while his colleague, Mr. Stone, questioned Mick. Mick could see Vincent smirking in the corner, and Dominic's face looked tight and fearful. Mr. Stone followed Mick into a small parlor, the agent flinging his black briefcase on the round table in the middle of the room. Sunlight filtered in through the Venetian blinds. Four hardback wooden chairs surrounded the table, the oak floor polished to a sheen.

Stone asked, "Ready for a grilling, Brother?"

Mick didn't know what to say as the agent pulled a form from his briefcase and shoved it in front of him:

"Brother, please state your full name, place and date of birth."

Mick did so.

"How long have you been in the United States?" Mr. Stone asked.

"Five years," Mick replied.

"Before you joined the brothers, how were you supported?" Mr. Stone asked.

"My Uncle Dan is a dockworker in New York. He brought me here from Ireland," Mick replied.

"Is he Red, a Commie? The dockworkers' union stinks with them," Mr. Stone said.

"No."

"Parents?" the agent asked.

"They're deceased."

"How did they die?"

"Killed in a train accident in Dublin when I was a baby."

"Why did you and your uncle come to America?"

"Better education, more chances for a job."

"Do you like it here?"

"Yes, Sir."

"Damn right, the good old U.S. of A., better than living in the muck and mire over there. Now let's cut to the chase. Have you or any members of your family ever been members of the Communist Party, the Nazis, the IRA, or any other subversive organization?"

"No," Mick lied.

"Aw, now, Brother, with a brogue as thick as yours, you can't expect me to believe the IRA boyos never recruited you."

Mick drew back but said nothing.

"Do you have allegiance to any foreign government or power?"

"No."

"Really, No Sinn Fein——"Ourselves Alone"——no shamrocks popping out of your ass?"

Mick didn't reply.

"If asked to defend the United States of America in time of war, would you be willing to do so, aside from your religious exemption, that is?"

Before Mick could reply, Mr. Stone continued, "That religion thing saves a lot of your asses, doesn't it? Better in here poncing around in a black dress than having the Germans or Japs taking potshots at you."

"Look here to me, Mr. Stone. What war did you serve in?" Mick asked. The man turned pale.

"I thought so," Mick said. "Aren't you the lucky one then to go parading around in a suit and tie and driving your big car rather than getting shot at in Italy or the Philippines?"

"Listen, wise guy, collar or no collar, I can make trouble for you," Stone asserted.

"And I for you. You're only second in command here trying to push your weight around. I wonder what your boss and the Novice Master will have to say about your insults," Mick fired back.

Stone responded, "Your word against mine, Irish punk. Whom do you think they'll believe?"

"Let's find out," Mick said.

Sweeping Stone's briefcase to the floor, Mick walked out to Mr. Kozicki and the Novice Master who were chatting by the front door.

"Mr. Kozicki, Brother, Mr. Stone has been kind enough to point out to me how lucky we brothers are to be able to wear a black dress and not have to fight in the war because of our 4 D religious classification."

Bright roses sprang into the Novice Master's cheeks, and Mr. Kozicki glared at his partner.

"Now just a minute," Mr. Stone said. "I didn't mean that seriously, just as a manner of speaking."

"How did you mean it?" asked the Novice Master.

"Well, that a young man was lucky to be a religious here rather than a soldier in the front line," said Mr. Stone.

"There's no luck involved," the Novice Master answered. "A man chooses to work, study, and pray to become a Christian Brother. And the community opts to accept or reject him. What do you think happens when a young man leaves? By law we notify his draft board immediately of his changed status, and often he's right into the war. I am offended by your remarks, Mr. Stone. This is a house of religious, not draft-dodgers."

"Brother, thanks much for your time and hospitality," Mr. Kozicki hastened to interpose. "You've been most kind. Goodbye."

After the two agents left, the Novice Master said to Mick, "I'm glad you stood up for yourself—-and for us."

That afternoon as he worked by himself to clear the railroad underpass of broken glass and rocks, Mick had time to reflect on the visit from the Secret Service. He had done well to be aggressive with Stone. Thank God the Novice Master had supported him.

But Mick was worried about the lie that Uncle Dan wasn't IRA. Also, Mick had covered up the murder of his parents, telling Stone their deaths were accidental, so that there would be no suspicion of a motive for revenge.

# Chapter 28

Captain Miller realized that the key to the incidents at St. Paul was the boy and his uncle. There had been no more trouble since the summer. Except for the Cardinal, who had summoned Police Commissioner Dolan to his residence for failing to solve the case. In his turn, the commissioner called Captain Miller downtown to his office.

Dolan had survived the cross fire between the mayor's administration and the police for fifteen years. A horseshoe of gray hair crowned his head, a contrast with his red face. On the knotty-pine paneling of his office, a gaggle of official photographs showed a smiling commissioner with President Roosevelt in an open car during a parade and other pictures with several New York mayors. Almost hidden by the other photos was one of Dolan with J. Edgar Hoover faking a smile, looking like a stuffed frog with his protruding reptilian eyes. The Police Commissioner looked like he was about to have his pocket picked.

Dolan knew and trusted Captain Miller: "Charlie, the Cardinal called me to his residence for the official iron glove treatment: 'No city in the world has had its priests attacked. In public too. Your department is a disgrace. Find the criminals—and soon.' These worry lines on my puss

161

are well earned, believe me. The old bastard treated me like crap, didn't even offer me a cup of coffee while flaying me. He called the mayor, too, just to make sure I got the message. What do you actually have on this St. Paul's thing? By the way, do you want a cup of coffee?"

Captain Miller chuckled, "No thanks, Chief. We have no solid proof, but there might be IRA involvement.

"Something's wrong between the Slattery kid and his uncle, whom we think is IRA. I can press the uncle and go see the boy in the seminary; but if we confront those Irish bastards without proof, they'll only stonewall us."

"Yeah, you're right," Dolan commented.

"Because the priest wouldn't break the Seal of Confession, we could get nothing out of him. And now he's moved to Rome. The Irish boy, Mick Slattery, up and joined the Christian Brother's novitiate just after the shooting, and he never said a word to me about it."

"Charlie, I know this thing is a pain in the ass.

Thank God there's been no more trouble. Meanwhile, I'll inform the Cardinal about the IRA. That's a can of worms for him too—-his Irish constituency. At least it'll get him off our backs for a while."

\* \* \*

The policeman decided to question Mick's uncle at his apartment after he got home from the docks. With the days getting shorter at the end of September, the kids playing outside felt a greater sense of urgency. As he walked down the four blocks to the Slattery flat, he came across a game of street hockey just in front. Two red plastic traffic cones marked the goals at either end of the "rink," twelve boys slashing away at a puck coated with black electrical tape. The tall blond figure in full uniform caused play to halt momentarily for gawking.

As play resumed, two stick-handlers hit the puck from opposite sides, and it floated high above the sidewalk where the policeman snagged it out of the air. Mimicking a professional referee, he walked into the street with the puck in his hand, motioning a player from each side for the face-off. The kids played along, and he flung the puck between the two skaters and scurried out of the way.

The vestibule of the Slattery brownstone was open, so the policeman walked up to the door and knocked, leaving his quarry less time to prepare himself:

"Who is it?" the uncle asked.

"Captain Miller, Police."

The uncle opened the door as surprised by the visit as the policeman had hoped.

"I'm sorry, Officer, but Mick is gone, off to join the Brothers' seminary upstate."

"I know, Sir. It's you I've come to see."

Dan led the officer to a kitchen chair, first having to clear away a plate with bacon and charred toast and a tea cup stained a dusty rose: "I don't see how I can help you, Captain."

The kitchen was a mess. Crusty dishes battled for space in the sink, and pages from The Irish Echo covered the other chairs.

"Just a few questions, Mr. Slattery. Wasn't your nephew's departure for the seminary rather sudden, just after the trouble at St. Paul's? He didn't tell me he would be leaving when I saw him last."

"I suppose. But he's of age and didn't give me much warning either. Sure, I couldn't stand in the way of his call."

"Of course. As a Catholic I understand. It's just that the two of you weren't getting on well."

Dan flushed, his face bright under his salt and pepper hair, "I don't know how you can say that."

"The two of you had been fighting. Mick's knuckles were bruised and your face marked up."

"I'm not sure about his knuckles, maybe from playing street hockey. I had a bit of trouble with a dago on the docks as I told you. Nothing special."

"Mick and you never came to blows?"

"God, no. I'm his uncle, sure."

"Have you been to the seminary to visit the boy?"

"Not yet, they have rules about that."

"Has he written you?"

"A few times, Officer. I've thrown the letters away. What's this all about?"

"Still investigating the attempted beating and shooting at St. Paul's this summer. It all stopped when the priest was transferred and Mick went to the seminary. Are you a member of the IRA, Mr. Slattery?"

"In the Old Country we all were, but not here," Dan lied. "I know some of them in the tavern."

"Which one?"

"Not to inform against anyone, but the Cork and Kerry."

"Well, enough of your time, Mr. Slattery. I'll be questioning your nephew up at his seminary. Do you have his address?"

After much fumbling about, the uncle read off, "Christian Brothers Novitiate, West Park, New York."

"Do you have a phone number for him?" The policeman asked as he wrote the address in a black notebook.

"No, but the brothers at Power must have one."

"Thanks, Mr. Slattery."

When the policeman left the building, the hockey game

was still raging. He walked down the block and ducked behind the stoop of a nearby brownstone, his patience rewarded when the uncle raced from his apartment and headed toward 10th Avenue, the quickest route to the Harp and Shamrock.

# Chapter 29

D ominic wondered if he was meant for the novitiate, more physical than religious. Thin, almost cadaverous, he had to endure digging ditches and sawing down trees and mandatory sports like baseball, football, soccer, and basketball. He bruised easily, was frequently out of breath, and had the night sweats. He had come all the way from Chicago for this.

The Novice Master was assigning jobs for the afternoon: "Dominic and Mick, go cut down that overgrown bunch of pine trees to the south of the cemetery." Armed with ax, saw, and rakes, the two novices headed for the trees.

Outwardly hesitant and shy, Dominic concealed the fire burning within: he ached to become a full-fledged Christian Brother.

"These trees are so dirty with gluey sap," Mick remarked. "They won't cut easily."

"Full of cobwebs, too," Dominic replied.

They first had to cut down the large branches to get at the trunks.

"Do they have pines in Ireland?" Dominic asked.

"Some, and Sitka spruce" said Mick. "The Tudor armies cut down the hardwoods—-oak, maple, and the rest——to use for themselves as ship's timbers, barrel staves, and charcoal, with the added benefit of stripping Irish rebels of their cover."

"Terrible," said Dominic.

"Right devils, Cromwell and his armies left Ireland the least wooded nation in Europe. With the trees went deer, wild boar, and wolves," added Mick.

"I remember my grandparents telling me the land in the middle of the country, like Limerick where they were from, was rich farmland."

"Good for growing wheat and cattle grazing, like here in New York State," responded Mick. "We had a couple of cows in Ballyristeen, but the land is rocky, more suitable for sheep."

"Do you miss your mother and father even more being away from your own home?" Dominic asked.

"No. In a way now it's easier, not having my uncle with me every hour of the day to remind me of their deaths," Mick replied.

"In our family we have a terrible problem. My mother is an alcoholic," said Dominic. "What they call a 'sneaker,' burying bottles in kitchen drawers and other odd places."

"How do you know?"

"My brother and I would smell whiskey on her when we came home from school. I even think part of the reason I came here was to escape her drinking. Then I feel bad that I left my father and little brother to face it alone."

"Does your father know?"

"Yes, but pretends not to. He won't touch a drop himself," Dominic said. "I tried to talk to her about it a few times myself when we were alone, but she became guilty and hysterical."

"Ireland's a nation of alcoholics, you know. I bet it's in your mom's family too. We Irish even talk of alcohol in capital letters——"The Drink."

"You're right, Mick. Some of my uncles and cousins are drunks."

The two continued to saw off and rake up branches. "I often think about The Drink with these brothers. The Novice Master never discusses it," Mick said. "We had a great math teacher and track coach at Power, Brother Edmund. And we could smell whiskey on him during school. He was very good to us, but was so lonely."

Dominic said, "I don't know what made me think of it, but when my brother Dennis didn't get accepted into Leo High School because he had failed the entrance test, things in my home were awful. He was beside himself, crying, swearing, and running through the house. Then my Mom talked to some of the Old Country biddies who gave her a solution."

"What?" Mick asked.

Dominic laughed: "I was to bring up a card with $10 and a bottle of John Jameson whiskey to my homeroom teacher, Brother Ailbe, an old Irishman who doubled as Vice Principal."

"Weren't you embarrassed bringing a bottle to school?" asked Mick.

"Mortified. But my mother made me," Dominic explained. "I had to bring the bottle on the bus in a brown paper bag and hide it in my desk when we went for First Friday Mass. I kept imagining the round bottle rolling out of the desk and exploding on the floor. As soon as Mass was over, I bolted upstairs, and rushed the bottle up to Brother Ailbe before any other kids came back into the room."

"I'll bet he took it," Mick said.

"As if he had known it was coming. The next week Dennis got a letter of acceptance."

"Great story," chuckled Mick. "The old Irish ladies sure knew their man."

"He was a fine teacher. Later he directed us in a play, Arsenic and Old Lace, and he was good to us," Dominic explained.

Mick and Dominic attacked the pine trunks with the ax, and soon had the trees ready for pick up. After they had finished, Mick and Dominic stopped to pray for the brothers buried in the cemetery, a custom the Novice Master encouraged.

The cemetery, twelve crosses of Vermont white marble rippled with veins of purple, shone in the afternoon sun. Simple and unadorned, each cross bore the brother's name, birthplace and dates of birth and death. The cross that aroused the most interest was inscribed "Brother Edward Rudolph Cassidy aged twenty."

As Mick and Dominic gazed down at the cross, Mick said, "He was three years ahead of me at Power, a nice kid and a great street hockey player."

Dominic replied, "He's the first American buried here."

"What a waste of a young life. He never had a chance to get his degree and become a teacher and coach."

"What do you mean 'waste'? He suffered and died as a brother for Christ. They even let him take his first vows early, before he passed away," said Dominic.

"Yeah, but only twenty. Full of cancer. They cut out a lump from behind his ear and gave him radiation every two weeks. Then lumps broke out all over his body. Must have really been a blow to the Novice Master," commented Mick.

"He suffered for Christ is what he did. Remember that Psalm 116 we read today: 'Precious in the sight of the Lord is the death of his faithful ones.' You've got it all wrong," said Dominic. "The Novice Master is a very spiritual man and would have accepted it."

"Mother of God. What about the kid's parents? How did they accept it? They send their son to West Park, entrust him to God, and he dies," countered Mick.

"It was God's will, Mick."

"I'm sick of hearing about God's will. God's will always happens to somebody else. Like it was God's will that Tom Beasley be shot by a madman."

"I don't understand you, Mick. Please God, I'll be buried here some day," Dominic said. "Don't you believe in Christ and the value of suffering? That's what He did."

"Are you off your head altogether—-thinking about dying, your whole life in front of you?" asked Mick.

"This place is so holy and peaceful. I want to die a brother and be buried here, like Rudolph," Dominic said.

"For Christ's sake, Dominic. No need to rush it."

"Swear all you like. I do want to be buried here. And yes, for Christ's sake."

\* \* \*

"Like a fly buzzing against the window," Brother Theodore yelled at Mick after he had read aloud the spiritual text for the day. At the end of the meal, Brother Theodore had asked the rest of the faculty to leave and then closed the two doors of the dining room. He took it upon himself to monitor the oral reading of the novices during meals, Mick his first victim.

"Mick, return to the lectern and read again. You're reading sounds like a fly buzzing against a window. Read the text again—-loud and slow."

Conscious of his brogue, which thickened with pressure, Mick stammered through one page, the book shaking in his hands.

"No, read it again. You're still swallowing your words."

Mick felt two feet tall. Even when he was a kid in grammar school in Dingle, no brother had ever embarrassed him like this. Then a voice cut through the tension in the room: "Brother Theodore, this is wrong. We have Speech 101 next year at Iona College. You're embarrassing a novice in front of his peers. You treat your dog better."

The kindest, mildest of all the novices, Dominic had spoken up. The old brother growled, "I'm just trying to help him improve his reading."

"No, Brother, what you're doing is humiliation," responded Dominic.

"What would you do?" asked the old brother.

"Work with him privately. Listen to him read to you and teach him proper breathing techniques for oral reading."

"This is how I was taught," Brother Theodore snarled.

"Brother, what would Jesus, the greatest teacher, do?"

Brother Theodore stiffened and marched out.

Mick went over to Dominic and shook his hand: "Thanks, Dominic, you really put yourself on the line for me. He still might go running off to the Novice Master."

"Let him. He was wrong. A man has to stand up for what's right. The worst they could do to me is throw me out. Before you read next time, we'll sit down and practice the text, so you can learn to take a breath and enunciate your words."

# Chapter 30

From a secretary at Power Memorial Academy, Captain Miller got the phone number for the Christian Brothers' novitiate and spoke to the brother in charge of the seminary, the Novice Master, Brother Chapman, explaining that he wanted to interview Mick as a witness in the shooting the previous summer at St. Paul's Church. The Novice Master was cordial, setting an appointment for the following afternoon and providing the policeman with directions. The policeman would ask Mick hard questions.

To appear less formal, the policeman wore civilian clothes, blue pants and gray sports coat. As Road 9W twisted and turned on the last leg of the drive, it offered spectacular views of the Hudson, a third of a mile below. On the left side of one of the curves stood a sign "Christian Brothers, Novitiate." The policeman took a circular drive up a hill to a house built of yellow frame atop a stone base.

Mick was pacing in front wearing a black habit. "Hello, Mick," said the policeman shaking hands, "or should I call you 'Brother?'"

"Just call me 'Mick,' please, Officer," the young man said, as he ushered him into a small parlor with three stuffed chairs and a coffee table. The wooden floor was buffed to a fine gloss, and Christ peered down at them from a pine crucifix high on one wall.

"A long drive for you, Captain, over two hours. Can I get you some coffee, tea, or kool-aid, which we make here by the barrels?"

"Tea would be fine, Mick——cream and sugar."

"I'll be a few minutes. There's a bathroom next door. The Novice Master will drop in later to meet you."

"Thanks."

The policeman thought Mick more polished than when he had seen him two months ago. After using the bathroom, he walked to a window and saw a number of young men in work clothes raking leaves and beyond them what looked to be a cemetery.

Even though this wasn't a woman's house, it was clean and neat. Outside, the landscaping and grounds were like a park.

Mick returned with a brown plastic tray on which rested a teapot, cups and saucers, spoons, napkins and a small silver jug of real cream. After allowing the tea to steep for a few minutes, Mick poured for them both saying, "Captain, I can't see why you drove all the way up from New York to speak with me. I have nothing to tell you."

"A few questions, Mick. Why did you join the seminary so soon after the trouble at St. Paul's?"

"I wasn't sure I had a vocation, but I wanted to try it and find out."

"You didn't say a word to me about going away this summer. What changed?"

"New novices enter in July, and I didn't think you had any further need of me."

"Why did you beat up your uncle?"

"Well, we had an argument, like. I lost my temper and hit him."

"Why?"

"He wanted me to quit seeing my girlfriend."

"Why?"

"Thought she was a distraction to me."

"Distraction from what?"

"School and studies."

"But the school year was over."

Mick didn't reply.

"Why is your uncle a member of the IRA?"

Mick prayed that the Novice Master would come to rescue him: "I don't know, Sir. You'll have to ask him."

"Are you IRA?"

"Never."

"Have you written to, or seen your uncle since coming up here?"

"I've written him a few times. But he works on visiting Sundays and can't make it."

"Have you heard from Father Ryan?"

"Yes, he wrote me that he's happy studying in Rome, and I answered telling him how I was doing."

"And how are you doing?"

"Well enough. We have a crowded schedule. They keep us on the run."

Mick poured them both more tea and said, "Captain, these questions are personal, about me. I don't see what they have to do with the shooting last summer."

"Mick, you're lying, covering up. I don't know what or why, but I'll find out. This thing is about your uncle and the IRA. I'm a Catholic, too, and I don't understand how you can pretend to serve Christ while hiding a criminal who could have killed people, one of them a priest, and yourself. Here's my card again. I expect to be hearing from you."

There was a knock on the door, and a handsome middle-aged brother walked in. He had a kind face, red from the outdoors: "I'm Brother Chapman, Captain Miller. I wanted to meet you."

The policeman rose to shake hands: "Glad to meet you, Brother. Mick and I have finished our interview." Turning back to Mick, the policeman said, "As I said, if you think of anything more, give me a call. Thanks for the tea."

The Novice Master and the policeman chatted as they walked to his car, "What a great view of the Hudson, Brother. Do your men swim there?"

"Oh, yes, the strong swimmers can go back and forth, but the river can be treacherous too. A few years ago on a visiting day we lost the younger brother of one of our novices. Then when we went to inform the boy's mother, she had a heart attack and died on the spot, a double tragedy—-a story we tell all our young men so they respect the river."

"That's sad, Brother." As he glanced around, the policeman commented, "Your house and grounds are kept beautifully."

"Thanks, we have thirty-six young men, and we work at it."

As the two men gazed at the valley below, the Novice Master said, "I never tire of looking at the river. That white-columned building on the left on the other side is the Vanderbilt Mansion where the Secret Service lives, and the President's home in Hyde Park is just to the right, hidden by some trees and a turn in the river. The first Irish brothers came here and fell in love with the place because it reminded them of home."

"Will most of your novices stay, Brother?"

"Yes, but they're free to leave at anytime before taking first vows in the fall when they promise to remain for a full year. Those men then go to Iona College for teacher training."

"I went to La Salle High School in the city and later graduated from Manhattan College. Those De La Salle Christian Brothers were great teachers and fine men. I have the utmost respect for them and for you."

"Thanks. That's kind of you to say. Was your interview with Mick satisfactory?"

"Yes and no, Brother. I feel like I'm shadow boxing with him. He's the only witness we have to the shooting at St. Paul's because the priest, Father Ryan, has since been transferred to Rome, partly, I suspect, to escape danger."

"You seem honest and understanding, Officer, so I'm going to go with my instincts and speak to you openly. Mick has seen too much violence for a young man. More than most of the novices, he's waging some internal war. He needs peace."

"Yes, Brother. You're right. He doesn't get along with the uncle, his only family here."

"An unusual thing, Captain. Recently Mick received some pictures of a girl he had dated." Pulling an envelope from his habit, he gave the four snaps of Katie to the policeman. "There was no message or return address. As you can see, the photos were unposed. Mick says the girl wouldn't send them. I believe him."

"Brother, may I keep these? I'll find out who the girl is and interview her. This is strange."

"Certainly. I hope they help in your investigation."

"There's a lot going on in Mick's life that we just don't know. If I learn anything that might help him, I'll call you. You've been kind. Would you allow me to tour these beautiful grounds?"

"Of course, I can find a guide for you, or you could just ramble on your own. No one will bother you."

"Thanks, I'll walk around by myself. I just wish my wife and children could see how beautiful the Hudson

Valley is."

"There's the brothers' cemetery to our right and the farm beyond that. At the bottom of the drive is an underpass opening on a path to the river. Anytime you'd like to visit with your family, just call ahead. We'd be happy to host you."

"I've often heard of the hospitality of the Brothers. Now I understand."

After taking his leave from the Novice Master, the policeman wandered over to the cemetery and inspected the names carved into the white tombstones. He then crossed a road to the farm. Cows were scattered on the hills with blue skies overhead, a few white clouds scudding by. A red barn stuffed with hay dominated the yard, machinery parts scattered here and there. An old brother was sprinkling chicken feed into a tin-roofed coop enclosed with wire mesh.

The seminary was its own world, cut off from the war raging in Europe and the temptations of New York City. There was much more Mick could tell him, but the young man wasn't ready yet.

* * *

Caught off balance by the policeman's aggressiveness, Mick had revealed too much. Miller was tenacious and smart, but still didn't know why he was up here. Mick liked the man.

* * *

Captain Miller reported to Commissioner Dolan about the pictures sent to Mick: "My hunch is that the IRA sent them to remind Mick he must stay up there, a warning that the girl could be hurt if he doesn't."

"What I can't figure out is why the IRA wants the kid up there in the first place."

"Chief, you're right. There's something right in front of us we still aren't seeing."

"By the way, His Eminence has retracted his claws about St. Paul's when I mentioned the IRA as suspects. He would never want to cross a sizable portion of his flock."

The Captain's first step was to find a friend of Mick's at Power Memorial who would know the girl in the photos. Following protocol, he made an appointment with the principal to interview one of Mick's friends. Brother Hendry summoned Terry Kelleher to speak with the policeman. Wiry with wavy red hair, he stood first on one foot, then the other. The policeman waved the boy to a side chair while he took one next to it: "This the first time for you in the principal's office?"

"Yes, Sir."

"You're in no trouble. I have some questions about Mick Slattery and the church shooting last summer. I've been up to see him and wonder if he told you anything right after the fireworks that he might have forgotten."

"Talking on the stoop, Mick told Katie and me it had something to do with the IRA."

"Who's Katie?"

"Katie Muldoon, from the neighborhood, his girl."

"Is this the girl?" the policeman asked, handing over the pictures he had received from the Novice Master.

"Yes, Officer."

"Did Mick's leaving for the seminary surprise you and Katie?"

"Yes, he gave no hint of it. But these brothers are always badgering the good kids to join up. It's like a feather in their cap if one of their own students joins the order. Katie was devastated."

"How did he tell you?"

"Talking one night after he had given Katie the news. He gave me the phone number and the address of the novitiate, warning me to call him if Katie had any trouble. In fact I almost called just last week. Some older creep was taking pictures of Katie—-probably these---from across the street between the brownstones. I ran after him but he made it to the subway. Because he didn't talk to her or harass her, I didn't inform Mick, but I let Katie know."

"What did he look like?"

"Old Country with that bumpkin look, pants too short with white socks over black shoes. In his twenties."

"Mick felt Katie was in danger?"

"He suspected the IRA."

"Here's my card, Terry. If you ever see the guy with the camera again, call me anytime. By the way do you have her address?"

"Right across from me, 211 West 46th Street."

The policeman got the Muldoon's phone number from information and called. He reached a lady with a soft brogue: "Mrs. Muldoon, this is Captain Miller from the police, and I have some questions about a seminarian, Mick Slattery, a witness to an incident at St. Paul's last summer. You know the boy from going with your daughter."

"Yes, Officer, but I don't see how she could have any information that would help you."

"The boy may have told her something he wasn't even aware of that could assist us."

"Well, Captain, you're welcome to speak with her. She should be home from school around 3:00."

"Thanks, Mrs. Muldoon. See you then."

\* \* \*

The policeman was welcomed by a middle-aged woman with dark hair, a boy of four attached to her leg like a limpet.

"Can I see your gun and badge," the boy blurted out.

"Here's my badge," said the policeman, withdrawing the star from a black leather folder, "but the gun is too dangerous to take out."

"Are you going to arrest someone?"

"Eddie, you're being too fresh altogether. Now go into the kitchen and wait until your sisters come home for your snack. Don't mind him, Officer. He's been too doted on I'm afraid."

The policeman was invited to sit in the 'dad's' chair in the front room. Mrs. Muldoon sat opposite him on a long couch of blue mohair: "Katie will be home soon, and then we'll have some tea if you like."

After some pounding on the stairs, two chattering girls a year or two apart and wearing identical blue plaid uniforms, burst into the apartment, their charge slowed by the appearance of the tall policeman in his uniform.

"Bridge and Mary, say hello to Captain Miller."

The girls smiled shyly as they each kissed their mother.

"There's nothing wrong with Dad, is there Mom?" asked Bridge.

"No. Girls, go put the kettle on for tea, and give your brother his snack. No fighting, mind."

"Now, Officer, how can I help you?" asked Mrs. Muldoon, straightening a circular lace doily on the arm of the couch.

"We're wondering why Mick left so suddenly for the seminary after St. Paul's," said the policeman.

"God knows, Officer. He broke Katie's heart."

"Well, I'd like to talk with her about it. I'll be gentle with my questions, and you can stay with us the whole time."

"Well, come into the kitchen while I start your tea. By the time it's ready, Katie will be here."

In the kitchen over a long white metal table with parallel lines of black running through it, the two sisters were jousting with their brother: "You've had four already, and you'll spoil your dinner," Mary complained.

"You're not the boss of me," Eddie retorted.

"All right," the mother directed, "split the cookie three ways. Eddie, go play in front where I can watch you. Girls, go do your homework. When Katie comes home, tell her we have a guest."

"Wow, Mrs. Muldoon, your kids do what you tell them."

"Sometimes."

"We have three girls of our own at St. Agatha's. With the costs of uniforms, tuition, and books, it sure cuts into our budget. Strict German nuns run the school; I wish they'd run our house."

Mrs. Muldoon laughed: "Ah, here's Katie now."

A young woman with hair the color of coal, a replica of her mother, knocked on the door, nodded at the policeman, and entered the kitchen to kiss her mother.

"Katie, this is Captain Miller. He's investigating that shooting at church last summer."

"Mick mentioned your name," Katie said blushing.

"We'll have some tea and cookies," Katie's mom said, and reached behind some cereal boxes and brought down a plate of cookies stuffed with chocolate chips. "I have to squirrel these away or Eddie would have them all devoured. I don't know what I'll do when he gets big."

"They look great," the policeman said.

"Katie, I'll let Captain Miller speak for himself; but if any of his questions make you uncomfortable, speak up, and he can come back when your Da is home. I'll stay right here."

Katie nodded: "Mick told me you interviewed him after the shooting in church."

"Yes, and I saw him in the novitiate last week."

Katie colored and asked, "How is he?"

"Physically all right, but evasive and nervous."

"Officer, I do have some information that might help, but I want to bring no more trouble to Mick."

"Katie, I'm on Mick's side, your side. When I interviewed him in West Park, he admitted his uncle is in the IRA and that the two of them had come to blows before he left. He's lying about why he went up there."

Katie looked to her mother: "Didn't I tell you, Ma? Officer, before I say any more I want a private word with my mother."

When Katie and her mother stepped into the living room, the young girl said, "Ma, I've something serious to tell you about Mick. When he was a boy in the Old Country, he accidentally shot and killed a home invader, a tinker. His uncle covered the shooting up, hid the body, and left Mick feeling guilty all these years."

"Mother of God. What about the dead lad's family?"

"Never came back. Probably gave him up for dead."

"Why did his uncle do this?"

"He wanted to have something to hold over Mick so that he'd come to America and work for the IRA."

"God, the man is right vicious."

"We'll talk to this policeman some more, Mom. I like him and can tell him."

The policeman said, "Before we go on, Katie, I assume that Terry Kelleher mentioned the man taking pictures of you from across the street"

"I thought he was joking."

"No. I think the IRA mailed four pictures of you up to Mick in West Park with no note or return address."

"Why?"

"To warn Mick that he had to stay in the novitiate or they would hurt you."

"Mother of God, I can't imagine why they would harm Katie," her mother said.

"We don't know," said the policeman.

"Well, Captain. I'm going to trust you." Katie repeated the story of the home invasion in Ireland and Dan's threat to reveal Mick. "After he went to confession and told the priest about the blackmail, the IRA wished to scare off the priest and him. His uncle had buried the boy's body where he could retrieve it."

"That explains a lot," said Captain Miller.

Mrs. Muldoon said, "Officer, I would like to meet again tomorrow night here at 7:00 with Katie's Da and my brother, Mike Quinn."

"The man from the Transport Workers' Union?"

"Yes. Even though he quit the IRA when he came here, he's kept an eye on them. He may be able to help us."

"Okay. Now I know this has been a grueling session for you both. Thanks for your honesty. Mick is a very good young man, and I hope with some prayers we'll sort this out. Katie, here's my card. If you notice some stranger, call me anytime. I'll see you tomorrow evening."

* * *

As he walked back to the station, the policeman realized that he had at least one leg up on the IRA. They mustn't know that the union boss was Katie's uncle-- because they would never mess with the niece of the most powerful labor official in New York.

183

* * *

The next evening Katie admitted the policeman to their apartment, the other kids banished to a neighbor's for the evening. The captain greeted her mother and shook hands with her Dad, a heavy-chested man with a halo of blue pipe smoke crowning a head of graying hair. Mike Quinn, the transport union boss, looked like a bulldog with glasses. Enthroned in the dad's chair, a cup of tea next to him, he wore a brown suit and a blue tie peppered with shamrocks. In his signature brogue, Mr. Quinn announced, "Well now, Officer, seeing as we're all here, what do you have to say for yourself?"

"Katie has told us from speaking with Mick that the incident at St. Paul's was aimed at blackmailing him for the killing of a home invader in the Old Country."

The girl nodded agreement.

"We've only the boy's word for the killing. Maybe he lied," said Mike Quinn.

Katie broke in: "Why would he lie, Uncle Mike? And if the uncle hid the body, there would be no police report."

"Sure, that's something easily checked. Look into that with the Dingle Gardai, Officer," commanded Mr. Quinn.

"I already have. There's been no report of a violent death in Dingle for over twenty years since the war over the Free State."

Katie said, "Mick told me Father Ryan had gotten him a lawyer who thought the shooting would be ruled an accident. He was very relieved. Two weeks later he leaves for the novitiate. I don't understand."

"Maybe the boy does have the call," Mike Quinn said.

"He has no call," Katie shouted. Realizing she had shocked the group with her outburst, she went on, "I'm sorry."

Captain Miller said, "I agree with Katie. When I interviewed Mick in the novitiate, I knew he was lying about why he was up there. Any thoughts, Mr. Quinn?"

"Not a one. Eileen and I have an older brother, a Christian Brother, living in retirement at the same novitiate in West Park. I'll get on to him and see what I can learn."

Speaking for the first time, Katie's father said "Have these IRA sunk so low as to threaten an innocent girl?"

"I'm afraid so. Those Irish boys killed five innocent people in Coventry," said Mr. Quinn.

"Please come into the kitchen and have some tea and soda bread," announced Katie's mom.

As they were the last two walking down the hallway into the kitchen, Mike Quinn clamped his meaty paw on the policeman's arm and warned, "I'll have you know Katie's my goddaughter. If anything happens to her, I'll hold you personally responsible."

Shaking off the man's grasp, the policeman flared, "That's an insult. I'm treating this girl like my own daughter. Instead of trying to bully me, why not check into your IRA boyos. They're your people, not mine."

The group sat down for their tea and soda bread after Katie, as the youngest, said Grace.

Katie's mom passed around butter and strawberry preserves.

"Mrs. Muldoon, your bread is sweet and light, not like our heavy German pound cake, which goes right to our stomachs."

Everyone laughed.

When they had finished their meal, the policeman thanked Mrs. Muldoon and told Katie, "Call me any time day or night you feel in danger, like this guy taking the pictures. You're a fine woman, and Mick's a good man. I have a feeling this will all work out."

When Katie's mom and brother were alone in the kitchen, Mrs. Muldoon said to him, "Mike, look here to me. You may be boss of the Transport Workers Union, but you're not boss in this house. You were rude to that policeman, cutting him off, issuing him orders, just about provoking him. And I saw you strong arming him. Thank God he was a gentleman. Here we are in a crisis and you play Boss Tweed."

"But, Eileen, I want the man to be on his toes."

"You don't do that by stomping on them."

# Chapter 31

In the Catholic Church the month of May has always been designated to honor the Blessed Virgin Mary, the novices praying an additional rosary each day. A different novice in rotation gave a short meditation on her life every evening. This night the task fell to Dominic. Standing by the grotto of the Pieta' at the rear of the cemetery, Dominic turned to face his peers and then pitched forward gently onto the grass, out cold. Bending over him, the Novice Master asked, "What's wrong?" but got no response.

The Novice Master took him into St. Benedict's Hospital in Kingston. A nurse found a pulse, but Dominic's breathing was labored and ragged. When Dr. Larkin came, he shooed the brothers from the room to examine his patient. After some time, the doctor joined the Novice Master, Mick and Ambrose in the waiting room, "I don't know what's wrong. He's still unconscious with a high fever. What happened?"

The Novice Master explained that Dominic had fainted: "How sick is he, Doctor?"

"I can't tell yet. We'll watch him overnight and give him a battery of tests tomorrow."

"He's from Chicago. Should I call his parents, Doctor?"

"No, let's wait, but could someone spend the night here with him?"

"I'll do it," volunteered Mick. The Novice Master agreed, but wanted to wait until Dominic had awakened before leaving.

Finally after a nurse had been mopping his brow with a wet towel, Dominic moaned and looked around, myopic without his glasses. He choked out, "Where am I?"

The doctor checked his vital signs once more: "Well, he's perked up, but we'll observe him tonight and tomorrow."

Dominic remained conscious but too weak to talk. "Mick, here's the phone number for my room," said the Novice Master. "Call me anytime if there's a change in him." He walked over close to Dominic and gently laid his hand on the young man's forehead saying goodbye.

A nurse brought Mick blankets and a pillow, settling him into a chair. Mick was stunned at Dominic's sudden collapse. Like all the novices, he had had a physical exam just a few months before entering the congregation. Now he lay sick in the hospital dreaming.

Dominic was standing on the brothers' dock praying his rosary as hard as he could. In front of him, the Hudson was a golden river of whiskey. His mother was drowning, bobbing up and down in the liquid gold, clinging to a bottle of Jim Beam. Churning through the whiskey until he reached her, Mick released the bottle from her grasp and embraced her in a body carry. Holding her head up, Mick brought her to the dock and deposited her in Dominic's arms.

Writhing in pain, Dominic woke up in his hospital bed, globules of sweat covering his face and head. "You saved her," he told Mick as his friend wiped his face with a cold cloth. "You saved her from drowning, thanks, Mick.

You're kind." Aided by a shot of morphine, Dominic fell into another uneasy sleep, the beads of perspiration popping right back.

Confused by Dominic's ramblings, Mick could only pray: "Please, Jesus, help him."

The next time he awoke, Dominic found Mick patting his forehead with a towel: "Mick, I dreamed that you rescued Mom from a river of whiskey. If I die, who'll pray for her?" Dominic sobbed.

"Who said anything about dying? You fainted, and the doctor is keeping you overnight as a precaution," Mick replied.

Throughout the night, the nurses came in to check Dominic's vital signs and massage his feverish brow. Even with all the comings and goings, Dominic fell asleep, Mick keeping a watchful eye on his friend.

The next day Dominic was better, talking a bit, and the doctor felt he was strong enough to take some x-rays and blood tests. The Novice Master returned with Vincent, and Mick left for Santa Maria and some sleep.

On Mick's next trip to the hospital, he found his friend sitting up in bed ready to talk: "I'm coming home tomorrow. No test results yet, but doing better."

"Thank God, Dominic. Sure threw a scare into us."

"These purple blotches. Thought it was acne, kids' pimples along with the paleness and vomiting."

"Too much of the sports and work?"

"Mick, where do you go when you leave the house at night?"

"What?"

"That night I caught you sneaking out of the house."

"I told you, I get nervous sometimes, and I work it off by going for a swim."

"Across the river at night?"

189

"Yes, been swimming all my life."

"How do you see?"

"Flashlight to the river. I wrap it in plastic and bring it over to the other side."

"What about the river? Isn't it dangerous with ships going by?"

"There's light from the highways on both sides of the river, so I can see any craft. Crossed a few times already."

"It's against the rules. The Novice Master would go crazy."

"My business. He won't know about it."

"Mick, it's wrong. Can't you get exercise some other way?"

"I'm sorry I told you."

"It's still wrong."

The next day the Novice Master brought Dominic home, and he would stay in the infirmary room until he got stronger. He would have to return to the hospital periodically for blood transfusions.

\* \* \*

After a few days, Dominic was feeling much better when he met Brother Quinn out for a walk and spoke to the old man: "Brother, do you have the room next to Brother Angelus?"

"Yes."

"Why are you spying on Mick Slattery?" asked Dominic.

"What?"

"Are you putting Mick into danger, Brother?"

"I don't know what you're on about, but are you making some charges against me?"

"Yes, Brother, I am. You're watching and reporting on

Mick," Dominic said.

"Are you the novice who's sickly? You have nothing better to do with your time than make wild accusations. I have half a mind to go to the Novice Master right now and report you."

"Go ahead, Brother. I imagine he would like to know why you're playing informer on a novice."

# Chapter 32

B ig day coming soon, Mick," Brother Light said. Already nervous, the cook was bouncing from one end of the kitchen to the other, dumping peeled potatoes into an industrial-sized masher that looked like a cement mixer.

"What's that?" Mick asked as he sidestepped the cook to sweep the red stone kitchen floor.

"Brother Quinn's 60$^{th}$."

"He didn't say a word about it to me," answered Mick, "and I just talked to him."

"Probably shy. He's a humble old guy."

"Not always," Mick said as he thought of the old brother's yearly pilgrimage to Hyde Park to irrigate Roosevelt's property.

"Will his family attend?" Mick asked.

"Oh sure. His brother is head of Transport Workers Union. And there'll be priests and brothers from all over. Few brothers make sixty years in the Congregation."

As Mick walked out to work, he was filled with dread and anticipation. Would Katie come? She was Brother Quinn's niece, but she wouldn't want to see Mick. He didn't have the courage to ask the old brother if she were coming.

\* \* \*

"Mom, I can't go to the jubilee," Katie announced.

"Why not," her mother asked. "Barney is in his seventies. Who knows how much longer he has. And you're one of his favorites."

"Mick is there," Katie answered.

"Good God, I forgot. Your Uncle Mike mentioned it. But, love, this is family. Uncle Mike is renting a bus for the whole lot of us."

"Mom, I won't see that fake. He's a liar and I hate him," Katie replied.

"I know. But the place will be filled with our own. Besides you'll be minding the little ones, and all your cousins will be there for you to gossip with. Maybe even some good-looking fellas to scout out."

"Mom, please," Katie begged.

"Let me talk to your Da, but 'twas your Uncle Mike got Dad his job, and Barney has been so kind to us. Remember the glass rosary he gave you for your First Holy Communion? Think about it, love, will you?"

\* \* \*

On Jubilee Day the novices were assigned all the grunt work: directing traffic, serving food, and minding the kids. One even had charge of the glass tureen from which he ladled out old Brother Joachim's manhattans, sweet, syrupy—-and potent. Afraid to face Katie, Mick had started his day retching the gray glob of oatmeal that had been breakfast.

His first task was parking the cars in the high-school lot below Road 9W. After helping to shepherd the first few cars, Mick realized that many of the old folks with canes would have a tough time climbing the hill, so he suggested to the Novice Master that one of the brothers park the station wagon in the lot to ferry the elderly up the road.

As the morning wore on, the butterflies in Mick's stomach multiplied. At noon a blue and red Greyhound bus approached, sleeker than the battered yellow school buses the brothers from the city schools had come on. Mick's heart lurched. The first person to alight from the bus was Mike Quinn, the transport boss, easily recognizable from his newspaper pictures. Short and stocky with a boxer's build, he bore no resemblance to the ascetic figure of his brother, the Jubilarian.

"Good morning, Brother," he roared at Mick, his trademark brogue in full voice.

"The same to you, Mr. Quinn. A great day for you and your family."

Pleased that Mick knew who he was, he shook hands easily. "Mr. Quinn, do you have any old folks on your bus that might wish to be driven up to the Novitiate? The hill is right steep."

"Yes, Brother, old widow Maloney, though I'll have a job to talk her into it. Thanks."

Forty-one people of all ages exited the bus, among the last the Muldoon Family, who treated Mick as if he were a leper, all except for Eddie who gave him a tiny wave in remembrance of some past treat.

"Hi, Katie," Mick croaked to a dark-haired girl with freckles who glided past him like Lot's wife, only she didn't look back. He had pictured her a thousand times before this moment. She wore a blue dress and was more beautiful than in his dreams.

As the bus had pulled into the driveway, Katie's heart jumped when she saw the fool with his brown hair in a crew cut and more weight filling out his black habit. She wanted to hit him. Her Mom gave her hand a squeeze as they went down the stairs of the bus.

Before the outdoor Mass, there was a reception line for Brother Quinn, relatives and friends queuing up to offer congratulations and to drop a card in the offering basket on the altar, alongside him, his brother Mike guarding the treasure and taking careful note of the contributors. The old brother hoped that there would be enough for a trip to Ireland, probably his last.

In the invitations to the jubilee, the brothers had mentioned that there would be plenty of activities for kids from the city, like touring the farm to see the horses, cows, and pigs; going for a walk in the woods, playing softball; and swimming in the river—-all under the supervision of the novices, thus providing a break for the parents.

The Novice Master chose Ambrose and Mick to supervise the swimmers, the Newfoundlander taking six older boys, Mick the four younger, Katie's brother, Eddie, among them. Some of the boys wore trunks under their good clothes, and others chose from among the supply bought by the brothers for the occasion. Eddie grabbed Mick's hand as the group made its way down to the Hudson, the blue sky and open water spread before them like a new world:

"Mick, why were you wearing that black dress thing before?" Eddie asked.

"It's called a habit, the clothes brothers wear, like priests and nuns," Mick answered. "I guess Katie's still mad at me."

"She hates you, says you're a fake brother. Sometimes she cries."

"I suppose she has a new boyfriend," Mick said.

"No. Mom tells her to get one, and that Ryan boy down the block is always mooning at her, but she's like me, waiting for you to come back——-and bring us treats."

Mick laughed.

Ambrose took the bigger boys, all comfortable swimmers, out to the raft sixty feet away where the water was just over their heads. He permitted them to dive from the raft back to shore, but not farther out into the Hudson where the current was swift. Anchored by four empty barrels, the raft had a square wooden frame with red roofing shingles for traction on top.

Mick kept his group near the dock where the water was only two to four feet deep.

"The water's warm, Mick. I'm going to swim to the raft," said Eddie.

"No, it's too deep altogether, and I've these other boys to watch too. Look off to the left there across the river. That's the Vanderbilt mansion with the big white columns. Belongs to one of the richest families in America," Mick explained.

"I'm going to swim to the raft."

"No."

"I'll ask the other man then. He's not afraid."

"No, Eddie, those boys he has are bigger and stronger."

"Then I'll go by myself," Eddie insisted.

"No, Goddamn it!"

"A swear. A swear! Real brothers don't swear. Katie's right, you are a fake. "

Just then Mr. Muldoon was walking down the path to check on Eddie.

"Hey, Dad, watch me swim to the raft," Eddie yelled up and waved.

With Mick's head turned away for a second, Eddie struck out for the raft and sank like a rock.

"Christ, Mick, get him," Mr. Muldoon yelled.

But Mick had already dived after the boy, a blob of

white sinking fast in the dark water. Mick dove as deep as he could and then came up from the bottom. No sign of him. He knew the undertow was taking Eddie out deeper into the river towards the raft. The little boy was about to go under the raft when Mick spotted him, grabbed him from underneath, and carried him past the raft, without hitting his own head or Eddie's on the support barrels. Mick dragged Eddie out of the water and flung him on top of the shingled surface. Eddie was retching brown water, crying, and kicking as Mick held him tightly so he wouldn't roll off back into the river.

"Eddie, you're going to be okay," Mick soothed. "Just keep spitting out the water."

"Shall I swim out to help ye get him back?" Mr. Muldoon yelled from the dock.

"No, watch the kids. Ambrose, come out and we'll take him back in."

Each grabbing an arm and holding Eddie's head above water, the two novices brought him to the dock where still choking and crying he jumped into his father's arms.

Tears in his eyes, Mr. Muldoon thanked them both: "I saw the whole thing from the path. You're great lads. This one's a corker, afraid of nothing. More trouble to me than all three of the girls put together."

Mick tousled Eddie's hair and said, "Well, you swam to the raft and on your own too," prompting the beginnings of a smile from Eddie.

By the time Mick and Ambrose rejoined the celebration up at the novitiate, they had become heroes. Mrs. Muldoon, Eddie buried in her side, walked over to Ambrose and him: "Thanks. He'll be the death of me, this one." Mick turned and there was Katie standing stiffly: "Thanks, Mick. I wonder had I been in the water, would you have saved me?"

Her words like a kick in the stomach, Mick started to tear: "Oh Good Jesus, Katie, why don't you just shoot me and be done with it?"

"I've considered it," she responded; but seeing Mick's tears, relented.

"Katie, I'm hoping you'll forgive me. I'll come back to you."

"We'll see," she answered, and kissed him.

Mike Quinn had been observing the scene as he walked over to thank Mick: "You're a Dingle man right enough, the way you saved my nephew. I don't know what's between yourself and my niece, but it can't be a bad thing. I've watched you all day even before the rescue, helping the old folks walk, fetching food and drink, kind to old and young alike. If you ever need anything from Mike Quinn, you've only to ask."

As Katie was about to rejoin her family, a tall brother so thin he was almost lost in his black habit approached her: "Katie, I'm Dominic, a friend of Mick's. I know he's put you through a hard time by coming up here, but he's being forced. The IRA has threatened to hurt you if he doesn't stay here. He really loves you, you know."

"Strange way he has of showing it, Brother."

"Katie, I don't know the whole story, but he isn't up here to run from you. He wants nothing more than to come back to you."

"Brother Dominic, you must be very close to Mick for him to confide all this to you. I feel he's in danger. Please try to keep him safe."

"Yes. I've been sick. Mick has been by my side both here and in the hospital, and we've become good friends."

"I'm saddened by your illness, Dominic. I'll pray for you. I can tell that you're sincere and good."

"He'll return to you, I promise."

"Thanks, Brother," Katie replied, her eyes misting. "I believe you." As she touched his habit and kissed his cheek, Dominic turned flame-red.

\* \* \*

As the celebration was winding down, Mike Quinn and Brother Quinn were sitting together under the shade of an oak tree, the swag lying in a briefcase at their feet. Dominic walked over to the two men and looking at Brother Quinn said, "Sorry to interrupt, but I want to find out why you're spying on Mick Slattery?"

Brother Quinn's face darkened as he said, "Get away from us. I don't know where you're getting these wild ideas. I know you've been sick, but that's no excuse."

Mike Quinn interjected, "Brother, what are you on about? Do you mean Mick Slattery who just saved our nephew from the river?"

"Yes, Mr. Quinn."

"Mike, this poor brother is off his head entirely."

"No, I'm not," said Dominic. "You told someone on the phone that you were watching Mick Slattery leave the house to cross the river and come back. Was it you, Mr. Quinn? Are you part of this IRA business?"

"Indeed not." Turning to his brother, Mr. Quinn asked, "Why would you be doing such a thing, spying on a young brother, and what does the IRA have to do with it?"

"I told you to pay him no mind, Mike," Brother Quinn pleaded. He then rose and rushed for the house.

"Brother," Mike Quinn said to Dominic, "I don't know what's going on, but I'll find out."

\* \* \*

"Mick, don't go across any more," Dominic said as they cleaned up after the celebration.

"Been there twice."

"You're just tempting fate. Katie doesn't want you putting yourself at risk," Dominic continued.

"How do you know what Katie wants?" Mick retorted.

"She wants you safe. I just talked to her," Dominic replied. "I told her you'd come back to her."

"I hope you're right," Mick said.

# Chapter 33

Uneasiness simmered between Dominic and Mick over his evening swims. Sitting with Mick one afternoon in the infirmary, Dominic confronted him:

"Are you going to leave, Mick?"

Fighting his impulse to lie, Mick replied, "I'm not sure."

"All this sneaking out. What's really going on?"

"I told you. Exercise."

"You're lying. Nobody gets more exercise than you."

"Know everything, don't you?" Mick walked out in a huff.

The next day Dominic was feverish and had chills. Even his bones ached. In just a few days he had lost more weight from his skinny frame.

As he entered Dominic's room, Mick pretended nothing was wrong between them:

"How are you today?"

"Be a lot better if you weren't lying to me."

"Give it up. Nothing to tell."

"Ok, then. I'll tell you something."

"What?"

"I'm dying."

"You're crazy altogether. You had a physical a few months back."

"The blood test in Chicago didn't catch it. Dr. Larkin told the Novice Master and me. Leukemia, cancer of the blood."

"Damnit, it's your own fault. All that talk about the cemetery and Rudolph."

"You're being stupid, Mick. It's a disease."

"Will you go home for treatment?"

"No. Told my parents I want to stay here. They'd only worry and feel helpless."

"What can they do for it?"

"Blood transfusions for a while to prevent anemia."

"Oh God, Dominic. And all I've been doing is fighting with you."

"Now you can help me."

\* \* \*

In the infirmary Dominic had started to retch uncontrollably, so he returned to the hospital. One night Mick was keeping lonely watch, the only light a red vigil lamp before a statue of the Blessed Virgin in a corner. A bronze crucifix stood sentinel on the wall above Dominic's head, which glistened with the night sweats. Only an occasional "Oh, Jesus" pierced the silence and revealed Dominic's torment, even in repose.

That afternoon as Dr. Larkin was making his rounds, Mick followed him into the corridor. He had seen Mick by Dominic's side so often that he had no reservations about speaking openly with him: "Doctor, why is he so bad?"

"His spleen. The leukemia has invaded his spleen."

"Does he have any chance at all?"

"No, Brother, I'm sorry. As I told Brother Chapman, his spleen will gradually become swollen and displace other organs in the stomach. Very painful.

Then he'll fall into a coma."

"Can't you do anything?"

"Only shots for the pain to try to keep him comfortable. You're good with him, Brother. Stay and keep him company." The doctor patted Mick on the arm and entered the room. Mick thanked him and later sat by Dominic's side, dozing lightly.

Dominic's voice startled Mick: "What are you doing here? You ought to be out practicing your swim across the river."

Mick helped his friend sip from a cup of water, holding his head forward while tipping the water into his mouth. Even Mick's hand gently caressing his neck caused him pain, his back damp and warm to the touch.

"Mick, what's this sneaking out for. Tell me the truth."

"Get some rest," Mick said.

"I'll get plenty of rest soon enough."

"Jesus, you're morbid tonight," Mick said.

"Nice word choice, Mick. You're hiding something."

"You never give up, as sick as you are. All right, you win. It's part of a plot for the IRA. I'm supposed to swim over to Hyde Park and assassinate Roosevelt and Churchill."

"Mother of God. Why?"

"Churchill's English. Roosevelt is helping him. With their deaths the IRA fools think the war will turn against the Brits."

"Security would kill you."

"Maybe. Made the trip to his house a couple of times already. The bastards have threatened to break Katie's legs if I don't go. They fired warning shots over her head in broad daylight last week."

"What about the Secret Service, those guys who were here."

"A coincidence."

"Simon was telling us about the Coast Guard patrol."

"They're looking for boats, not a lone swimmer. I've never even seen them."

"Something else, Mick. I discovered who Brother Spy is."

"How did you find out?"

"I confronted him. Brother Quinn."

"Jesus God, and I thought we were friends. We went to the same school, and he's Katie's uncle," explained Mick.

"Why's he watching you, Mick?"

"To make sure I swim over to Roosevelt's. Then he reports to the IRA in New York."

"Mick, do you mean to tell me this whole year's been a fake?"

"Yes, I'm here to protect Katie, but I like it more than I had thought. Learned a lot about myself and made some good friends like you."

"I hope I die rather than see you killed by the Secret Service over there."

"You're not going to die."

"You're a better actor than liar. I heard what Dr. Larkin told you."

"Dominic, I'm sorry."

A young nurse glided into the room to check Dominic's vitals allowing Mick to escape to the corridor. As she was leaving, the nurse asked. "Everything ok with you two? Usually you're a real comfort to him."

Mick said, "No, but I don't know how to make it any better."

"Ever try praying, Brother?" she asked as she went down the hall.

Returning to Dominic's bedside, Mick said, "The nurse told me to pray."

"Maybe she thinks you believe in it."

"Why all the sarcasm?" Mick asked.

"I'm jealous of you. Here I am falling apart, not a thing I can do. I'll never be in a classroom. For months been practicing writing on a blackboard for students I'll never teach. What a joke! And here you are flirting with a hare-brained assassination plot to satisfy your uncle's need for revenge for a tragedy of twenty years ago. As if your death or those of the two old men across the Hudson will make one goddamn bit of difference. You're the dumbest Irish bastard I've ever known."

"Blast you, Dominic. I'll kill you." Mick made a rush at Dominic, jouncing his bed so hard that his friend moaned in agony. Dominic didn't even flinch and fell back exhausted.

"Oh God, Dominic. I'm sorry."

The nurse came in to give Dominic a shot of morphine enabling him to resume his uneasy sleep. Depressed, Mick curled up in the hospital chair and fell into a dream.

This was the final trip. Mick snuck out before afternoon prayers. The day was hot, the water in the seventies. No patrol boats dotted the horizon, just a slow-moving barge laboring from the north.

When he reached the eastern side of the river, he drew out the canvas ducks, work pants and shirt from his plastic bag and then clambered up the bank. The white stones of the New York Central railroad tracks were still hot under his shoes. Up ahead was the red "Churchill special" train car. The British bulldog was here.

Entering the woods, Mick saw a brown-clad military policeman at his phone station, so he slithered off to his left through the wetlands to avoid the man, and then turned south where the woods were thickest. He moved in slow motion, conscious of every footfall, afraid of stepping on

205

branches. After twenty minutes he reached the waterfall, pond, and brown boulder. From behind it he dug out the canvas bag with the black cassock and gun. He shook the wrinkled habit and threw it on over his work clothes, stuffing the revolver under the back of his belt.

Mick had to dash the hundred feet from the wooded path to the fields that lay below the house. Diving on his belly, he lay in the corn stubble and waited before starting his crawl up the hill. The afternoon sun on his black habit pinioned him to the ground. The spikes of corn cut his hands and cheeks. Startling both himself and Mick, a red fox shot through the hay hunting mice.

His sweat had stirred up mosquitoes that dive-bombed into his ears, Mick stopping to dig them out with his fingers. Dogs were a threat that had never entered his mind, but there was no sign of the President's black Scottish terrier Fala, smarter than the humans by remaining in the house and keeping out of the sun.

Through the spikes of the harvested corn, he finally saw the two figures a few hundred feet away deliberating on the future of the world, as they sat in the shade of a garden near the house, just a wooden picket fence away. Long before he saw them, Mick smelled the President's cigarettes and Churchill's fat Cuban cigar, only a drinks' table between them. Because his cassock was getting snagged in the stubble, Mick had to go even more slowly. Churchill was a white whale with skinny legs like Babe Ruth. Roosevelt looked tired, but raised his cigarette holder at a jaunty angle skyward above his straw hat. Both men had their backs to the sun and to him. They were two old men, grandfathers, like those he saw in Dingle enjoying a smoke and a pint.

Three Secret Service guards stood talking on the far side of the garden, instructed to give the great men space.

As Mick inched closer, tugging the gun from his pants,

he sneezed: "Ah choo, ah choo. Mother of God, a sneezing fit." Mick buried his face in the ground, squeezed his nose hard, and spat snot and phlegm into the hay beside him. The sneezing stopped, but it had a life of its own and could return any time. For minutes, afraid to look up, he buried his face in the sleeve of his habit.

Hearing no commotion, he resumed his crawl, images of Katie and Dominic flashing before him. Still lying down, Mick balanced the gun on his left arm and sighted it. He would take Churchill first because he was a little farther away and then the President immobile in his wheelchair.

Then the same young nurse roused Mick, whispering, "Why are you fighting with him? Don't you know how sick he is? You're always the best with him."

Dominic had never spoken to him like that before. His stomach distended by the enlarged spleen, Dominic looked like a skeleton with a beer belly. For months Mick and the other novices had thought the purple bruising, the vomiting, and the bleeding were symptoms of a wimp, not of a leukemia victim. "Some fag," Mick thought.

While his friend slept, Mick followed the nurse's advice and prayed for Dominic, Katie, and himself.

# Chapter 34

**M**ick usually hated First Fridays of the month because they were designated days of silent retreat stuffed with extra prayers and meditation. Just what he needed. But now he welcomed a day cut off from others because it gave him time to think. His feud with Vincent seemed endless, Captain Miller was hot on the chase, and old Brother Quinn was charting his every move. Dominic was dying before his eyes each day, and his mission date was closing in on him. Everything was against him. During the afternoon, three hours were set aside for the novices to meditate, providing Mick time to go for a hike and lose himself in the woods, a temporary respite.

Mick was already feeling Dominic's loss, praying to Jesus to release him from the pain of the bloated liver and spleen. Blue pincushions of pain, Dominic's fingers were purple, so swollen with needle pricks from drawing blood that he tried to hide them under the sheets from visitors. But Mick saw them. Even though Mick wanted Dominic free from suffering, he would lose his best friend, the only one he confided in, even about his mission. Strange how Mick had come to like someone so different. There was more to being masculine than kicking a football--or an opponent. Like Katie, Dominic was his own person and had integrity, a commitment to his own values. When Brother Theodore was excoriating Mick about his reading, Dominic had spoken up with a moral authority that even the old crank had recognized.

When Mick reached the cemetery, he knelt to say a "Hail Mary" before the white crosses of Vermont marble reflecting the sun. Soon Dominic would get his wish and be buried here. And this good man was determined that Mick not make himself into a killer, trying to save his life even as his own ebbed away. But couldn't Dominic understand that he had to save Katie? Murder for love. First it had been his parents he would kill for, and now it was Katie.

Why did Dominic care so much? Mick had placed a terrible burden on him by revealing the plot, yet he knew implicitly that he could trust his friend. But why? What was Mick to a dying young novice from Chicago, more than a friend? Then it hit him: Dominic was his <u>brother</u>. As much family to him as Katie and Aunt Elizabeth, one of the three people in the world who loved him.

The afternoon wore on, hazy and warm, Mick finding physical release by running. Reaching Murphy's Road, Mick turned west up the hill. On the left, trees shaded the asphalt, but on the right sticky pools of fresh tar bubbled with a smell Mick had always loved, part oil and part licorice. All his life Mick had to watch out for something as he ran, road kill like a dead raccoon compacted into a mass of black and white fur, a crushed possum all ugly snout, and in Ireland once a dead cow lying frozen on its back, all four legs pointing stiffly heavenwards as if Oscar, the giant of Celtic lore, had lifted it up, flipped it over, and dumped it on its back, dead.

Aunt Elizabeth, Katie, and Dominic had told him he couldn't make a life built on hatred. Mick had to find a way around Uncle Dan and those old whiskey heroes at the

Harp and Shamrock. Otherwise, Mick would be destroying Katie and himself. Two more victims, maybe more if the mission were to succeed. Dominic was right: no one murders for love. Besides hadn't he already given enough for The Cause---both his parents?

The road was quiet except for the pounding of his sneakers and the hum of insects. Occasionally a dog barked. After four miles of running, all uphill, perspiration drenched his shirt. To lose himself even more, Mick angled off the road into the shade of the woods where he found stonewalls. The low fences of piled fieldstone built over two hundred years ago, even deep in the forests, had always fascinated him.

Dutch farmers had to rebuild their walls every spring because the winter cold heaved up new stones to the surface. In the woods the walls were used for boundary markers. How presumptuous these Dutch must have been to think their walls conferred a lifetime claim to the land they had marked out. In his own country, stonewalls were built higher and not only demarcated boundaries, but also penned in sheep, cows, and horses.

Stepping around some wetlands near Gugan Barrow, an oval pond used for ice-skating in winter, Mick picked up a white boulder and with two hands heaved it at some low brush directly ahead when a mass of snarling teeth and fur exploded back at him. Summer vacationers often abandoned dogs when they had grown tired of them and were about to return to the city, many of the strays developing rabies caused by bites from infected raccoons, foxes, and other animals.

More startled than afraid because he had grown up around dogs in Ireland, usually border collies for minding the sheep, Mick realized that these dogs were wild and dangerous. The alpha male, the leader of the pack, was a mixed German shepherd with patches of pink skin where the mange had eaten the hair away, making him look even more menacing.

Because direct staring was an invitation to aggression, Mick kept casual eye contact with the leader while the rest of the pack yelped and danced around. In classic attack mode the leader's hackles stood on end, chest thrust forward, ears and tail erect, teeth yellow, dangling silver bubbles of saliva. Images of Katie, Aunt Elizabeth, and Dominic flashed in front of him. Would he ever see them again? Had he gone through all this torture to become meat for dogs?

Fearing being encircled, Mick cut off the alpha b male, a brown and white collie, sliding around to his left, all the while keeping the leader in view, as he retreated toward the road, fearing that moving faster would incite the pack's chase instinct. He reached down and grabbed a thick branch, the length of a baseball bat, making the dogs hesitate for a moment.

Tense but showing no fear, Mick was working his way backwards when he stumbled over a half-hidden log covered with green and white moss, the sudden movement triggering a leap from the leader. Recovering his balance in time, Mick thrust the branch upward with both hands like a jousting pole into the dog's teeth and chest, deflecting it to the left. Bouncing to his feet, he grabbed the stick like a bat and smashed the leader across the snout, its teeth and bones cracking, driving it whimpering backwards. "Take that, you son of a bitch," Mick screamed. Enraged, he waded into the nearest dogs and lashed out at them too, so that they began to skulk away from this animal with the stick.

Mick was almost glad of the attack, the energy and emotion purging his fear and anger. From now on he would take no shit from anyone.

A few feet more and Mick had backtracked onto the road, the dogs melting into the woods. Inspecting himself for dog scratches that could lead to infection, Mick found only a bruise from his fall.

From another world, a blue station wagon honked at him. The driver, venerable old Brother Light, the cook, pulled up and yelled: "You'll be late for prayers. What in the name of God are you doing in there anyhow?"

Sliding in beside the old brother, Mick slammed the door and said, "Shut the fuck up."

# Chapter 35

I n June, with the beginning of a heat wave, the Harp and Shamrock stank of cigarettes and old beer. The three conspirators in the back room had done little since mailing the photos of the girl to Mick.

"Dan, is that cop Miller still nosing around, the one who called at your house?" asked Joe Murphy. "Biddy O'Hearn reported seeing a blond copper visit the girl's house two days running."

"Could be," replied Dan. "If so, that's bad for us because it means he hasn't given up, the bastard, and he could be putting things together."

"But the girl doesn't know anything," said Tim Moore. "Maybe it's time to send another batch of pictures up there."

"We've done that," said Joe. "We've two months. Maybe there's another way to put the fear of God into him, just to be on the safe side."

"We had such good results from the church shooting, the priest leaving and the boy going to the seminary, we could try something like that again," said Tim.

"What do you mean?" asked Dan.

"A shot across the bow of a ship, a warning like. Some morning I could fire a couple of rounds over the girl's head," replied Tim.

"Jesus," said Joe. "If anything went wrong, we could be done for."

"Yes," Dan said, "but Tim did a good job last time. And if the police are getting close, it would be a timely reminder to Mick," Dan said. "But the bastard is so unpredictable, he might come back and kill us all."

"A chance we'll have to take," Joe said. "We could send him a letter that there'll be a warning like, only a warning just. Dan can do that."

"I'll write him. Tell us your plan, Tim," said Dan.

"According to my nephew who took the pictures, the girl leaves for school at 7:45 when most of the men have gone to work. I'd wait across the street in a gangway and fire two or three shots in the air as she comes down the steps," Tim said.

"Jesus, you better not hit one of those brownstones for fear of a ricochet," Joe warned.

"I'm not a feckin' eejit," Tim replied.

"And no drink taken like last time, mind," Joe cautioned. "You'll need a clear head. I'll have the car parked on 10th Avenue for a fast getaway. And wear a mask."

"All right, all right. Bejeezus, you're worse than the wife, the two of you," barked Tim.

"Tim, all our lives are at stake here. You might do a reconnaissance the morning before," said Joe.

"I was planning on it," replied Tim.

\* \* \*

A few days later on a Tuesday morning, Tim had his first look around. An old lady with gray hair and glasses gazed out on the street from her first-floor window, with no curtains or blinds to conceal her presence. Old Biddy O'Hearn, Joe's informer, who kept track of all movement on the block. Joe would have to warn her to keep her yap shut after the shooting the next day, better would be if he warned her off her post altogether.

The next day he arrived at his station beside the stoop at 7:30 but not before stopping for an eye-opener or two of Paddy's Irish at McCluskey's on 9th Avenue, a bar where he was not known and where Joe Murphy wouldn't catch him out. Only a few early drunks were nursing shots served by a stout woman of late middle age with a face like a hatchet. She wore a clean white apron and made no pretense of being friendly. Her scowl suggested she disliked her job, her patrons, and probably her husband who was upstairs sleeping after the night shift.

Ten minutes before Katie was to leave the apartment, Tim made his way to his niche alongside the brownstone. He had cut slits in the black watch cap for his eyes and pulled it down to cover his face.

When the girl opened the door of her building and began to walk down the stairs, he pulled the revolver from his overalls, took two steps into the street, and fired over her building. Boom! Boom! Gray and black pigeons flew from the rooftops. Out of the corner of his eye, he registered someone flashing from the building on his left, an Irish terrier at his heels. Distracted, Tim fired his third shot too low, gouging a large chunk of masonry from the cornice of Katie's house, showering it on the street below. Even in the open air, the shots were like cannon fire as the three flats on both sides of the street bounced the noise down the concrete canyon.

"For Mother Ireland," the thick man yelled.

Then a red-haired boy was on him, Terry Kelleher, Mick's friend from Power, knocking the much bigger man off balance against a wrought-iron fence, the dog and his leash entangled with them both. "Are you daft, boy? I'll blow your feckin' brains out," Tim yelled as he shook the boy off, but the terrier had grabbed hold of the man's pants leg. "Goddamnit," the big man cursed and brought the gun down on Terry's shoulder to fend off another charge. He then fired into the dog's chest leaving it quivering on the sidewalk.

All this time Katie had stood chalk-white before recovering and dashing across the street. She threw her books at the man, knocking off his mask. He screamed at her, "You little hussy. Sure, you're the cause of all this."

He pushed her away and then limped towards 10th Avenue out of sight.

"Oh, Terry, are you ok?" Katie asked as she rushed to help him to his feet.

"Yeah, just some bruises and a knot on my shoulder," he replied. "But he killed Casey." The dog lay on its side just a few yards away, blood leaking from its brown and shaggy fur into the street. The boy cried.

"I'll call Captain Miller," Katie said.

Katie's mom came tearing across the street, Eddie in tow: "What happened?" As she looked around at the gathering crowd, she noted that for the first time in living memory Biddy O'Hearn wasn't at her window.

Just a few minutes earlier, with his black Ford running, Joe Murphy had been peeking around the corner during the shooting and scramble afterwards. He helped push Tim into the car, screaming "Where the feck is your mask?"

"The bitch knocked it off. And a wee shite of a kid pushed me into a fence. Had to belt him with the revolver."

"Either of them hurt?"

"No, the boy's got a few bruises, and I had to shoot a Goddamned dog."

"Did they get a good look at you?"

"Once the mask came off."

"You'll have to keep your head down. Grow a beard and change your hair."

\* \* \*

Captain Miller arrived at the scene mad. At least no one was badly hurt. Weeks of interviews, trying to stitch the story together and now this. At least this time they should have a better description of the shooter from both Katie and Terry. Both pictured the man as Irish, thickset, and gray, reeking of whiskey, as Father Ryan had mentioned about his assailant, probably the St. Paul's gunman again.

Huddled with Katie and Terry in the Muldoon's flat, the policeman drew from them the sequence of events, the man's firing over Katie's head, suggesting that this was another warning. But for whom, Katie or Mick? It had to be Mick because Katie didn't know enough.

On impulse the policeman decided to drive straight to West Park to deliver news of the shooting to Mick and to gauge his reactions. Leaving an assistant in charge at the scene, he headed up the West Side Highway.

The drive of two hours along the Taconic Parkway gave the policeman time to think as he wove through the trees and flowers in mid-bloom, not as beautiful as when they had changed colors in the fall six months before. When he reached the novitiate, the novices were heading out for sports. Seeking out the Novice Master for permission to speak with Mick, he met a tall thin brother who asked him his name and directed him to the parlor while he fetched the Novice Master.

Wearing a flannel shirt and overalls, the Novice Master greeted him with a handshake: "Captain Miller, this is a surprise." The two men sat down after the Novice Master had closed the door.

"On purpose, Brother. I have to explain. I've come directly from Hell's Kitchen where a man fired three times over the head of the girl in those pictures sent to Mick—Katie Muldoon. We think Mick may know this man or know about him, probably an IRA thug, perhaps the one from St. Paul's."

"That's strange, Captain, because just the other day Mick received a letter from his uncle, the first one I think. Just a few lines. 'There will be a warning to you coming very soon.'"

"That fits, Brother. I came unannounced to judge Mick's reactions if you'll permit me to speak with him. I believe Mick has no knowledge of the shooting, but may know who's behind it. His uncle is in an IRA cell and is putting pressure on him. Why we don't know."

"Captain, I trust you. Certainly you can speak with him. He has a new worry. Another novice is very ill, and Mick has been the main caregiver."

"A tall thin brother with big glasses and bruises on face?"

"Yes, that's Dominic. I'll fetch Mick."

"Thanks, Brother. We can talk after."

Mick had just finished infield practice when the Novice Master told him that Captain Miller was waiting to see him. It was just a few minutes' jog from the field to the novitiate. Mick breezed into the parlor determined not to let the policeman catch him off guard like their last meeting. He would give nothing away.

"What can I do for you, Captain?" Mick asked.

"Tell the truth," the policeman replied.

"What?"

"This morning a gunman fired three rounds over

Katie's head in front of her house, probably the same Irish lug from St. Paul's."

"Oh Jesus God, is she okay?"

"Shaken but unharmed."

"Those dirty bastards. Dan sent me a note." Getting madder as he spoke, Mick blurted out, "Take me back with you right now. I'll go and kill them all. I warned Dan."

"And how will that help Katie? I told you she's ok. This is all IRA, right Mick?"

"Yes, a cell from the Harp and Shamrock, my uncle the worst of them."

"What do they want from you?"

"Officer, I can't tell you. Please, please don't make me. They've threatened to break Katie's legs if I say a word."

"I've met her, you know. She's a lovely girl. Why don't you get the hell out of here and go back and take care of her? This life is not for you."

"I know. They've forced me to be here. Does Katie think I had a part in this?"

"No, but why stay? There's nothing but religious and cows and the river."

"Captain, you're a good man, but for Katie's sake I honest to God can't tell you. Please trust me." Mick shook the policeman's hand and left.

In a few minutes the Novice Master returned to the parlor: "Captain, I can see by the look on your face that you had little success."

"Yes, he's under siege from his uncle and the IRA, but he won't unburden himself to me."

"I've never met the uncle. According to Mick, he's always working on visiting days."

"I hope so. Thanks again, Brother, for letting me speak to him."

# Chapter 36

Mick had to borrow a book from the high school library, and he had the place to himself because the seminarians were in class. At the end of a row of books, he noticed a picture that seemed out of place with the rest of the room. It wasn't religious. In a studio picture with a background of trees and a lake, Thomas Ashe, the Irish martyr and Nellie's beloved, was sitting on a stone bench. His flowing, curly brown hair framed a thin face with a trimmed moustache. Dressed in a kilt with a yellow sash over his left shoulder, the Irishman radiated a quiet authority.

This was a photo new to Mick. He wondered how the picture came to be there in the same room with St. Joseph and his carpenter's tools and the Angel Gabriel announcing to Mary that she was to be the Mother of God. Some Old Country patriot now buried in the cemetery had probably hung the photo there years ago, and it remained undisturbed because later generations of young brothers were afraid to touch it. What a nice present this would make for the old lady across the river. With his handkerchief Mick lightly dusted the space where the picture had hung and sandwiched it between two books. He had to find a way to keep the picture dry on his swim across the river.

\* \* \*

That evening sneaking out of the darkened novitiate, Mick made his way to the river and entered the warm water. He wondered if Brother Spy were making his phone call at this very moment. When he had reached the eastern shore, he was below and a bit north of Springwood, the Roosevelt estate. He had brought with him his flashlight, and a pair of canvas shoes and work clothes tied in a waterproof bag strapped onto his back. In the bag he had also wrapped the framed photo of Thomas Ashe in layers of plastic. Because it was a weeknight, Roosevelt was away in Washington, and there were no Coast Guard patrols to worry about.

Putting on his clothes, Mick climbed up the bank and over the New York Central railroad tracks. From here he found the path to the house, a mile and a half away, much of it wetlands, even in the heat of the summer.

When he reached the boulder where the blue bag was buried, he looked around for the Irish lady who had caught him napping months ago. Hearing a footfall, Mick blended into the trees.

"Well, lad, you've been on my conscience," Nellie's brogue penetrated the silence of the woods. With her gray hair tied back in a severe bun and wearing a check-patterned apron, the Irish lady stepped closer. "You're not a killer. I knew that the first moment I laid eyes on you. I don't give a pin for Joe Murphy and his plot. I'm just a silly old lady who couldn't say no."

"Miss, I brought you a present."

"Mick, it's time you called me by my name, Nellie, Nellie Keyes. What's this then?"

"I wrapped it up in plastic and carried it in a bag on my back. It's dry," Mick said, handing her the package.

221

Nellie unwrapped the layers of plastic and focused her flashlight on the picture: "Mother of God, my Tom. I've never seen this one."

"I think it was taken just after his capture of the police barracks at Ashbourne."

Nellie's face melted into tears. Unable to speak for a few minutes, she pulled Mick to her and sobbed on his shoulders: "What a wonderful gift. Bless you, lad. You're kind, aren't you, not like those in the city dreaming only of violence. Sit down here on this boulder next to me, and give it out how they pulled you into this business."

Mick unfolded to her the history of his life: the death of his parents, the tinker, and his uncle's blackmail threat to cripple Katie unless he shot the two Old Men. "Just the other day they fired warning shots over Katie's head right in the open street," Mick explained.

"I never knew they could be so foul. And here I signed on to their plans without a thought in my head, silly old woman that I am," Nellie explained.

"What would Thomas Ashe want you to do?" Mick asked.

"You're no fool. The right question, Mick. It pierces my heart. Not to have an innocent young man slaughtered and a girl crippled."

"Nellie, take the bag with the gun and bury it somewhere else. Tell no one."

"I'll do it. I'll do everything I can," Nellie answered.

"There's a city cop closing in on the plot. I have only two months until early August when Churchill comes. I'm to shoot them both."

"There's not a spark of human decency in them. Your uncle must be a devil altogether."

"What's hardest on me now is I have to find a way to fake the mission to protect her."

"I'll help you. Those six German spies were executed and never got near the Old Man. Your life and that of your girl are more important than the pipedreams of some old men full of whiskey in Hell's Kitchen."

"Nellie, my uncle wouldn't care for a minute if I was killed."

"By the way, one of them brothers over there is watching you. Joe Murphy gets a call from him whenever you leave the seminary to swim over. Then Joe phones me that you're coming. That's why I knew you would be here tonight."

"Yes, an Old Country brother from my own school in Dingle, and I thought he liked me."

"And they call themselves 'religious.' Mick, not a word about our talk, mind. Be careful of your every move. Where can I reach you?"

The two exchanged phone numbers.

"Mick, I love the present, and I love you for bringing it to me." Clutching the picture to her breast, she gave Mick a final hug and headed up the path to the house.

Nellie had given Mick hope as he swam back over the Hudson, no tankers this evening, not a boat on the river. He reached shore and climbed the hill to the novitiate, always walking behind the oak trees adjoining the asphalt road for cover. That same light was on in the corner room of the third floor. Brother Spy.

\* \* \*

A phone call originated again from that room: "Joe, it's me. He's just come back home. An hour and ten minutes. Getting faster."

# Chapter 37

Elizabeth had had enough. From her cousin Norine in New York, she had received clippings from the New York papers about Mick's heroism in the Power Memorial tragedy and the shooting at St. Paul's. In his letters he had revealed that he loved a girl, Katie, whom he had been seeing for over a year. Then Katie herself began to write her with the news that Mick had decided to join the Christian Brothers.

Like Katie, Elizabeth couldn't understand Mick's sudden change of heart, unable to picture him as a celibate Christian Brother. She would come to America and find out what was going on with her Mick.

At the same time after an absence of many years, her nightmare had sprung back into life. In Dublin's Kingsbridge Station, Elizabeth was clutching Sean under one arm, while with the other she was rooting beneath her sister's body, to pull free the screaming infant, so blood-spattered that she feared he had been shot too. Clasping both babies to her chest, she could hear herself whispering to her dying sister, "I'll take care of him, Mary."

Sending letters to Mick and to her cousin in New York to arrange her stay, Elizabeth then wrote to the Novice Master:

Dear Brother Chapman,

I am Mick Slattery's aunt from Dublin, his deceased mother's sister. I have not seen him for five years and have missed him greatly, so I plan on coming to America and spending a few days with him in West Park. I love him, the last living reminder of my sister.

Please make no special arrangements for me other than a ride back and forth to a hotel close by. I'll be arriving in July.

Sincerely,
Mrs. Elizabeth Long

\* \* \*

When the Novice Master had digested Elizabeth's letter, he was glad. He hoped the visit from his aunt would help relieve some of Mick's tension, freeing him from whatever demons pursued him.

The next day the Novice Master approached Mick:

"Your aunt will be visiting for as long as she likes. The Mother Cabrini nuns will give her accommodations at their convent, and she can eat all her meals with you. Be sure you plan some activities for her."

"Yes, Brother, perhaps the historical sites across the river, so she won't be bored."

\* \* \*

Before going up to West Park, Elizabeth met with the Muldoons, attending a war council after the shooting on the street. Katie's mother introduced the guest, a tall woman with black hair speckled with gray: "Captain, this is

Elizabeth Long, Mick's aunt, come from Ireland to visit him. Katie and she have been writing to each other for the past year."

"Mrs. Long, I'm pleased to meet you. You're here at a crucial time to be a help to Mick and to us."

"Captain, I love him. He needs me now. Katie and the Muldoon's have filled me in about the violence and the pressures his uncle has put on him. I'll do anything for him."

"Great" said the policeman, "we need your help. I drove immediately to West Park once I knew Katie and Terry were okay. Mick had no knowledge of the shooting but had received a letter from his uncle that a warning was on its way."

"Why would they warn Mick up there?" asked Mr. Muldoon. "The trouble was here."

"I think they have a healthy fear of Mick. When I told him, his first instinct was to come back with me and slaughter them all. When he calmed down, he begged me not to press him about why he was up there because they had threatened to hurt Katie should he tell."

"Mother of God, they would hurt an innocent girl," Katie's mom said.

"Captain, why can't you arrest these fellas now that you have Terry and Katie as witnesses?" asked Mr. Muldoon.

"We want to get them all. Mick says his uncle is the worst of them, and he's kept his head down," explained the policeman.

"What kind of an uncle is he to torture the lad like this," asked Katie's mom.

"The devil's own," interjected Aunt Elizabeth. "He wants to kill Brits to avenge the deaths of my sister and brother-in-law over twenty years ago."

"With your permission," the policeman nodded to Katie and the Muldoons, "I'd like to have a plain clothes policeman shadow Katie until this is over. He'll be as unobtrusive as possible."

"Please do this for us, love. It'll bring us peace of mind," pleaded Katie's mom.

"Yes, Mom."

"An odd thing, Captain," offered Katie's mom. "There was no sign of Biddy O'Hearn, an old woman across the street, the morning of the shooting. Usually, she's like a hawk. Not a squirrel can cross the street that she doesn't see. I wonder could she have been tipped off so as not to be a witness."

"By God I'll go right over and ask the old witch myself," said Mr. Muldoon.

"I know how mad you are, Mr. Muldoon, but I would rather do that myself. Tomorrow morning I'll surprise her and threaten to haul her into the station if she's not cooperative," explained the policeman.

"All right," replied Mr. Muldoon. "Your threat might work."

"Officer," said Aunt Elizabeth. "I haven't understood Mick's going to the seminary from the beginning. We wrote often, and he never even gave a hint of it."

"You've hit the nail on the head, Mrs. Long," replied the policeman. "Mick tells me he's up there to safeguard Katie from the IRA, and I believe him. But why there?"

Aunt Elizabeth replied, "I hadn't known about the tinker killing until Katie told me. Neighbors, the Ahernes, wrote me that Dan had had a visitor from New York, a cousin named Pat Condon, supposedly IRA. Dan is obsessed with striking some dramatic blow for The Cause. The visit seemed to set everything in motion."

"That name is new to me. I'll check him out," answered the policeman.

"So I'm thinking that the IRA paid their way over, getting Dan a job and an apartment," reasoned Elizabeth.

"That all fits, Mrs. Long, but why West Park," answered the policeman.

"God knows, Officer," said Katie's mother. All my brother, retired up there in the novitiate, goes on about is Hyde Park and Roosevelt across the river."

The policeman bolted upright: "Good God, that could be the answer. They want him to go after the President. Is Mick a swimmer?"

"Sure, he saved our Eddie in the Hudson," Katie's mom said.

When Katie began to cry, Elizabeth consoled her, "He hasn't done anything wrong, love."

The policeman went on, "That plot would explain why he's so conflicted about being up there. They're holding Katie hostage. If they're after Churchill, who visits there, there might be a leak despite the news blackout of his movements. I'll find out."

"Mick's no assassin," Katie blurted out.

"You're right," said the policeman. "But the IRA is forcing this on him to protect you. His uncle doesn't care about him. That explains the pictures and the warning shots."

"But sure a lone man would have no chance," said Mike Quinn. "He'd have to swim over and have a gun there waiting for him."

"As I said, Mr. Quinn, as improbable as this plot seems, Mick is simply a pawn. His uncle and his friends are willing to sacrifice him. He didn't tell Katie why he was up there to protect her. Our job is to prevent this. Mrs. Long, when you see Mick, you've got to question him directly.

You can reveal to him what we know. I have a feeling he'll unfold it all to you. Then we can get him out of there, keep Katie safe, and capture these IRA guys before they do any real damage."

"Captain, I'll do what you say, but you must guarantee a way to keep Mick out of trouble," said Aunt Elizabeth.

"That's what I intend, Mrs. Long. We'll meet as soon as you return from West Park. One final point. There could be a brother up there with IRA leanings spying on Mick. Any thoughts?"

Mike Quinn said, "As I've told you, my eldest brother lives up there retired, I'll get on to him and see what I can learn."

"Fine," the policeman said. "Let's enjoy some tea and Mrs. Muldoon's fine cookies before we go."

\* \* \*

That same night less than a mile away the conspirators were tense despite the freely flowing whiskey and beer.

Joe Murphy was angry: "Tim, you cocked the shooting up. Those two kids saw your face."

"That bitch knocked my mask off with her books," Tim whined.

"And I asked you to lay off The Drink. I could smell it off you at 7:45 in the morning, which I'm sure sharpened your wits wonderfully," attacked Joe.

"You've become a threat to us," Dan said. "Those kids identify you, and they'll clap you in jail. The Drink makes you a handicap to us."

"All right, Tim. Your last chance. We need you but not half-drunk. The Cause is bigger than any of us."

"All right, I won't disappoint," Tim replied.

* * *

The next morning the policeman approached Biddy O'Hearn's flat by coming from her side of the street out of her line of sight, leaving her no time to prepare a story. Propped up on a rocker, the old lady was manning her window like a watchdog. He got to her door quickly and knocked.

"Who's there?" Biddy called.

"Police."

It took the old lady some time to get to the door, which she opened only a sliver keeping the chain latch on.

"Yes?"

As she peeked through the crack, the policeman said, "I've some questions for you, Mrs. O'Hearn."

"Officer, I can't let you in because the house is not ready for visitors, especially at this early hour."

"That's all right, Mrs. O'Hearn. Get dressed and I'll have a patrol car here in a few minutes to take you to the station."

"Glory be to God, what would the neighbors think? Let me tidy up here first."

When Biddy finally admitted the policeman, he found the apartment neat, but overstuffed with old furniture. A gallery of religious art adorned every wall with a large picture of Jesus bearing a heart radiating flames the centerpiece. The widow's gray hair was covered with a rose kerchief. She wore a blue housecoat and shuffled about in pink slippers. Her most prominent feature was her blue eyes magnified by thick glasses like two azure shooter marbles. She turned her rocker from the window to face him as he sat on a wooden chair with a seat of green leather.

"Now, Officer, what can I do for you?"

"The neighbors tell me you keep a sharp eye on the street," the policeman began.

"That I do. Not much gets past me."

"What did you see when the shots were fired the other day?"

"Oh, that morning I was in the kitchen making tea and didn't come out until most of the commotion was over. I saw some policemen and the neighbors milling about."

"The shots and screams didn't attract your attention?"

"My hearing's not what it used to be. I'm eighty four."

"Someone didn't warn you off your window beforehand so as not to be a witness?"

"No, Officer. I don't have any truck with them IRA."

"Why would you suspect the IRA?"

Caught out, Biddy answered, "Sure, they're always causing trouble, like at St. Paul's last summer."

"Mrs. O'Hearn, all I want is a name, whoever drew you from your watching."

"I'm sure I don't know, Sir."

"I'll call for that squad car, so that we can question you properly at the precinct. I'll wait outside while you dress."

"Well now, come to think of it, a man did call, an Irishman, about some danger on the street."

"Who?"

"An Irish fella with a brogue."

"Well, Mrs. O'Hearn, get dressed for the station house. We'll have some tea there, and it'll give you time to remember the man's name."

"Now I recall. It was Joe Murphy, a friend who spends a lot of time in the neighborhood."

"What did he say?"

"To stay out of the window because he had heard rumors of some trouble."

"Thanks for your help, Mrs. O'Hearn."

"Please, Sir, these IRA can be right vengeful, so I'd rather them not know you talked to me."

One more name of the cell.

* * *

When he had returned to his office, the policeman called Commissioner Dolan: "Chief, I think we have a lot of this business figured out, but you aren't going to like it."

"Tell me."

"They sent the Slattery kid up there to kill Roosevelt and Churchill—-just across the river. They're holding the girl hostage. That's why the fireworks in front of her house, to scare him into it."

"Oh good Christ."

"We need to find out if someone's leaking the President's schedule and Churchill's despite the news blackout."

"There I can help you. The answer is 'Yes,' Charlie. We know that Churchill curries favor with his own press by slipping them his schedule. It drives F.D.R. crazy because the American papers are left out."

"Boss, we have to learn if Churchill is going to visit Hyde Park soon because that would be their target date. But we don't want to alert the Secret Service or Hoover. They'd just take over and the boy would be caught in the web."

"Charlie, you're right. Better we handle this. I'll get back to you with the date."

# Chapter 38

As Elizabeth rode the bus to West Park, she thought of Dan with deep resentment. His heart had become stone. He was willing to have the boy he raised die or be ruined for revenge. He had no love for Mick.

Along Road 9W, the last part of the ride, the Hudson shone brightly below. The Novice Master himself drove Mick to the station, and hovered in the background when Mick and Elizabeth greeted each other. Mick forgot his nervousness when he embraced his second mother. "My, Mick, but you've grown healthy and husky," Elizabeth said. Mick introduced the Novice Master, a handsome man of middle age with cheeks red from the outdoors and blue eyes the color of the sky above the Hudson: "Mrs. Long, you've come a long way. We're happy to have you."

They drove her first to Mother Cabrini convent to drop off her luggage and to freshen up before continuing on to the novitiate. Impressed by the Novice Master's kindness, Elizabeth told him, "Thanks very much, Brother. You've been most considerate. This is a beautiful place you have here, so well kept."

"Thanks, Mrs. Long. We have a house full of workers."

Mick took his aunt for a tour of the grounds, ending with a walk to the river, giving them privacy. "See that place with the white columns across the river to the left? An interesting story. That's the Vanderbilt estate, one of the richest families in the world. When Frederick Vanderbilt died in 1938, he left the estate to his niece who wanted to sell it. Father Divine, a black minister from Harlem with a large following, wrote President Roosevelt asking if he would mind his buying the estate and becoming the President's next-door neighbor. Roosevelt did mind, and then convinced the heiress to donate the estate to the National Park Service."

Elizabeth remarked, "You've always had a keen eye for history. Now tell me, your novice master seems a nice man. Do you like him, Mick?"

"He's fair minded, but can be demanding and bossy. He hasn't one qualm about any decisions he makes. Around you he's a different man, courteous, but reserved. He acts like that with all the women, the sisters and mothers of the novices on visiting days. As soon as the women leave, he's back to being Napoleon."

Elizabeth laughed, "Sure the priests in the Old Country are the same, afraid to talk with us or even look us in the eye. They consider us another species altogether, sisters of Eve, all of us temptresses."

As Mick and his aunt walked down towards the river, Mick said to her: "How is Uncle Dave with his job?"

"Guinness has promoted him from driver to supervisor. Sean was just accepted into Dublin University, and Michael is in his last year at Christian Brothers High School. As their mother, I wish they had as keen an eye for their books as they do for the colleens. I have to keep a close watch on them both. Neither of them is the natural scholar you are."

"Yes, but living in the back of beyond, I had fewer girls to distract me."

"Well, you sure found a lovely girl in Katie."

"You know her?"

"You mentioned her in your letters and we began to correspond."

"Does she hate me?"

"No, she loves you, but your coming up here has made her crazy altogether. I met her parents, lovely people, with Captain Miller after the shooting outside her building. So I'm pretty much up to date on what Dan has done to you. I hadn't known about the tinker lad until Katie told me. He's a devil from hell, your uncle, blackmailing you and all for The Cause, ready to sacrifice you. He's done this your whole life."

"Yes, and it's taken me until the last year or so now to figure it out."

"And now he's holding Katie over you, isn't he."

"Yes, he'll cripple her if I don't kill those two old men. Since she came into my life, she's brought me love and hope." Sobbing, Mick embraced her, "Aunt Elizabeth, what can I do?"

"Well, love, you haven't done anything yet. Captain Miller has all this figured out, no fool that one. He's got a watch on Dan and the boyos in the Harp and Shamrock, and has several of them identified, including Dan, of course. Miller has some plan, but he's keeping it to himself. He thinks the IRA have a Christian Brother up here spying on you and some help from the Roosevelt house."

"He's right. But Nellie Keyes from the Old Man's staff is on our side and will help us. We'll drive across to see her," Mick said.

"Over the next few days we'll pray to Our Blessed Mother. We'll just act normally so as to keep hidden that we're on to them."

"Aunt Elizabeth, you're my second mother."

During her stay Elizabeth met quite a few of the

novices. At lunch next day she was their guest. Next to the novitiate stood a pine grove with trees ordered neatly in rows, leaving space for chairs and tables laden with mounds of peanut butter and grape jelly and platters of bologna. Stacked like cordwood, loaves of bread stood on every table with dented metal pitchers of milk and different flavors of kool-aid. The Novice Master said Grace and introduced Mick's aunt. The novices broke out in applause, the brothers' custom for welcoming visitors. Elizabeth turned crimson and whispered to Mick, "Mother of God, I don't have to say anything, do I?" Mick laughed and said, "No. That's a greeting, like."

Mick told her, "I'd like to introduce you to Dominic, a Chicagoan, my closest friend. I've told him everything, and he's given me good advice. He's wanted to meet you."

"Is he the pale, thin brother?"

"Yes, he's very sick but never complains. He has to go back and forth to the hospital in Kingston for blood transfusions. He has leukemia, cancer of the blood. We don't know how long he can last."

"Poor lad. Dominic, come over and sit next to me. I'm glad to see you. Mick tells me you've been a great companion to him."

"Thanks, Mrs. Long, but he's been the friend, going out of his way to take care of me when I've been sick."

"With your family so far away, this must be very difficult for you."

"Yes and no. I miss them, but it would only be harder for them to see me so sick."

"You've been in hospital then?"

"The longest stay two weeks, then several days at a time for transfusions."

"Are they painful?"

"Not so much, but I'm always having needles stuck into

me, like a pin cushion. Worst are the long nights in the hospital. When I wake up with the night sweats, Mick is always there to mop my forehead."

Tears formed in Elizabeth's eyes and in Dominic's as she said: "Even here in this Garden of Eden we still carry Christ's cross."

"I don't think I'll have to suffer much longer."

Mick butted in: "Stop that. You've already buried yourself."

Elizabeth leaned over and touched Mick on the arm: "Be quiet now, love, why don't you. Dominic and I want to have our own chat."

"Yes," Mick said, and moved off to join the others.

Elizabeth and Dominic sat quietly holding hands like a mother and son.

From a distance the Novice Master observed them and was reminded of the Pieta', Michelangelo's marble sculpture of Mary caressing the body of Christ in her arms.

"Your parents will come when you get very sick?" Elizabeth asked.

"Yes, the doctor will let us know when I'm close to the end, and they'll come by train. But, Elizabeth, I dread their visit even more than dying. My mother is an alcoholic, and my parents hold their emotions in. It'll be hard knowing that we'll be seeing each other for the last time. My brother is two years younger and will be a distraction to them."

"Love, try to think what they'll be going through and be kind to them. They're suffering too. Feeling for them might help with your own pain."

"Why, Elizabeth? Why does God allow so much hardship in our lives?"

"I don't know. When Mick's mother and father were killed, I snatched him as a baby covered with blood from under their bodies. Even with my own baby in my arms, I wanted to run away and die. But somehow I accepted Christ's cross. We have to believe He loves us and will bring us to a better life. There's a meaning to this we can't see but only sense."

"I believe that too. I want to die a brother and be buried here."

"You've been a godsend to Mick with all his troubles with Dan and the IRA. For a young man he has endured the loss of his parents and being raised by his uncle to be a killer. Somehow with your help and that of his girl Katie, he has kept his goodness. He'll find his way."

"Yes."

"Dominic, the two of you are in my heart. I'll be thinking of, and praying for, you every day. If there was any more I could do for you, I would."

"Thanks. Just talking with you has been a great help."

Dominic was about to give her a perfunctory kiss on the cheek, but she reached out and embraced him tightly. "I love you," she said, "not for your pain, but for you." Both sobbed.

As Elizabeth was walking away, the Novice Master intercepted her: "Thanks, Mrs. Long."

"He's as fine a young man as I've ever met, Brother, a saint among us."

"In just a few minutes, you've caught him perfectly," he said. "In our way of life, we miss a mother's touch, despite how much we pray to our Blessed Mother. Somehow I wonder if I have failed him in some basic human way."

"Brother, there's goodness written all over you. You've acted like Christ. There are some things only He can do."

"Thanks for the kind words. You've been a blessing to all of us."

Later talking with Mick, Elizabeth said, "Sorry to shoo

you away from us like that, but Dominic wanted to talk more freely and empty his heart. He's a good, good man."

"I understand. He's gone through so much. The constant nausea. The night sweats. Spells of fainting. The pain from his enlarged spleen. And the terrible disappointment that he'll never become a teaching brother. Only a few weeks ago he finally stopped practicing his handwriting with chalk on the blackboard."

Elizabeth decided to take a walk by herself. Drawn to the cemetery with Christ the King guarding the entrance, she marveled at the care lavished on this holy ground, the grass manicured, the white marble gravestones neat and glistening in the sun, a God's acre with the Hudson down below, quite a contrast to the cemeteries in Ireland, grown wild and untended. Only the contributions of their Yank children had provided headstones for most of the native Irish buried in local cemeteries. On a stone bench in the shade, Elizabeth prayed for her husband and boys back home and for Mick and Dominic. She noted the gravestone of Rudolph Cassidy who had died at twenty, and felt a shiver that Dominic might join him soon. She prayed hard for an end to Dominic's suffering and a resolution to Mick's troubles.

The next morning, the last day of Elizabeth's visit, Mick suggested to the Novice Master that Brother Light drive them across the river for a tour of the Vanderbilt and Roosevelt estates. A Dubliner, he was charmed by Elizabeth on the ride over the Poughkeepsie Bridge to Hyde Park. "Tell me, Brother," she asked, "how long since you've been home?"

"Since before the war. I first came in 1919 when we were fighting the English. I was a young pup during the Easter Rising in 1916 and then joined the brothers."

"A strange thing, Aunt Elizabeth," Mick intervened.

"Brother went to one major league baseball game, and it was the only game in which a player was killed."

"Yes, in New York, 1920. A Yankee pitcher, Carl Mays, hit a Cleveland shortstop Ray Chapman in the head and killed him. I never went to another game."

"How long have you been in West Park, Brother," Elizabeth asked.

"Almost twenty-five years."

After a drive of some twenty minutes, Brother Light dropped them off at Vanderbilt's, open to visitors this day. Acres of flower gardens, ponds, gently curving lawns, and a white mansion crested a hill overlooking the Hudson. "Sure, an entire town could fit in here," Elizabeth said to Mick. "It seems wrong for one man to own so much while the poor starve in the city."

"'Robber barons,' they called them," said Mick. "They made their money on monopolies: railroads, ship building, oil, and steel." The entrance hall to the mansion had a marble floor with wall tapestries of medieval hunting scenes and carved wooden furniture from Germany. A chandelier sparkled two floors above them.

From there the two walked to Springwood, the Roosevelt complex, the outside of which was open to tourists because the President was away.

"I called Nellie to tell her we were coming over," Mick said.

At the top of the road leading to the house, military police were on duty for visitors to sign in and receive identification badges. A walk of a mile ran alongside a field for riding horses. As Mick and his aunt approached the house, there was a rose garden next to the Presidential library. A columned portico with a balcony above served as the entrance to the main house with a carved stone balustrade marking the perimeter of the front.

The house was impressive but much less grand than Vanderbilt's, a point that during his life the President often made, deriding Vanderbilt's as a Renaissance museum while his own house was to be lived in.

A tall Secret Service man in a blue suit stood sentinel at the front door, politely informing the tourists that the house itself was off limits for the day.

In her lilting brogue, Elizabeth asked the man, "Sir, Nellie Keyes is expecting us."

"She was making coffee for us an hour ago. Walk around to the back by the kitchen and the guard there will fetch her for you."

"Thank you, Sir."

The sentry at the back of the house was a mirror image of the first man, tall, all business, and wearing a blue suit: "May I help you," he asked.

"We're visiting Nellie Keyes. The guard in front said to come here and ask you," said Elizabeth.

"Please wait here. I'll see if I can find her. Whom shall I say is calling?"

"Mick Slattery and Elizabeth Long. She knows we're coming."

After a few minutes a lady with graying hair came through the kitchen door in an apron sprinkled with shamrocks. "My Mick, good to see you."

"Nellie, this is my Aunt Elizabeth here on a visit."

"Grand," Nellie said. "The house is shuttered for the day. But I'll make us some tea, which we can have in the garden. We can have a good talk there." Turning to the Secret Service man, Nellie asked, "Would you care for a cup of tea, Mike?" "No thanks, Nellie. You've got me about poisoned with tannic acid," he laughed.

The two guests walked to a garden that had a glass-topped table with wrought iron chairs covered with cushions bearing the Presidential seal. A harvested cornfield lay next to the garden. Neatly trimmed hedge roses in varying shades of red formed the perimeter of the garden interspersed with purple bearded irises. Bearing a large wooden tray embossed with the image of a flag and the American eagle, Nellie placed before them a blue tea cozy, cups and saucers, and lemon cookies: "We'll let the tea steep for a bit. Elizabeth, I'll bet you're from Dingle too."

"Actually from Lispole, and your man Thomas Ashe. As a little girl I saw him riding a giant black horse once in a parade. He was tall with a fine head of chestnut hair. My great uncles were taught by him in school, a wonderful teacher, smart and kind."

The old lady's eyes turned glassy: "Would to God he had stayed at that instead of being sucked into Ireland's romance with death. I'd be a grandmother today. You know we had only a few days to ourselves, at Benner's Hotel in Tralee. I cherish every second. As a lover he was grand, kind and gentle. Sorry to scandalize you both, but we had to steal our time."

"Of course," said Elizabeth. "It was war."

"I was his only--both before and since. No other man has touched me. What an awful thing to love a martyr, in and out of jail, rushing here and there to give speeches. I lived in constant fear they'd shoot him. Every time a man came up our road, my heart was in my mouth that he would bring me terrible news. One day he did."

"We're a land of loss," said Elizabeth. "My poor father spent twenty years in Chicago living in exile, returning a husk of a man. He missed our childhood. As I'm sure Mick told you, his parents, my sister and brother-in-law were killed in Dublin before my very eyes."

Nellie poured the tea.

"Best cup of tea I've had in this country, and your cookies are light and delicious," Elizabeth praised, bringing a blush to the old woman's cheeks. "What terrible memories we have. Nellie, we need your help to stop these fools in New York. All they've done is export the violence. They'd make fresh martyrs out of Mick and his girl Katie."

"Mick told me. I've hidden the gun and clothes. I'll do anything for ye."

"Keep putting off your IRA man by not taking his calls," Mick said.

"That's easily done. His name is Joe Murphy, and I wish to God I'd never met the man. They can't get at me if I stay up here."

"Don't tell him where you've put the gun and clothes. We may have to give it to Captain Miller for evidence later," Mick said. "You're right brave, Nellie."

"I'm an old lady. If I can protect you and the girl from these devils, I would die happy. Don't worry about me. Remember to watch that Brother Spy over there. He'll be in a great hurry to tell them about Elizabeth's visit."

"The police have a bodyguard on Katie, so right now she's ok," Mick said.

"Elizabeth, don't you wish in your dreams that us women had been in charge of our country. We wouldn't have fallen in love with killing and death."

"As sure as God. The men go for glory. It's us that suffer and mourn."

"Brother Light will be waiting for us on the highway. We'll have to go soon, Aunt Elizabeth," said Mick.

"You will not. Finish your tea first. I have a thermos of it in the kitchen and some cookies for your brother driver."

After finishing their tea, Elizabeth and Mick moved to help clear the table. Nellie ordered, "Stop. Away with you. I have the whole day for this."

243

As Mick and Elizabeth hugged and kissed Nellie, the old lady said through her tears, "Please God, we'll meet in happier times."

* * *

When they had made the trip back to West Park, Elizabeth told Mick, "I won't go home until all this is settled, and Katie and you are safe and happy."

Packed and ready to leave, Elizabeth said to the Novice Master, "Brother, thanks again for all your kindnesses. One last favor: I'd like to say goodbye to Dominic." Even as she asked, tears danced in her eyes.

Dominic lay in the stuffy infirmary with a fever, globules of perspiration matting his face and forehead. His rosary beads on the sheets next to him, Dominic lit up when Mick brought Elizabeth into the room. She sat on a wooden chair next to him holding his hand while Mick brought a towel to wipe his head. She gave him some ice water in a straw: "There now, my love, you're doing the best you can. Jesus and Mary will help you through this. Mick and I have made some progress in this awful business. Keep praying for us."

No longer trying to restrain her tears, Elizabeth bent down and kissed his cheek: "Goodbye, my love."

"Thanks, Elizabeth," Dominic croaked. "I love you."

Elizabeth broke down completely on the front steps in front of Mick and the Novice Master, but she was unembarrassed: "Thanks, Brother. No one could have been kinder."

"Your visit has been a godsend to us," he said.

"And to me," she replied.

His own eyes glistening, the Novice Master said to Elizabeth, "If you don't mind, Mrs. Long, I'll have Brother

Light and Mick drive you to the bus station. I want to sit with Dominic."

Unable to speak through her tears, Elizabeth hugged the Novice Master. Aside from his family, no one did this. He didn't resist.

# Chapter 39

T he IRA had gotten a tip from the British press corps that Churchill would visit Roosevelt at Hyde Park the weekend of August 16th before accompanying the President to Quebec. The two men would discuss Operation Overlord, the cross channel invasion of Normandy the following summer, both of them concerned that Stalin wouldn't be participating in the conference. The Russian leader cited the demands of his leadership of the war, but there was the niggling suspicion that he could pull another about face and make a separate peace with Hitler as he had in 1939.

Joe Murphy and his two cellmates had the date of their mission: Saturday, August 17[th.] The end was in sight after six years of planning. But there was apprehension with the group.

Dan Slattery asked, "Joe, what's wrong. You're so fidgety you'd make coffee nervous."

"Something's changed. I can feel it," Joe said. "Nellie won't take my calls, and I haven't heard from our scout up there in the novitiate. Even Biddy O'Hearn has clammed up, if you can believe it."

"I'll bet it's that bloody copper, always nosing about," said Tim Moore.

"I think you're right," Joe replied. "He must have scared her into silence because she'd be reporting to me about his sniffing around across the street at the Muldoon's."

"If worse came to worse, I could always do for the cop and get him out of the way," Tim declared.

"Good Jesus, has the alcohol robbed you of your wits entirely? Shoot a cop, and you'd bring the whole city down on us," Joe shouted at Tim.

"Hush up, the two of you," Dan said. "They'll hear us in the bar.

\* \* \*

Upon her return to the city, Elizabeth called Captain Miller to set up a meeting at the Muldoon house. The night of the meeting was hot, with only the gentlest of breezes cutting through the fog of Mr. Muldoon's pipe smoke. The policeman, Katie, her mother and father, and Mike Quinn joined Elizabeth. In the kitchen Katie's mom had the kettle going. Never too hot for tea.

Elizabeth began: "Captain, your analysis was spot on. The plan called for Mick to shoot the two great men with a gun planted by Joe Murphy of the IRA through Nellie Keyes, a domestic on the President's staff. On his trial runs, Mick met the lady several times, and his goodness so impressed her that she has renounced the plot and has hidden the gun somewhere else. Mick and I visited her at the President's home, and she'll do anything for us. We told her to fob off her IRA contact, Joe Murphy, to give us time for your plans."

"The two of you have done great," the officer said, "and just in time because Churchill will be up there in five days. Katie, no trouble with anyone following you since your bodyguard has been on the case?"

"None."

"I was going to remove him, but with things heating up I would like him to stick with you."

"Yes," said Katie's dad. "We're grateful."

"A bit of dispiriting news from our family, Eileen," said Mike Quinn. "But it might yet work out to the good. The brother spy in the Novitiate keeping an eye on Mick's comings and goings across the river is our own brother, the fool."

"Oh no," she gasped.

"He admitted it to me. This Joe Murphy co-opted him too. But he swears he had no idea about Katie being in danger, and I believe him. However, he did know about Mick being in the frame."

"How could he, Uncle Mike. He knew Mick and I were friends," said Katie.

"The daft old man has always wanted to do something for the IRA, our own three brothers killed in the Old Country. He saw this as his chance. He's the watcher on the river for them. I spoke to him roundly, and he's very remorseful. He's to take no phone calls from Joe Murphy until we tell him to."

The policeman then explained his plan: "Just before Churchill visits Hyde Park on Friday, we'll have Brother Quinn and Nellie get back in contact with Joe Murphy and tell him all is set. On the day itself, Saturday, these guys will be meeting at the Harp and Shamrock glued to the radio for a report on the assassinations. We'll wait until dark, say eight o'clock, when it's obvious there has been no attempt at Roosevelt's, and then swoop down and arrest the lot of them. Mick won't go across the river. We'll fake the whole thing."

"Captain, what charges will you have against them?" asked Mr. Muldoon.

"For starters we have the shooting on the street here with Katie and the Kelleher boy as witnesses. At a trial for the actual conspiracy we can use Brother Quinn and Nellie. Also, there was a dropout from the original cell, Pat Condon, Dan's cousin, who went to Ireland to recruit Mick and him for the IRA. If we can prove all this, these men will be charged with treason, punishable by death."

After these last few words, the mood in the room was somber.

"Let's have our tea," Mrs. Muldoon said.

\* \* \*

When the Novice Master opened the mail for the day, he discovered another picture for Mick. It was a long shot of the girl with an "X" scratched through her legs, with the words "Saturday, August 17th." He summoned Mick to view the letter, and then Mick called Captain Miller in New York: "Captain, I've just received another photo of Katie with a threat about next Saturday, the target date. I know you have a detective watching her. This is an especially dangerous time."

"Thanks for the call, Mick. We know that Churchill will be up there this weekend, and we'll get these guys. We'll keep Katie safe."

When the Novice Master wanted to know what was happening, Mick replied, "Brother, I'll tell you the whole story in a few days. Right now we have enough on our plate with Dominic."

# Chapter 40

Captain Miller aimed to arrest the conspirators at 8:00 that evening. At six o'clock that evening the brownstone windows of Hell's Kitchen danced with the last rays of the setting sun as Aunt Elizabeth, Eileen Muldoon, and Nellie Keyes, clothed in Sunday dresses, strode arm in arm like the three avenging Furies down 10th Avenue. Hardly exchanging a word and focusing only on their task, they invaded the male Irish preserve of The Harp and Shamrock, carving out a path through the smoke.

"Bejeezus, look at these hoors will you?" one Irish drinker muttered to his companion as the ladies marched by the men at the bar. "Sure they should be home minding their kids or washing the dishes."

Elizabeth stopped and asked the bartender what the complainer was drinking. "Guinness," she was told. "Bring me one, please Sir," she said, dropping a bill on the bar. The barman complied, and Elizabeth picked up the pint and dumped it on the offender's head, remarking, "Now perhaps you'll mind your mouth." The other barflies guffawed. The three ladies made straight for the back room.

Inside, the three conspirators were in a frenzy. "By Jesus, it's almost sunset. We should have heard by now, unless there's a news blackout," said Tim Moore as he, Joe

Murphy, and Dan Slattery sat hunched over the Philco radio, waiting for news of the assassinations. The three men smoked non-stop, packs of Fatima and Camels lying amid glass ashtrays flanked by empty shot glasses.

Elizabeth knocked as the bartender yelled, "That's a private party in there, Miss." Ignoring the man, Elizabeth knocked again until Tim Moore opened the door, a cloud of smoke escaping from within: "What's this then?"

The women pushed by him to find Dan Slattery and Joe Murphy listening to the radio. When he saw Elizabeth, Dan reddened and said, "What in the name of God are you doing here?"

"News for you," said Mrs. Muldoon. "Probably what you're waiting for on the radio."

"What?" Joe Murphy growled

Elizabeth responded, "Roosevelt and Churchill are unharmed, and Mick is safe in the novitiate."

"Goddamnit, how do you witches know that?" snarled Dan.

"A phone call from my brother, Brother Quinn, in West Park," said Mrs. Muldoon.

Nellie spoke up: "We're here to find out what you'll do to Katie now that Mick hasn't carried out your mission."

"Like I said, break her legs. I'll do it myself," Dan barked.

"Indeed you won't" said Mrs. Muldoon. She then opened the door and said, "Mike, they're all yours. No hope of reform here."

The three ladies marched back through the now empty bar as Mike Quinn and six workmen in bib overalls carrying toolboxes passed them. They crashed through the green door, wood splinters flying everywhere. The three conspirators jumped up, shocked to find a small man with glasses dressed in a gray suit with a blue tie marching in like a general. Impassive sentinels, the workmen stationed themselves against the walls.

"Mr. Quinn, Sir, what are you doing here?" asked Joe.

"As my sister has told you, we've had a phone call from my brother in West Park. Our President and his British guest remain healthy and sound, thank God, and your brother sleeper agent is at home in the novitiate," explained Mr. Quinn.

"'Tis true then. God help us," said Tim.

"You'll need His help soon enough," replied Mr. Quinn. "This President you wanted to murder has been good to us workers, including yourselves. I've gotten work for all of you. Where would you be without American jobs? Back home with your arses shining through the back of your pants like tinkers. Since we founded the union in 1934, the President has always been on our side. And you want to do for him."

"But he's helping the Brits," Tim objected.

"You jackass, even Ireland is neutral in this war. As you know, back home I was big on the IRA, but this is a different place and time. Thousands of sons of Irishmen are fighting and dying in this war. And you want to kill their Commander-in-Chief?" Mike questioned.

Silence enveloped the room.

Mr. Quinn took out his black wallet and extracted from it a small picture: "I want each of ye to study on this."

With trembling hands, the three men passed around the Communion photo of a small girl in a white dress and veil, her hands wrapped around a pair of glass rosary beads.

"Isn't she a darling girl in her First Communion dress?" asked Mr. Quinn.

The three agreed.

"This is my niece and godchild," Mr. Quinn continued, "Katie Muldoon, the lass whose legs Dan intends on breaking, the daughter of my sister who just spoke to you."

"Oh Jesus," Tim groaned.

Joe responded, "Sure, Mike, we didn't know she was anything to you."

Tim chimed in, "Mike, you know we'd never hurt anyone belonging to you."

"But I suppose it would have been all right if the girl came from more humble origins?" Asked Mr. Quinn. "You were attempting murder and treason against the government of the United States. The poor dago Zungara who tried to shoot the President in Miami in 1933 was electrocuted within a month. The six German spies who landed here from the U-boats suffered the same fate. If I call the Secret Service, that'll be your end too."

"What are you going to do with us?" Asked Joe.

"A choice: Either we turn you over to the police, or you receive the same blows you were going to inflict on my Katie," Mr. Quinn answered.

"Jesus, Mike, you'd break our legs" whined Tim.

"What a different outlook on leg breaking when it's your own legs!" said Mr. Quinn. Consulting a gold pocket watch, he said "Well, lads, it's getting late. I want this sorry episode behind us. You'll have to choose."

The three conspirators all chose the leg breakers.

The customers in the front bar had all been chased home, the doors locked, the lights dimmed, and the keening Irish music turned very loud.

"I believe in justice tempered with mercy, so only one leg, and my men here are so skilled as to make it a clean break, no shards or splinters," the union boss said. "In time ye may even be able to return to work. Just to be absolutely clear, if there's even a sniff of a threat to my family or to the lad, you're dead men."

Drawing a pint bottle of Paddy's Irish whiskey from his

suit coat, he passed it to the three prisoners: "Take this for a bracer, like, and face up to it as best you can. I'm leaving now. I'll call for ambulances to take you to the hospital. Tell the police the dagos did this to you. They'll believe you."

As he left, Mr. Quinn beckoned to his workmen. Carrying wrenches and hammers wrapped in towels so as not to break the skin, they advanced on the three men, two of them yanking each conspirator off his feet one at a time and laying him lengthwise on the scarred table swept free of debris. A third worker swung a railroad monkey wrench, twenty-three pounds of dark steel, each blow causing a sharp crack followed by screams and curses. Heedless of the cries of their victims, the workers lifted each man from the table and gently laid him on the tiled floor. In five minutes with three swings, the operation was concluded and the workers departed.

At 6:30 that evening the phone rang in Captain Miller's office:

"Captain, you'll find your IRA plotters in the back room of the Harp and Shamrock," Mike Quinn said. "They're a bit worse for wear and will wait for your arrival. You'll be needing ambulances, but will meet no resistance from them. Their fates are in your hands, but you'd do well to consult His Eminence before bringing the feds in."

Within the hour Captain Miller and his men found the scene at the tavern just as Mike Quinn had described, an empty bottle of Paddy's on the floor with three writhing, cursing men. They were taken to nearby Roosevelt Hospital with police guarding their rooms. The policeman called Commissioner Dolan at home: "Chief, we've got the IRA guys, each with a broken leg. Said the dagos did it."

"My Irish ass, Charlie. Mike Quinn, right?"

"Yes."

"Well, at least we'll get the Cardinal off our backs. Come downtown in the early afternoon. By that time the phone calls will have been made."

The next afternoon the policeman met with the Commissioner: "Charlie, after all your hard work, you're not going to like this," the Chief said while the two men sipped coffee. "I've already heard from the Cardinal. To not upset his Irish following, he wants these thugs treated as victims of a turf war with the Italians rather than as spies. J. Edgar, the little bastard, would love to get his mitts on them and make a spectacle of himself as the President's protector. If we keep this local, we can avoid a pissing contest with the feebs. Hoover will learn of it, of course, but won't cross the Cardinal."

"I was afraid of something like this, Chief. I interviewed each of them today at the hospital. They stonewalled me. This is all Quinn."

"Your instincts are good, Charlie. But whatever plans the fools had, have collapsed. Quinn saw to that. We're best dropping the thing now. We don't even have to warn them. They'll limp until the day they die."

"Yes, Chief."

# Chapter 41

Religious vows are public promises made to God usually as part of a Mass, but Dominic was so weak that he had to make his in the infirmary surrounded by his family and the novices. He whispered, "I, Brother Dominic, make the vows of poverty, chastity, obedience, Perseverance in the Congregation, and Gratuitous Instruction of youth, and I promise and vow that with the grace of God, I will observe them faithfully."

The Brother Provincial, the head of the brothers in America, held the document for Dominic to sign, and then inscribed it himself. In a few days the vow sheet and his Congregation rosary would be placed in his hands at his wake and burial.

In a room full of weeping men and Dominic's parents, a sad peace settled. Still in pain, Dominic fell into a coma, lingering a few days more. Though they had said their final goodbyes, Mick took much of the deathwatch for one last word. Dr. Larkin had told the novices that even the comatose retained the power of hearing. Late one night, the two of them alone, Mick reached out to pat Dominic's arm: "Thanks, Dominic. You're the kindest, most courageous man I have ever known."

On Saturday at noon, his parents, the Novice Master,

Mick, and other novices surrounding him, Dominic quietly passed away, ending his suffering. His body was brought down to the chapel later that day, the novices standing guard in pairs by his coffin for the next two days.

Mick was one of the pallbearers who carried Dominic's coffin the few hundred yards to the cemetery. His friend had gotten his wish: dying a brother and being buried in West Park.

\* \* \*

The day after Dominic's burial, Mick went to see the Novice Master: "Brother, you've been very good to me, but I've decided to leave."

"Dominic's death have anything to do with it?"

"Actually the opposite. Wanted to stay with him until the end."

"You were wonderful with him, Mick. A real brother."

"Thought I knew toughness and courage. He suffered quietly, sweet and kind to the end. Poor family."

"Yes."

"Once they realized how much pain he was in, they knew he should go. First time I ever prayed for someone to die."

"Mick, I've seen a lot of great brothers die, none holier than Dominic."

"Yes. As for myself, Brother, two favors."

"Sure."

"I want to enlist in the army right away after leaving. Need to know which draft board would be quicker, up here or the West Side."

"You sure, Mick? I think up here because of fewer draftees. But I'll call and find out. You'd be going into action pretty soon."

"My time here has changed me. I want to serve my country and then marry Katie Muldoon and then get on with my own life."

"You'll do well in marriage and in life."

"Your vocation is so lonely, Brother, I can't take it."

"Some days neither can I, Mick."

"A second thing. When I come home, I want to enroll in the brothers' college, Iona. Become a teacher. Like you and the good men who taught me. Like Dominic would have been."

"Certainly. You're a good student and will make a fine instructor. I'll write a letter of recommendation to the registrar. There will be a place waiting for you when you come back."

"Thanks. It'll take me a day or so to get ready. Keep it to myself. All right?"

"Yes."

"Be careful, Mick. A hard war. Trust in Christ to keep you safe. I'll miss you. You always had my attention. Sometimes too much so." They both laughed.

\* \* \*

On Mick's return to New York, he went straight to the Muldoon's. Katie was out doing the shopping for her mother, so Mick and her mom had tea in the kitchen. Mick told her everything, and she filled him in about the last act at the Harp and Shamrock. The front door opened, and a voice called out, "Ma, whose suitcase is this?"

"Come in and find out," Mrs. Muldoon answered, "but don't drop the groceries."

Katie popped into the kitchen and Mick rose to help her with the bags. "Mick," she said.

"Will you forgive me?" he asked.

She didn't reply but embraced him, the only answer he needed.

"I'll tidy up the house for your father, and let you have your chat," Mrs. Muldoon said.

Eddie burst into the kitchen, "Did you bring me some treats, Mick?"

From his pocket Mick pulled out a fistful of penny candies. "I have some for Bridge and Mary, too," Mick said.

Mick and Katie held hands. "Let me tell you the full story. I've been practicing with your Ma," Mick said.

When he finished, he said, "Do you have any questions?"

Katie shook her head "no," tears drowning her freckles.

"I have one for you. Will you marry me?"

More tears.

"I've registered for the draft and may be called up soon. I want to lock you up before I go. I'll talk to your Dad tonight."

Katie said, "Yes."

"Go and tell your Mom, so she can warn your father."

\* \* \*

Mick Slattery survived D-Day and the war. With the GI Bill he paid his way through Iona College and became the teacher he had aspired to be. There were days in class when, as he approached the blackboard, he thought of his friend practicing with chalk in a lonely classroom and of his friend's favorite Psalm: "O Lord, how great is the depth of your kindness which you have shown to all who love you" (30:20). The memory inspired Mick to infuse his own work with some of Dominic, buried in that quiet cemetery above the Hudson River.